THE CRAZY SCHOOL

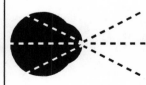 This Large Print Book carries the
Seal of Approval of N.A.V.H.

THE CRAZY SCHOOL

CORNELIA READ

THORNDIKE PRESS

A part of Gale, Cengage Learning

Detroit • New York • San Francisco • New Haven, Conn • Waterville, Maine • London

GALE
CENGAGE Learning™

LIBRARY OF CONGRESS CATALOGING-IN-PUBLICATION DATA

Read, Cornelia.
   The crazy school / by Cornelia Read.
     p. cm. — (Thorndike Press large print reviewers' choice)
   ISBN-13: 978-1-4104-0551-7 (hardcover : alk. paper)
   ISBN-10: 1-4104-0551-6 (hardcover : alk. paper)
    1. Women teachers — Fiction. 2. Boarding schools — Fiction.
   3. Berkshire Hills (Mass.) — Fiction. 4. Large type books. I. Title.
   PS3618.E22C73 2008b
   813'.6—dc22   2007051036

Published in 2008 by arrangement with Grand Central Publishing, a division of Hachette Book Group USA, Inc.

*To all the kids who attended
the Desisto School,
especially those of you
who were my students,
thank you for all that you taught me.*

■ ■ ■ ■

PART I
WESTERN MASSACHUSETTS, 1989

■ ■ ■ ■

"As a matter of fact, I've always had a theory about anxiety. I've decided my anxiety always increases in direct proportion to the absence of Richard Nixon in my life."

Julie began to smile. She knew where I was headed.

"When he was around, lying, cheating, trying to destroy the Constitution, I was furious, but I had no anxiety. Then he resigned in '74, and I swear that's when my anxiety got really bad. What's more, I bet I'm not the only person who is walking around psychologically crippled by the

absence of Richard Nixon in their lives."
— Barbara Gordon
I'm Dancing as Fast as I Can

1

Halfway to Christmas, Forchetti stated the obvious: "You can't teach for shit."

The other six kids went quiet, looking from him to me — teen-angst scratching and hair twirling and pencil chewing arrested for once.

He cracked his gum, noise reverberating off the jaundice-yellow cinder block.

It was an ugly room. Demoralizing. I didn't want to be in it, either, only you're not supposed to say that when you're the grown-up.

The trees outside were losing their last Robert Frost touches of burnished brass and copper — sorry leaves ready to drop from maples and elms and whatever the hell else kind of East Coast trees I still didn't know the names of, twelve years after leaving California.

I dragged my eyes back from the window and crossed my arms. "Did you read the damn chapter?"

Forchetti smirked and pincered the spit-warm raisin of Juicy Fruit off his tongue. He held it up, pretending to sight down the damn thing, straight at my forehead.

I stared right back at his narrow face, at those baby features overwhelmed by black eyebrows he hadn't yet grown into. "*Did you?*"

Without looking down, Forchetti opened his copy of *I Know Why the Caged Bird Sings* at a random page. He dropped the little gum wad inside and mashed the paperback shut against his chair's faux-wood paddle of desk.

"I wouldn't read this piece of shit," he said, "if you dropped to your knees and blew me."

Wiesner hissed, "Shut the fuck *up,* Fore-skin."

Good-looking kid, Wiesner: six-five, white-blond hair slicked back, gray eyes with long dark lashes. He was just back from eight days in county lockup, after holding a teacher and a couple of students hostage with a carving knife so he could call his girlfriend long-distance on the principal's office phone. Now I had him for two out of three classes.

Forchetti dropped his eyes to the carpet.

"She *is* a shitty teacher," he whined, "and you owe a dollar to the Rape Crisis Fund for saying the F-word, Wiesner."

Which was true. Big-time rule here at the Santangelo Academy, because Dr. David Santangelo felt that "fuck" was a word fundamentally linked to violence against women.

It was, in fact, the only word the students weren't allowed to say. Or the teachers.

Wiesner pulled a crisp five from his pocket. "Four to go, then." He lifted his right hand, waggling the digits in Forchetti's direction.

"Madeline is not a *fucking* shitty teacher," he said, folding his index finger down on the stressed word. "You, on the other hand, are a *fucking*" — middle finger — "suckbag *fuck*" — ring finger — "and if you don't leave her alone, I'm going to *fucking*" — pinkie — "stomp your skinny ferret ass the next time I catch you alone in the showers."

Wiesner wadded up the money and tossed it at Forchetti's feet. "Be a sweetheart," he said. "Put that in Santangelo's little jar for me."

Forchetti blushed, but he picked the bill up off the floor and put it in his pocket.

I would have told Wiesner to lay off threatening a foot-shorter kid he had fifty pounds on, except Patti Gonzaga started growling, which was what happened the first week, right before she chunked her chair at my head.

The lunch bell went off, thank God. They stampeded into the hallway, all except Wiesner, who just stretched his legs out, still in his seat and grinning.

One last door slammed down the hall.

He ambled over and sat on the edge of my desk. "Penny for your thoughts."

"I think you'll be late for lunch."

"Figured I'd walk you over," he said.

"I still have to do everybody's marks."

We were supposed to rate how each kid behaved, right at the end of class. Forchetti'd racked up three straight weeks of zeroes — winner and still champion.

Wiesner lounged back on an elbow. "I can wait."

I pulled open the top drawer, looking for a pen. "They'll get all pissed if you're not there for the meds."

"You just seem kind of shaky," he said, voice all soothing. "I want to make sure you feel okay."

The drawer was full of crap, souvenirs of my predecessors — paper clips, barrettes, dental floss, half a roll of TUMS, and a screwdriver.

12

Teachers left this place in a hurry.

Wiesner leaned over, perusing the contents.

I looked up. "Of course there isn't a single fucking pen."

He smiled, extracting a Bic from his jacket.

"Trade you for that screwdriver," he said. "I need to make a phone call."

Wiesner and I angled across the lawn toward the dining hall. I didn't want to get there. I wanted to cut off into the woods and have a smoke, alone, only I couldn't because the other teachers would have smelled it on me and narked.

I shoved a hand deeper into the pocket of my leather jacket, fishing through its torn lining to grip my crumpled pack of Camel straights.

I hadn't even thought about cigarettes since college. Now they were the focus of my existence, along with caffeine. We weren't allowed to have that, either, which didn't stop me from sucking down thick-walled cups of the tepid institutional decaf, hoping in vain they'd missed scrubbing the kick from a bean or two.

The Santangelo Academy air was crisp and fresh after a week of rain, edged with wood smoke and rotting leaves. There was even a sweet breath of cider drifting up from the weed-choked orchard, planted back when this had all been some Bostonian nouveau magnate's country place, before the Civil War.

It was beautiful here in the Berkshires. I'd give it all that much.

"I like that *Caged Bird* book," said Wiesner.

He was lying. I shouldn't have cared.

"The lady who wrote it," I said, "I knew her brother Bailey. He used to come to our house."

I was going to tell Wiesner about this one time when I was little, maybe 1970, and Bailey saw me cutting dry rot out of a tree trunk in our backyard with a paring knife. He told me he'd bring me a switchblade as a present the next weekend he came down from Berkeley. Said he wanted to make sure I'd be okay "come the revolution," since I was pretty hip for a white kid.

I never got the knife. He never got the revolution.

Wiesner nudged my upper arm with his fist and said, "So, d'you do him, her brother?"

"Chrissake, Wiesner . . ."

14

He grinned down at me. "Can't kid a kidder."

"I was, like, eight years *old.*"

"Sure," he said, laughing now. "Sure you were."

I stopped walking. *"Seriously."*

He gave me a pat on the head.

"What the hell kind of thing is that to even *say?*" I said, batting his hand away. "To anyone, let alone a teacher. I mean, would you pull that shit with Mindy or Gerald or Tim?"

"Do I look like an idiot?"

"So why *me?*"

"How about because you look good in that little skirt, and you're blonde with green eyes, and you're wearing cowboy boots, and it's a gorgeous day."

I rolled my eyes. Started walking away.

"Are you sure you want to know?" he asked, behind me now.

"Whatever."

"Turn around."

I sped up.

"Fine with me," he said. "I'd just as soon check out your ass from here."

I turned around.

Wiesner was still smiling.

"We're late," I said. "If you want to say something that's not merely about pissing me off, I'll give you ten seconds."

He looked at the ground, a little embarrassed. "I say shit like that to you, Madeline, because I know I *can,* okay?"

I was touched. "Because you trust me."

"No, because you're too whacked to maintain appropriate boundaries."

He raised his eyes again, but I looked away. At the trees and stuff.

I'd always despised the shrink-sponsored murder of language — all precision and metaphor and beauty boiled away until there was nothing left but carbonized lumps of jargon.

"You have issues around authority," he continued. "I figure that's why you're here."

"That's why *you're* here, Wiesner. I'm here because it's a job."

He shrugged. "When you're ready to own your shit, you'll know why you're *really* here. That's what this place does."

"Cha," I said. " 'Good for the disease.' "

"What the hell is that supposed to mean?"

"It's from this book," I said. "*Magic Mountain.*"

"Books don't help," he said.

"You'd be surprised," I said, even though I'd never managed to finish reading it myself, back at Sarah Lawrence.

He took my elbow and started us walking.

"Can't kid a kidder."

Sometimes you can, Wiesner.

I was here because I'd killed a guy. And I owned the hell out of that.

The fact he'd been trying to kill me at the time hadn't helped me sleep any better since.

Neither had this place.

2

The dining hall had the acoustics of a hockey rink, the voices of a hundred-something students and thirty-odd faculty bouncing between thin carpet and low curved ceiling.

I sat with the teachers. Wiesner didn't.

The last open seat was next to Mindy, who was trying to explain to everyone around the circle of table how her TMJ was acting up again. She could barely open her mouth.

A friend of mine had that: temporomandibular-something-something.

"What does TMJ stand for again?" I asked.

Mindy turned and blinked at me, twice. "Tense mouth and jaw," she said, pronouncing the first word "tints."

"I'm so sorry you have to deal with that," I said.

"Aren't you *sweet?*" she said, blinking again, twice.

When not stricken with TMJ, Mindy

chewed gum with her mouth open. She was from Ohio. Every inch of furniture surface throughout her campus apartment was jammed with stuffed animals, all of them pink. She'd brought the canopy bed her parents gave her as a sweet-sixteen present with her all the way from Dayton.

We couldn't stand each other, but I hated her more. She was so shallow she couldn't even dislike people properly.

I despised her receding chin and her stupid fluffy perm and her stupid fluffy pink sweaters and her fucking giggle. It made me happy that she was fat, since I'd dropped twenty pounds doing time at Santangelo, having been too fucked up to eat much of anything.

I pushed the little piles of lettuce and cottage cheese around my plate, just to annoy her.

"Don't forget we have Sookie today right after lunch," she said.

"Thank you, Mindy," I said, "but I know we have Sookie today."

I chose to believe that our mutual loathing wasn't the reason the two of us got assigned to the same Santangelo therapist, though it wouldn't have surprised me. We went twice a week for an hour, along with Tim.

Mindy turtled her head forward, talking across me. "I know *you'll* remember, Tim. You're not passive-aggressive, like some people."

Blink. Blink.

Tim was a little guy, mostly harmless, with skin and hair so pale he was practically opaque.

Sookie reminded me of a golden retriever — big-pawed, blonde, and brimming with indiscriminate affection.

Everyone at the school had to do Santangelo-approved therapy — not just the kids but the teachers, the administrators, and the parents of every student. We did ours on campus. Santangelo had a traveling crew of shrinks who met with parents around the country. If they missed a session, they weren't allowed contact with their kid by phone or mail for a month. I couldn't believe that was legal, but they were desperate enough to suck it up without complaint.

They wanted to help their children get better — they wanted to believe Santangelo had the secret cure, that he'd fix everything so their kids could resist suicide, or heroin, or schizophrenia, or the urge to inhale fumes from glue and gasoline and hair spray and that stuff you spray on records to get the dust off.

I wanted to believe Santangelo could fix *me,* while he was at it. Who among us does not want to be shriven, to confess all, in the hope of being made clean and whole and new?

It's just that I was second-generation at this, one of those kids dragged along for the ride by parents trying to achieve escape velocity at Esalen or Woodstock or, God help us, Jonestown.

Forage through the five-for-a-buck milk crate at any midlife suburban garage sale, and you'll run across at least one of us in a photograph — captured frolicking, blond, and naked on some scratch-hazed, blunt-cornered old album cover. *Eat a Peach. Mc-Cartney.*

We were the ideal, pretty babies poised to inherit their fresh Eden after the war, after Nixon, after all the world's bitter, stupid old men stopped trying to pave paradise and put up parking lots and shit.

Not like I can blame my parents. Who wouldn't have wanted to get out from under the black-hole physics of Levittown and Eisenhower, the whole Herb Alpert–Republican death trip?

So there I was, November 1989 — Madeline Dare, age twenty-six and at a total loss, sitting on a hill in the Berkshires.

Locals called this Wifflehead Mountain: a single peak tucked into the lush hills and canyons just west of Stockbridge, a baby Matterhorn that had drawn to itself all manner of seekers and lost boys, wild girls and pagan sprites — a century-long parade of Adult Children with enough cash to kick and wail against the trammels of age and responsibility, mortality and the scientific method.

Santangelo's "therapeutic boarding school" was just one facet of the primary native industry.

There was the yoga center where you could pay a thousand dollars a week to subsist on watery juice and sleep on a mat no thicker than a dish towel.

There were grand Georgian sanitariums that had dried out the country's more artistic drunks and junkies, enough of whom stayed on to give the Berkshires a permanent bohemian foundation.

There was the detritus of untold communes and utopias — from the celibate Shakers, who'd died out through lack of breeding, to the wholly licentious latter-day acidheads who'd left behind nothing but their fleas and half-finished macramé plant hangers and lawnsful of broken major appliances.

Then there was this place, its stone gates surmounted by an ineptly welded arc of steel butterflies, mascots fluttering along the school motto: "Free to Be."

I pushed away my untasted salad and reached for the jug of fake coffee, suddenly exhausted.

Mindy put her arm across my shoulders. "Are you going to talk to Sookie about your issues around food?" she whispered sweetly.

"Are you going to talk to her about yours?" I whispered back even more sweetly. "There's probably some ice cream left."

Even Mindy didn't deserve that.

She jerked away, leaving fluffy pink angora lint all over my not-fluffy-at-all black sweater sleeve.

"Mindy," I said. "I'm sorry. That was an asshole thing to say. I slept about three hours last night, and my stomach is just a goddamn nightmare. That's no excuse, but I hope you can accept my apology."

"I'll accept your turn-in," she said, "at tonight's faculty meeting. Unless you think it would be more appropriate to fire yourself."

"She can't fire herself."

Mindy looked across the table at Lulu. Lulu taught Spanish, a language she'd picked up during a Peace Corps stint down

23

in Peru. She'd come home to the family farm in Pennsylvania, landing here after the only work she could find was checking in guests at the local Econo Lodge.

She was the saving grace of the entire Santangelo experience, in my opinion. Despite her fondness for show tunes.

"And why can't Madeline fire herself?" asked Mindy. Her jaw clicked with a sharp snap, like a pinball popping up to hit the glass.

"Because she fired herself yesterday," said Lulu. "You can't fire yourself if you've already fired yourself. It cancels out."

"Like Double Secret Probation," said Tim.

Lulu closed her eyes, exhaled through her nose, and rubbed her fists back and forth across her spiky dark hair. Not without gusto.

I knew what she was thinking. She was thinking, *No, Tim, that is NOT AT ALL like Double Secret Probation, as you would know if you understood ANYTHING, which you DO NOT, despite the fact that you have watched* Animal House *thirty-seven times, as you told us all in the faculty group therapy session at which Madeline fired herself last night.*

She opened her eyes and grinned at me.

And then we were saved by Dr. Ed's arrival with the stack of Med Plates.

He walked around the table, handing a disc of thick white dining-hall crockery to each teacher/dorm parent currently on duty.

These were preloaded with semicircles of tiny manila envelopes, a form of stationery I'd last seen stuffed with impotent Mexican dirt-weed on Fourteenth between Second and Third in Manhattan, circa 1983.

I still thought of them as nickel bags, which wasn't the kind of word-association thing I could've shared at that table.

Each envelope was marked with a kid's last name and first initial, followed by a list of medications contained therein: Haldol or imipramine or lithium or Thorazine.

Lulu, Mindy, Tim, Gerald, and the New Guy were dealt their respective plates by Dr. Ed, New Guy last.

Dr. Ed conferred with him, pointing from each envelope to its intended dosee.

The New Guy took it in with great seriousness. Then he caught me watching and winked. He was a babe — blond hair in loose curls that made me reminisce fondly about those portions of my youth misspent necking with surfers.

The plate bearers rose to make their appointed rounds. Each kid had to dump the meds into his or her mouth, hand the empty envelope back, take a sip of beverage, swallow, and then tilt his or her head back, open his or her mouth, and shift his or her tongue up, left, and right, so the doser could check that all pills had been ingested properly.

No hide-and-seek allowed. No save 'em, collect 'em, trade 'em with your friends.

I never got a Med Plate at meals because I was the only teacher who lived off campus. I was grateful to escape each night, but lately it had been hard to readjust to normal, like getting the bends because I'd come back to the surface too fast and didn't have a decompression chamber to get the painful "therapeutic" bubbles out of my bloodstream.

I leaned back in my chair to catch the sun coming down through a skylight, right when this big cloud cut across it.

Perfect. It was just going to keep on being that kind of day.

New Guy was the first member of the Clean Plate Club. He walked back to the table and sat down next to me, in Mindy's seat.

"Um," I said, "I think that's Mindy's seat."

"Are they assigned?" he asked. "It didn't seem as though the two of you were getting along, exactly."

"Um," I said, "no."

"No they're not assigned, or no, you two

aren't getting along?"

"Both."

"I don't want to freak out Mindy," he said, "you're just the only one I haven't introduced myself to yet."

Mindy would be freaked out anyway. She always was.

"I'm Madeline," I said.

"I'm Pete," he replied.

He had one of those really slow smiles, the kind that just kill you.

At that exact moment, the cloud moved on past the sun, and a big fat warm beam of light came down and hit all his blond curls.

I looked across the room and saw Wiesner tapping a butter knife against the edge of his glass, checking the two of us out.

3

Sookie's office was a slanted little room under the eaves of the Mansion.

Such a tacky word, "Mansion," though the building itself was a sadly perfect monument to that forgotten magnate's fortune, back when it was freshly minted.

His family crest still flanked the front door in twinned cement relief, so you wouldn't miss the credential even if you happened to be blind in one eye.

Santangelo claimed the place had been a stop on the Underground Railroad, but I found that hard to believe. The building's interior sagged under its sheer tonnage of embellishment: marble and parquet and stained glass and carved oak, gilt-scroll-encased ceiling murals crammed with ugly petulant cherubs, grand double staircase tortured into a frenzy of varnished pretension.

I pictured the flight of the man's horrified

offspring, shamed by this testament to their gentility's raw vintage.

The place had since housed third-rate spas and schools, each enterprise patching over another layer of furbelow with asbestos or gypsum board or fire-retardant dropped-ceiling tiles. The roof leaked. The faucets dripped. The ballroom stank of mildew and mouse piss.

I jogged up three flights to Sookie.

Mindy and Tim had claimed the love seat. Last one in got the rotten-egg wobbly chair by the radiator.

"Welcome," said Sookie. "Tim was just going to start us off."

Tim raised one hand slowly, placing his palm flat against the center of his chest.

Sookie nodded with approval. "Tim's feeling like he needs to nurture himself."

Mindy stroked his hair. We were supposed to touch each other a lot.

"I talked with my dad again?" Tim said, glancing down at his hand. "He's so . . ."

"Judgmental?" Sookie's forehead wrinkled with healing concern. Another nod, coaxing.

Tim teared up, nodding back with relief.

Mindy slid a box of Kleenex onto his lap.

At Santangelo, there was always a box of Kleenex.

"He wanted to know if I'd changed the oil in my car. And I couldn't even . . ." Tim dabbed his eyes with a fluffy blossom of tissue.

Mindy went for his hair again. "It's okay."

"Sookie?" he went on. "I wanted him to say something that didn't have all his disappointment around it. Just once."

"Let yourself feel that," Sookie said. "We're here for you. I'm here. Mindy's here. Madeline's here."

He closed his eyes. "My mom was on the other extension, you know? She didn't even . . . I mean, he told me to go out and write down what it said on the odometer. That he'd wait for me to come back and read it to him?"

I looked out the window. Not that I didn't feel for the guy. He was in genuine pain. The room fairly brimmed with it.

"Madeline?" Sookie turned to me.

I kept my eyes on the window.

Just the glass. Not the actual view.

"You're shutting down again," Sookie said. "I know it's hard for you, but can you try to let this penetrate?"

"Sookie, I'm *soaking* in it."

"You are so *cold*," Mindy said. "You are the coldest thing that ever lived."

I turned my head slowly until our eyes

locked, which got her started blinking again. I stared until she had to look down at the Kleenex instead of me.

Blinky bitch.

"Let's let Tim have the focus," I said. "He's hurting."

Mindy got pinker. "How can you even say something like that without any emotion at *all?* Like you're all . . . like you don't even have *anything* inside except, like, *words.*"

Sookie and Tim's attention snapped back and forth between us, like this was Wimbledon or something.

"It's cultural," I said.

"She's all, so, like" — Mindy flapped her free hand, trying to get the other two on board — "cold."

Some people are bi-polar.

I'm just polar.

I sighed. "It's an illusion."

"It's *disgusting,*" Mindy said, blinking at Sookie and Tim in turn. "Madeline's, like, this gross disgusting robot."

And you're like this repulsive inarticulate piece-of-shit tawdry butthead, so neener neener fucking neener.

Sookie turned toward me, crooning, "Madeline, how does it make you feel when Mindy says that?"

"Um . . ." I looked at the window again.

"Now, be *honest*," she said.

"Well, okay." I dropped my eyes. "I guess Mindy's saying that I'm 'a gross disgusting robot' makes me feel as though she only cares about Tim as a prop on which to, like, lavish utterly insincere gestures of affection, so as to mask her apparently crushing sense of generalized inferiority with a temporary veneer of ersatz empathy and concern?"

Silence.

"And *that*," I said, leaning over to squeeze Tim's knee, "that just makes me feel really, really *sad* for her, you know? Because Tim deserves to be *heard*."

"You are so . . . She is such a . . ." Mindy would have been blowing out flecks of spit if her jaw weren't still frozen shut.

Sookie turned to Tim. "Would you be all right if I followed up on this with Madeline for a little bit now?"

He mumbled assent.

"So, Madeline," said Sookie, "how are you?"

"Sookie, I'm terrified."

Then my eyes got all leaky and my nose started running, but that bitch Mindy didn't offer me a single Kleenex.

4

"Terrified?" Sookie leaned forward and rested her hand on my knee. "Tell us about that. What are you scared of?"

"I don't know what I'm supposed to be *doing* here. I just want —" My throat closed up.

Maintaining immaculate eye contact, Sookie started to nod, her head rising and falling so slowly that I flashed on those prehistoric-bird-looking oil derricks you see along desert highways, bobbing for sips of crude.

"This isn't about 'supposed to,' Madeline," she said. "Therapy is time for *you.* No judgment, no standard you have to meet . . . not in this room. Not with me. Ever."

Not exactly true. Ever.

But, okay, I smiled at her. "I appreciate that very much, Sookie. I do. Except I'm not talking about feeling terrified in this room, or with you."

"Mmm-hmmmm," she prompted.

"I'm talking about, you know, *working* here."

"You're terrified of working here?"

"Not, like, in a personal-safety sense. I mean whether I'm doing a good enough job. With the kids."

"Tell me what you're feeling about *that*," she said.

"I don't know if I'm helping them. I might be making it worse. I mean, the meds that get handed out at lunch? Lithium. Haldol. We are not talking about 'the worried well,' here."

"And that makes you feel scared?"

"It *matters* to me," I said, "the fact that my students are in crisis. In pain. I take that very seriously. I want to do right by them, to the very best of my ability."

Again with the nodding.

I wondered if it was something they taught in shrink school. Intro to Nodding 101. Advanced seminars on The Nod Through History: Freud, Jung, Adler, and Nodding and Nuance, a Feminist Perspective.

Sookie gave me the Empathy Smile. Sweetly enigmatic, with a touch of sadness around the edges. "What I'm hearing you say is that you're concerned about your ability to handle responsibility. Struggling to overcome feelings of inadequacy —"

I waited for the rest. I did not nod.

"And I'm *looking* at how you're sitting right now, Madeline," she continued. "How you're presenting yourself to us."

She paused, bringing in Tim and Mindy with a small swoop of her hand.

Tim plucked at the sofa's upholstery.

Mindy blew her nose.

"Sitting up straight," Sookie went on. "Ladylike, in a studied way. Earnest. Your back isn't touching the chair . . . exactly how I hoped I would look when *I* grew up."

She tilted her head to one side. Appraisal. "I'm just wondering who that's *for.*"

"I beg your pardon?"

"Someone *trained* you to sit that way, Madeline."

I fought the urge to cross my arms, knowing the gesture would be counted against me. A defensive move. An attempt at distance that Sookie would lap up as confirmation.

She gave me the curt nod. Zeroing in. "Someone made it very clear that you were required to cloak yourself in this sort of polished, impenetrable affect. This rigidity. Your parents?"

That made me cock a sarcastic eyebrow.

Couldn't help it.

Sookie leaned toward me, her face going all gentle again.

"Madeline," she said, "were you sexually abused as a child?"

Mindy and Tim snapped to attention.

I rolled my eyes. Shook my head.

Sookie was unfazed. "I know it's a tremendously difficult thing to talk about. If you'd prefer a private session, I can make time for you tomorrow afternoon."

"Oh, for chrissake," I said.

She got out of her chair and knelt before me, taking my hand in both of hers. Petting it. "Shhhhh," she said, "it's all right, sweetie, we're here for you. You're *safe* now."

"Sookie," I said, "I'm sure you have all the very best intentions, but you're way off base."

"You're in denial, Madeline."

I tried extracting my hand from her grip, but she just latched on tighter.

"Perfectly natural," she said, "under the circumstances. We often want to block out our most painful memories, repress them so we don't buckle under the sheer weight of shame and horror."

"Sookie —"

"What's important is that you know you weren't at fault, Madeline, and understand that *you* didn't do anything to encourage the abuse."

Mindy was nodding now, too.

Terrific.

I tried breaking through to Sookie again. "No offense, but on what planet does good posture indicate a history of molestation?"

"In fact," Sookie went on, "it's often that sense of having provoked the incidents which renders victims incapable of remembering them. And hostile."

"Of course Madeline's angry, Sookie," Mindy chimed in. "She must be sooooo weirded out now that she knows what's actually *wrong* with her."

"Mindy?" said Tim.

She looked at him. Blinky blinky. "Uh-huh?"

"Shut the hell up." He gave her a sharp finger poke in the arm for emphasis.

I wanted to hug him, but the warning bell for the day's last class went off, and we all bolted out of the room, except for Sookie.

"Come back tomorrow at one, Madeline," she called after me.

My third class was all boys, three of them. Wiesner again, but no repeat of Forchetti, thanks to a last-minute shrink appointment. American History B: Civil War to Vietnam.

We were kind of at Yalta, not that anyone was keeping track.

I was trying to get across why Stalin and Churchill and Franklin D. were so happy in the photo on page 192 of *We the People,* the archaic textbook Santangelo had probably scored at some other high school's tag sale.

We were all pretty dopey after lunch. The room's air felt thick and stale, bearing grace notes of mothball, sweat sock, and spilled root beer.

I had unfurled one of those giant window-shade world maps from above the black-board. Probably yanked it down so far that I'd have to get up on a chair and tweak it massively before coaxing the thing to reroll, especially now that I'd whacked a fist under the Crimea so many times, hoping to make something stick in our collective uncon-scious.

Yalta, for chrissake — stupid pick, but I was in too deep to give up now.

"So these guys agree to send out an invita-tion to anyone who might want to join the United Nations," I said, then started read-ing from the textbook: " 'The Government of the United States of America, on behalf of itself and of the Governments of the United Kingdom, the Union of Soviet

Socialist Republics and the Republic of China and of the Provisional Government of the French Republic invite the Government of *blank* to send representatives to a conference to be held on 25 April, 1945, or soon thereafter, at San Francisco. . . .' "

Sam Sitzman raised his hand. "Um, excuse me, Madeline?"

I liked him. He had this curly-headed Saint-Bernard-with-an-old-soul vibe. You knew right away there was a kind and wise and forgiving heart under the shaggy bits and the glasses.

Especially for a seventeen-year-old from Manhattan.

Especially here.

"Would it be okay if I stand up for a while?" he asked. "This is all really interesting and stuff. It's just sometimes my meds make me tired, and I don't want you to think I'm bored if I yawn or anything."

"No problem, Sitzman. Yalta is not exactly a thrill a minute, here."

He thanked me and got up, shaking out his legs.

Mooney LeChance cleared his throat. "Hey," he said, "isn't the UN in New York?"

LeChance was normally sparing with the classroom participation. A decent kid, just not hugely invested. He would have been homecoming king anywhere else.

"Yeah," I said, "the first meeting was the only one they did in San Francisco."

"Does any of this really *matter?*" asked Wiesner. "I mean, Madeline, do you actually wander around thinking about Yalta or why they picked San Francisco or whatever?"

I got up to crack a window while considering my answer. "I think it's hard to know what will matter, Wiesner." The window crank didn't want to budge. I tried hitting it a couple of times with the side of my fist to loosen it up.

"Stuff like this," I said, "it's all layers and layers, and most of it you'll forget, but maybe down the line you'll find what matters to *you.* Probably not Yalta specifically, just some wayward little snack-o'-trivia you won't even remember having filed away."

The crank gave suddenly, pinching my knuckles against the window's metal frame hard enough that I wanted to stick them in my mouth to quiet the sting.

The fresh air was worth it. Crisp, even bracing.

I looked over at Wiesner. "Dude, I don't have a damn clue what the Taft-Hartley Act was about anymore, or which numbers match most of the amendments to the Constitution."

"So can't we blow that stuff off?" he asked. "The teacher-geek trivia?"

"But you never know what *won't* matter." I flopped into my chair. "Like, here's the kind of thing I remember if someone talks about the UN: It's on top of the FDR Drive, on the East River."

"By my family's apartment," said Sitzman.

"Lucky ducky," I said. "Anyone know what's *under* the FDR Drive?"

No takers.

"Rubble from London," I said. "Chunks of all those buildings the Germans bombed to shit in the war —"

"Heinkels and Junkers and Messer-schmitts," said Sitzman, suddenly looking all blissed out and dreamy.

"Rubble that was dumped into the holds of U.S. Navy ships for ballast on the way home," I continued.

I looked at Wiesner. "Why did they *need* ballast?"

He shrugged, but he wanted to know.

"Because those ships were emptied out," I said. "All the tanks and planes and jeeps they'd brought over that weren't blown up got left there, in case Stalin tried taking over Europe after the war. A lot of bodies got left there, too. Two hundred ninety-five

thousand Americans didn't come home —
guys no older than all of you."

Wiesner looked stricken.

"I think about *that*," I said, "when I'm on
the FDR Drive. And I think about the
people killed in London when the buildings
were destroyed in the first place. Thirty-two
thousand civilians. Families. Little kids."

"How many people altogether?" asked
Sitzman. "The whole war?"

"There's probably a table in here." I
picked up the textbook. "Page two-thirty-
six: sixty-two million, five hundred thirty-
seven thousand, eight hundred deaths total,
military and civilian."

Sitzman looked at the page. "Which in-
cludes five million, seven hundred fifty-four
thousand Jewish holocaust deaths."

"Three million in Poland alone," I said.

They were quiet.

I heard footsteps in the hallway.

Sitzman said, "How could they *do* that?
Sixty-two and a half million people."

The footsteps slowed and then stopped
just shy of the classroom door.

"I have no idea," I said.

LeChance said, "And we *keep* doing it,
over and over."

"But people try to make it stop," I said.
"Like, even though there was the League of

Nations after the First World War — which, you might recall, didn't accomplish crap to prevent the Second World War — these guys were ready to try again. Roosevelt and Stalin and Churchill, in Yalta. They invited forty-six countries to San Francisco. The Germans hadn't even surrendered yet."

"Why San Francisco?" asked Wiesner.

"I always figured it was because people think of California as a frontier — new. The place to go when they want a fresh start, want to dump bad history. The gold rush . . . the sixties . . ."

My parents . . .

"Grateful Dead and all that, right?" asked LeChance, grinning.

"Sure," I said. "All that. Haight-Ashbury and the Summer of Love and *Go Ask Alice.* Pilgrims and dreamers. Peace marches. Pretty much the start of the history I was actually around for, as a kid."

"Tell us about that," LeChance said.

"Sure," I said, "when we get to Vietnam."

Whoever was out in the hallway started walking back in the other direction, no doubt relieved to discover I wasn't advocating global genocide.

I looked at the clock. "Five minutes, guys. How 'bout I give you a head start on finishing the chapter. Maybe we can get through the rest of this war tomorrow. Start talking about Korea and Levittown and McCarthy . . . the whole fifties trip."

When the bell was about to go off, I told them that anyone willing to help me get the damn map rolled up would get extra credit.

Sitzman took me up on it. For a second I thought LeChance would, too, but Fay Perry peeked around the doorway at him, all sylphy and golden, with those enormous gray eyes.

She touched the crescent charm that hung at her neck on a silver chain — his gift, a moon from Mooney — and the boy was gone.

It was getting colder out. I walked back over to close the window.

There were some guys with a truck across the lawn, unloading lumber and bags of concrete.

"Sitzman," I said, "you hear anything about them doing construction?"

He looked up, wistful. "Santangelo's buying a helicopter. He needs a pad to land it on."

"Nice for him," I said.

5

"That was cool today, what you talked about," said Sitzman.

I'd finished the daily behavior marks and shoved them in my desk. Now we were up on chairs, on either side of the wall map. The thing was still jammed, and we hadn't made any headway.

"Thanks," I said. "I like history."

"Me too. I think about the same kind of stuff you do, a lot. Sometimes even . . ." He stopped, embarrassed.

"Sometimes even what?" I asked.

"Well, sometimes too much."

We listened to the construction guys banging together a frame so they could pour Santangelo's helipad concrete.

I pulled my end of the map off the holder. "How do you mean?"

"It's a schizophrenia thing — all these weird connections. Like, well, tell me a random word. Anything."

45

"Um . . . Germany."

He considered that for a second.

"Okay, so before," he said, "I would have thought right away you meant all this deep stuff. Layers and layers, like you said. My family is German. We're Jewish. They all tried to come over here, but not everyone made it. I would've thought you were warning me about the Nazis coming back."

"Sure," I said.

"Before, though, it was always way beyond worry for me. I could hear something on the radio, some song when I got in a taxi — it would seem *important*. Like code. Messages."

"Before here?"

He nodded.

"So, Sitzman, stuff like that," I said, "does this place help?"

"My first month here, I ran away. I spent three days sneaking around the woods in my pajamas with no food. All I'd brought with me was my electric razor."

"To shave?"

He shook his head. "To keep in radio contact with the FBI."

"No shit."

"None. And it rained the whole damn time. I'm just lucky it wasn't snowing. I probably would've died."

I turned to look at him. "Dude, I'm really glad you're all right."

"I appreciate that."

"Do you like it here?"

"I miss flying," he said. "My dad used to take me up in his plane. Twin turboprop — Beech Super King Air 200. I almost had my license."

He toyed with the roller mechanism, then pulled the map down slowly, to see if it would roll back up.

First time didn't work. Second time he made it zip homeward like a champ.

"Sitzman, you rock," I said.

He blushed a little. "Can I ask you a question?"

"Fire away." I crossed my fingers that it wouldn't be whether I liked younger guys or what have you.

"Did you ever work in a hospital? Like Lake Haven?"

A lot of kids here came from Lake Haven. The equivalent of a feeder school. I shook my head and climbed down off the chair.

Sitzman followed. "It's just that when I mentioned the razor and everything, you didn't seem surprised."

I dragged my chair back in place and leaned against it.

"Most people would be," he said, perching on the edge of my desk, "even here."

"It sounded like my dad."

"No shit."

"Well, except he's more into the KGB."

"Oh, sure," Sitzman said. "Lot of that going around."

That made me smile. "He was in the Marine Corps. A John Bircher and everything. No warnings from the radio, though. Or at least he hasn't talked about it."

"He's probably just a delusional paranoid, then. With full-blown schizophrenia, you're all about the messages."

"Dad does occasionally get into sending me *Wall Street Journal* clippings."

With circles and arrows and a paragraph on the back of each one, explaining what each one was, to be used as evidence against us.

"Such as?"

"Oh, like he decided the Vatican Bank had assassinated John Paul I to cover up how the amount of money they 'couldn't locate' exactly matched the miraculously repaid national debt of Argentina or Venezuela or wherever."

Sitzman crossed his arms. "Sounds like they could get his meds dialed in a little better."

"Dad is not a meds kind of guy. Except for smoking dope."

"What is he, nuts?"

I sighed.

"Joke," he said. "But I mean, that's what this place did for me — got the dosage right. I'm relieved to finally discover that sometimes a razor is only a razor."

"Must be exhausting the other way," I said.

He nodded, thoughtful. "Have you ever talked to your dad about getting some help?"

I shrugged. Toyed with some papers on my desk.

"Even therapy," he said. "Just, you know, for a start."

"The thing is, Sitzman, he's got a perfect genius of a disease. It protects itself. Plus, the onset timing was particularly shitty."

"How do you mean?"

"It nailed him in the early seventies, which sucked in two ways. First, all the grown-ups were acting like lunatics generally, so he had a lot of camouflage. Second, he got into primal therapy."

"Don't know that one," he said.

"This guy Janov started it. He claims that if you're told to tough it out when something crappy happens to you as a kid, any emotions you repress end up rattling around in your body forever."

Sitzman shot me a smirk. "That's like saying 'The sky is blue and water is wet.' Big whoop."

"Janov took it further. He said that all illness is caused by repression — cancer, head colds, psychosis, you name it. He had this whole thing about how Western medicine only treats the symptoms, because the true cause of disease is repression. And so everybody's doomed to walk around poisoned half to death unless they 'have their feelings' about whatever happened when they were kids. But once you do, you won't need any other kind of doctor."

"People fell for this?"

"In droves," I said. "He set up these centers where the paying customers could work on dredging up childhood bummers, so they could cure themselves by weeping and strangling pillows and yelling their heads off in soundproof rooms. Like, I dunno, self-exorcism."

"You're shitting me."

"Sitzman, they ate it up with ginormous spoons, cross my heart and hope to die. Dad and the rest of them."

"That's just absurd," he said.

I shrugged. "It was the seventies — a decade during which you could count on one hand the entire gamut of things that

50

weren't absurd."

"And your dad drank the Kool-Aid."

"Dad paid extra for the Big Gulp," I said. "Besides which, they didn't drink Kool-Aid in Jonestown. It was this cheap knockoff crap called Flavor Aid."

"Teacher-nerd trivia."

Someone rapped twice on the door behind me.

"Might show up on your midterm," I said, and turned to see who it was.

6

Dhumavati smiled from the doorway.

She was Santangelo's dean of students — tall and rangy, with a thick silver braid down the middle of her back.

I rather liked her, not least because she'd encouraged me to get barefoot when we'd first met, while shaking my hand before she started my interview.

"How many jobs encourage you to take your shoes off?" she'd asked, wiggling her toes.

"Not nearly enough," I replied. "Especially before you're hired."

"My thought exactly," she said, laughing.

"So your name, is that Dhumavati as in the Mahavidya?" I asked.

"You're familiar with Hindu cosmology, then," she said, pleased.

"I grew up in California. Kind of comes with the territory, you know?"

She laughed again. "A guru picked it for

me. I'd been through a bad time, and he told me I didn't have to be that woman anymore."

Interesting choice: the mother goddess at the time of the deluge, also known as "the eternal widow," a deity invariably depicted as ugly and fearsome.

"Not sure how I'd feel about being named for 'the one who is without radiance,' " I said. "Doesn't suit you."

Dhumavati grinned — radiant indeed when she smiled, which was most of the time. "Beats the hell out of Gloria. What I started out with."

"Still, I'd have held out for Kamala. Tara."

And here she was, smiling anew from the threshold. "I thought you might like a little support with remembering that Teacher Reflection starts an hour early today, Madeline. Sookie mentioned you're still having some issues around the scheduling piece."

I was about to thank her for the heads-up when an explosive scherzo of shattering glass resounded down the hallway — fist vs. window.

Dhumavati bolted toward the source, with me and Sitzman close behind.

A small crowd of kids had gathered. We shoved through them to find Mooney LeChance standing pale and wide-eyed, right hand curled against his increasingly blood-soaked sweater, the window next to him all glittering spikes and daggers around a foot-wide hole.

Dhumavati hugged him from behind and got him to sit down. I squatted to raise his slashed hand in the air, wrapping my fingers hard around his wrist to stanch the bleeding.

Lulu came through the double doors at the lobby end of the hallway, saw the blood, and yanked off the sweatshirt tied around her waist.

"Pressure with that," she said, tossing it to me. "I'll call 911."

She took off toward the lobby.

Dhumavati put her hands on Mooney's shoulders. "You'll stay right here with Madeline, won't you? Don't try to get up."

Then she stood, walking over to Fay Perry, who was shivering and slumped against the wall.

Sitzman brought a chair from the nearest classroom. Dhumavati eased Fay down into it, then wrapped her own coat around the girl's slender shoulders.

Fay didn't say a word. She kept sneaking besotted glances at Mooney, her pupils so dilated with shock you couldn't see iris.

When she realized I was watching, she

dropped her eyes to the floor and just rocked slowly back and forth from the waist.

"Is Fay all right?" Mooney whispered. "Make sure she's all right. I didn't mean to scare her. It was just —"

He tried squirming around to see her.

I pressed a knee down against his thigh to pin him.

"Dhumavati knows what to do," I said. "Don't worry. The ambulance will be here soon, okay? Keep your hand up for me."

Blood seeped through Lulu's sweatshirt. My hands got hot and sticky with it. I clenched Mooney's wrist harder.

We waited, everyone quiet but for Dhumavati's murmured reassurances to Fay.

"They're going to send me to the Farm, aren't they?" asked Mooney.

The Farm was the punishment dorm. Off in the woods. It always made me think of Steve McQueen's "Cooler" in *The Great Escape,* only here they all got put on work detail instead of locked down with a baseball and mitt — plus which their parents were charged double tuition for the privilege.

Kids on the Farm weren't allowed out for classes. They didn't get mail or phone calls. The closest thing to leisure time was a study period at night.

"I'll make sure you get your assignments,

okay?" I said. "You won't be able to do any writing for a bit. This'll need stitches. But you'll be good as new in a flash."

The other kids were drifting toward the exit, watching for the ambulance.

Sitzman asked me if we needed anything.

Mooney was sweaty, but his teeth were chattering.

"Get me his coat?" I asked. "It's on that bench."

Sitzman brought it over and put it on Mooney's shoulders, trying to keep it clear of the blood. It was one of those letterman jackets, dark blue wool with white leather sleeves, the fuzzy first initial of some other school stitched over the left breast.

I nodded at Sitzman, and he backed away.

Mooney looked up at me.

"I'm going to move around a little," I said. "My leg's asleep."

I twisted to wedge myself against the wall. "Lean on me if you're dizzy."

"I might throw up," said Mooney. He was whispering, embarrassed.

"No biggie. I never liked this sweater."

He slumped against my shoulder. "So tired."

"Put your head down in my lap if you want."

"Yeah."

I helped him, keeping his arm up. "This is good," I said. "You're not really bleeding so much."

Mooney asked me under his breath, "Hey, so how come you always wear such big sweaters? You should get shirts that, you know, *fit*. We all think so."

"I figure you guys don't need any further distractions."

He smiled. "No offense."

"I'll chalk it up to you being in shock," I said. "Want to tell me why you took out the window?"

"Not really."

"I won't nark on you," I said.

He turned his head slowly so he could look straight up at me. "Serious?"

"Cross my heart and hope to die."

"Lean down."

I put my ear as close as I could to his mouth.

"Fay's pregnant," he said. "If Santangelo finds out, he'll make her keep it. He's a big-time Catholic, just like her family."

"She doesn't want to have it?"

"I'm nineteen. Her birthday's next week, and then we're both old enough to walk out of here. We could manage, but not with a kid. Plus, the meds Fay's on? She's afraid the baby's already too damaged."

Lulu was walking back fast from the other end of the hall.

Mooney measured her progress. "They won't let her stay here if they find out. But she can't go home."

"How'd the window get involved?"

"Fay thinks Mindy knows what's up. I just . . ." He closed his eyes. "She said maybe it was time to do a turn-in. She's scared."

"Isn't there anybody you guys can talk to?"

He shook his head. "There's you."

Lulu stopped in front of us and crouched down. "You guys holding up okay?"

"Kinda dizzy," he said.

"Just take it easy," she said. "Madeline's got you covered, and the ambulance is on its way."

"How long?" I asked.

"Maybe ten more minutes?" She stood up. "I'm going to go see if Dhumavati needs anything for Fay. Can I bring you some water?"

Mooney nodded.

Lulu came back with two paper cups. She gave one to me, then helped Mooney raise his head to drink.

It seemed like forever until I heard the distant siren, so faint at first I figured it was just wishful auditory hallucination. Then the sound came clear, growing louder and louder as help raced up the long drive. The wail cut out suddenly, and everyone was so quiet I could hear the wash of tires through gravel as the ambulance braked in front of the building, then the chunk-a-chunk of its opening doors.

I heard Dhumavati say, "Shhhh, sweetie, it's okay. Nothing to be frightened of. Help is on the way." She wrapped her coat tighter around Fay's quivering shoulders.

"Stay right here," she said, giving the girl one more quick squeeze before she stood up and started walking up the hallway.

Lulu rose from the floor to follow.

Mooney's eyes fluttered open. The first thing he did was check to make sure Fay was all right, then he looked up at me. "Take care of her while I'm gone, okay?"

"Of course," I said.

"You can't leave her alone."

"Listen," I said, "don't worry about anything else, just get through all this. They'll fix you up at the hospital. Concentrate on that."

Lulu and Dhumavati came back into view, holding the doors open so the paramedics could push through with a rolling gurney.

"Madeline?" Mooney touched my wrist

with his good hand. "Help us."

"Mooney, Jesus . . . I wish I could just load you both in my car and get you the hell out of here tonight."

He grabbed on to me. "Don't let them send Fay home. She won't survive. She won't even try."

Mooney didn't want to let go of me, not even when the paramedics collapsed the gurney down flat beside us and checked his cut hand.

"Promise me," he said.

They counted three and shunted him onto the thing, then jacked it up. The bleeding was under control now, but they'd given him a fresh compress.

He didn't blink once as they wheeled him away — just held my gaze until I nodded.

Lulu held the door open again.

Dhumavati told her to call Santangelo and let him know she'd be going to the hospital, then she grabbed the gurney's tail as the crew shoved through to the lobby.

I heard the ambulance doors chunk open and shut again outside. The siren powered up, loud at first but fading as they raced back out through the school gates.

I turned to check on Fay, watched her get up out of her chair and float over to the broken window, still wrapped in Dhumavati's coat.

Her face illuminated by a dreamy smile, she plucked a tag of Mooney's flesh from the icicle tip of the biggest shard.

Then she ate it.

Lulu came back inside after she'd called Santangelo. We steered Fay toward the library's glass doors, depositing her at the center of a worn old sofa before sitting down on either side of her. Lulu tucked her arm gently around the girl's shoulders and began to administer soothing, melodic doses of chatter.

We hadn't turned on the lights. The room's fluorescent panels would have been unnervingly harsh. Better the cozy second-hand glow from fading sun and well-lit hallway. Plenty to see by.

Fay hummed softly to herself, nodding occasionally, that dreamy smile still playing across her mouth.

She was all tiny bones and downy skin.

A watercolor girl.

An ivory fawn tipped with pink and gold and mother-of-pearl. Not quite tame.

She took my left hand in both of hers and raised it up a little, running a fingertip across the pale blue stone in my engagement ring. "Pretty," she said.

"Thank you."

"A candy made from ocean," she said.

"I like your necklace," I said. "The little moon."

"Mooney gave it to me."

Through the library's glass doors, I watched Dr. Santangelo coming down the hall, his mouth grim in its black nest of beard. The man was a walking J. Peterman catalog, arrayed in an opera cape and a billow of Jeffersonian shirt, the latter unbuttoned low enough to reveal a dark nosegay of chest hair between his flabby pecs.

It had grown just cloudy enough outside that he couldn't see us beyond the hallway lights and his own reflection. His cape lining flashed scarlet each time he swung to inspect a classroom.

Lulu stood up. "I'll let him know where we are."

Fay drew her feet onto the sofa and curled up against me. "Bet you the sun goes out right when he gets here. Bet you a million dollars."

"Bet you you're totally right," I said.

The door closed behind Lulu, and we watched her wave to get Santangelo's attention.

Fay lifted my hand again, started twisting the ring gently back and forth on my finger.

"Mooney told you," she said.

Not a question.

She raised her head to look at me, and I nodded.

"It's okay if Lulu knows," she said. "Just promise you won't tell anybody else. Not yet."

Santangelo and Lulu were heading for us. I didn't know what to say.

"I know it's not like we can keep this a secret forever," she said, "but Mooney's so fragile right now. If I just had a little more time to help get him calm . . ."

"How long until your birthday?"

"Five days."

"If Lulu thinks it's okay," I said, "we'll wait until then."

The sun dipped below a bank of clouds at the horizon.

Santangelo opened the door and slammed on all the lights.

7

Santangelo twitched his cape and lowered himself onto the sofa, knees apart to make room for the sheer mass of his belly.

Fay started shivering again, leaning against me harder.

"Poor kid," he said, patting her knee. "I know this must be awfully hard for you."

She turned her face into my shoulder.

Santangelo looked from Lulu to me. "I think Fay could use a nice cup of hot cocoa, don't you? A little break before she goes back to the dorms."

He shoved himself upright, groaning with the effort.

"Can't I stay here?" Fay asked.

One chubby paw emerged from Santangelo's cape in answer to that.

Fay ignored his open palm and rose to her feet. "I like the kind with marshmallows."

"I know," said Santangelo. "And there's even whipped cream."

He wrapped an arm around the girl's shoulders to gather her in, a gesture of supportive concern belied by his no-nonsense grip on her closer wrist.

Lulu opened the door, kicking down its rubber-tipped stop so she could move aside to let them through.

"We'll call the hospital," Santangelo told Fay. "Make sure they're taking good care of Mooney. Then you can tell me all about what happened."

"I will," she said, raising crossed fingers to the small of her back as they stepped across the threshold.

Lulu shoved the door shut behind them, fighting the tension in its hydraulic arm to get the job done faster.

"Jesus *Christ,*" she said, watching them go. "Please tell me you've got a couple of smokes tucked into that jacket, Madeline, because I need a few blessed moments of illicit-vice inhalation after all that *drama.*"

I patted my Camel-hiding pocket. "The woods or your place?"

"The woods are closer," she said.

We waited for Santangelo and Fay to reach the end of the hall, then hauled ourselves out a back window to make our getaway undetected.

■ ■ ■ ■

"Why the hell I ever left the old homestead," said Lulu. "What possessed me?"

She was hunkered down Indian-style under the abandoned grape-arbor hideout we'd stumbled upon our first week here.

The structure twisted in the embrace of its gnarled vines, hung with swags of shriveling black fruit that perfumed the air with a seder-wine Concord tang. The western sky sported streaks of orange and pink.

I shook a pair of Camels loose from my crumpled pack and lit hers first.

Lulu blew a stream of smoke into the shadows. "Dhumavati told me we'd hold off on the faculty meeting until she brings Mooney back from the hospital."

"*Fuck* me," I said. "I promised Dean I'd make it home for dinner tonight. Again."

"Poor Dean."

"A patient man, as husbands go," I said, "but getting testy."

"You can't blame him. With all these goddamn meetings, he barely sees you."

"I got home so late last night, he said he figures if I stay here one more week, they're gonna shave my head and make me sell flowers in an airport."

Lulu laughed. "He's a keeper, that boy."

"I just don't want to go back to Syracuse. Took me three years to pry him loose."

"Has he brought it up yet?"

"Any day now."

We'd moved here from Dean's hometown when the Southern Pacific told him they wanted two of the rail grinders he'd designed. He'd been antsy to start work ever since we arrived in August, but the contracts had to clear layer after layer of management first. When his inside-contact guy said final approval was a sure thing by the first of November, Dean began negotiations for shop space in this derelict factory outside Pittsfield. We met the out-of-town landlord there for a final walk-through exactly a month ago — October 17, just after dinner. The Loma Prieta earthquake must have hit San Francisco right about when Dean and I were first shaking hands with the guy.

An hour later, they agreed to meet the next afternoon to get the lease signed.

"I think that went really well," said Dean as we drove out of the parking lot.

I'd left the radio on and was just reaching to turn it off when the BBC News announcer said, "The two-tier Bay Bridge and Nimitz Freeway both partially collapsed, and rescuers are waiting to recover bodies from cars crushed by the quake."

"Bay Bridge?" I turned up the volume.

The BBC guy intoned, ". . . measured six-point-nine on the Richter scale . . ."

I hit the brakes and pulled over.

". . . what experts believe is the second biggest earthquake ever to hit the United States . . ."

Dean looked at me. "Bunny?"

I held up a hand for quiet.

". . . have reported unbelievable damage to infrastructure, with collapsed bridges and freeways, fires, shattered buildings, gaping cracks in roads, and landslides . . ."

Dean's guy at the Southern Pacific called the next morning. Damage reports were still coming in, but word was there'd be no budget for any new purchase orders.

"A year, at least," he'd said, "maybe two. Awful damn sorry to leave you swinging."

Dean was stoic about it. "I can always work construction."

The next week General Electric shut down their Pittsfield transformer plant, cutting loose some nine thousand factory workers. They all decided to work construction.

Dean looked for work every day, telling me each night how many hundreds of people had showed up for the same jobs he'd circled in the want ads: welder, mechanic, Sheetrock hanger.

The other guys were local, he wasn't.

He'd graduated summa cum laude from Syracuse and had experience as a stockbroker, too, but the competition for white-collar work was even fiercer.

"Look," I said, "we're okay. Our rent's not much. I'm making decent money at the school."

But I'd married a man who started working twelve-hour shifts the summer he was five years old. He could build or fix just about anything, from cars to train engines to houses. Now Dean was stuck pacing around our apartment while I freaked out at Santangelo. He'd rebuilt the vacuum cleaner three times already.

A month into his search for work, stoic was giving way to cranky, with scattered showers of bitter. He'd start rattling the *Berkshire Eagle*'s employment pages every day at dawn. "Bunch of listings for goddamn *boutiques* . . . part-time goddamn *real* estate . . ."

I kept waiting for the ax-fall moment when he'd finally come right out and say it was all my fault for dragging him to the Berkshires, that we had to go back to Syracuse.

But so far he'd just look up from the paper

and apologize for being whiny. "I go nuts with nothing to do, Bunny. I'm not wired for leisure."

"Maybe a temp agency," I'd said last week. "Get your foot in the door somewhere?"

"Sure," he said. "I'll start making calls."

Please God, let his interview today have garnered something. I can't go back to that place, to freezing in the dark.

The ground was cold under the grapevines. I shivered and turned toward Lulu.

She took another deep drag off her Camel. Blew it out slowly. "So. Any idea what all that was about with Mooney and the window?"

"Actually, yeah. But we can't tell anyone for a few days. They made me promise."

"I give you my word of honor," she said. "Spill."

"Fay's knocked up."

"Oh, those poor kids," said Lulu. "Jesus *Christ.*"

She stubbed out her smoke and buried it next to an arbor post.

I did the same, then lit us two more.

The faculty meeting was in Dhumavati's apartment, long after dark.

Lots of decaf. A platter of carob brownies.

We'd been there two hours already, what with everyone feeling compelled to weigh in on Mooney before we could get to the business part.

Thursday-night summary: how classes had gone this week, which kids were struggling, which kids each of us wanted to give a gold-star commendation in the next morning's announcements.

When it came around the circle to me, I said Wiesner was really pulling his weight.

"I'm very encouraged," I said. "He's polite, he's on time, he's pitching in after class."

I left out the part about his comments on the view of my ass.

Mindy giggled, her hand up coyly to her mouth.

"What?" I said.

She glanced across the circle to Gerald.

There was an air of maiden-aunt prissiness about the guy, but he'd toughed out at least a couple of years here.

I wondered why. Did it help, all this wallowing, or did he just have nowhere else to go?

Gerald sighed.

"Go on, *tell* her," said Mindy.

He rubbed his palms down his thighs.

"I thought Wiesner was doing really well

in my class last spring," he said. "For a few weeks there, he was all bright-eyed and bushy-tailed — asking if he could do extra reading, swinging by my classroom so he could walk me to lunch. Gold stars every Friday, let me tell you."

Dhumavati and Mindy nodded.

"And?" I said.

"And this," he said, reaching up to pop his four front teeth free, holding the plate out toward me, pink and white plastic bits glistening at the center of his palm.

"Wiesner walked right over and sat down on my desk one morning," he said, "happy as could be. I looked up, and he slammed a fist into me with all his weight behind it. No warning, no reason. He gave me a big grin the whole time, like he'd asked if he could help bang chalk dust out of the erasers."

Gerald looked twenty years older without his teeth. Lisped a little, too.

"Gerald," I said, "I'm so sorry."

He dropped his eyes and shoved his teeth back in. "Just be careful."

There was a needlepoint pillow next to him on Dhumavati's sofa, the words THOSE WHO DO NOT REMEMBER THE PAST ARE CONDEMNED TO REPEAT IT picked out in white on a dark red ground.

72

Gerald fussed with it, giving the thing little pats on either end to plump up the down.

"Let's end here," said Dhumavati. "We'll have our first meeting tomorrow at six-thirty sharp."

I looked at the clock on her mantel and bolted for the door. Quarter after ten, with a good twenty miles of mountain road between here and Dean.

On the bright side, I had recently inherited a Porsche.

I drove to the edge of campus, impatient with the school's five-mile-an-hour speed limit and egged on by the Violent Femmes in my tape deck, bass and volume turned way the hell up.

My headlights flashed across the school gate's stone pillars, the arc of rusted butterflies above them, the Santangelo motto: FREE TO BE!

Cha. More like *ARBEIT MACHT FREI.*

The second I'd passed beneath this odious load of hooey, I stomped on the gas and redlined toward Dean.

The Porsche shifted hard and steered harder, suspension so tight that running over a fingernail paring at eighty could have you pissing blood for a week.

I loved the damn thing, and I made it

73

blister through every last turn.

Home again, home again, jiggety-jig.

When I finally burst into our apartment, Dean was crashed out asleep on our sofa.

He'd set the table with flowers and candles — now wilted and guttering, respectively.

Linen napkins. Polished silver. A bottle of wine. The fancy yellow-rimmed dinner plates we'd received from Aunt Julie for our first anniversary — French ones with old fox-hunting scenes in the middle.

Had he meant all this for a celebration? Maybe the interview had gone well?

He opened his eyes and looked up at me. From the expression on his face, the answer was a resounding no — more like this finery was an effort to cushion the blow of bad news.

"I am so sorry to be this late," I said. "So so so so sorry."

"I got worried when you didn't call."

"They had to take that kid Mooney to the hospital," I said. "He punched out a window outside my classroom and cut himself all to shit, and then the faculty meeting got post-poned."

"It's okay." He got up and started bringing food out from the kitchen.

I poured us each a glass of wine. "How was your interview?"

74

"Thought I had it in the bag until the very last part," he said, putting down a platter of roasted chicken and carrots.

I took a sip of wine, then started arranging food on our plates while he went back for the salad.

"They said they were ready to sign me up," said Dean, taking his seat. "Everybody was slapping me on the back and all enthused to have me aboard, then they handed me a little container for the drug test."

"Um," I said. "So then —"

"So then I told them I took that as a goddamn affront to the deeply ingrained American tradition of guaranteeing personal liberty, not to mention my rights as a citizen of this great nation. Asked 'em how the hell they got off thinking the Constitution gave *anyone* the go-ahead for requiring me to whip it out on command and fill some plastic Dixie cup with my Purity of Essence. That's not why our boys died in Iwo Jima."

"*Please* tell me you didn't actually bring up Iwo Jima."

Now he was grinning at me. "Goddamn right I brought up Iwo Jima. Guadalcanal . . . Flanders Field . . ."

I tried to just roll my eyes in response, but I had this vision of him standing up on some battle-worn desk in his suit and tie, slamming fist against palm while ranting about the Halls of Montezuma and the Shores of Tripoli to a bunch of cowering temp-agency staffers, and I couldn't keep a straight face.

I raised my glass to him. "You are just fucked in the *head,* sweet boy."

He shrugged.

"Not like you would've passed, anyway," I said, "ya stoner."

"Like that's any of their business. Buncha damn pinkos."

I started cutting into my chicken. "Enough with the Semper Fi crap, already. Eat your dinner."

8

The clock radio cranked up in the dark, NPR pundits chatting about the Berlin Wall's remains getting hacked into fist-sized souvenir chunks.

I hit the snooze button too many times, trying to catch up on all the sleep I'd missed during the night, rolling around and fretting.

Dean's side of the bed was empty, already cold. I pushed away the covers and got up myself.

He had the paper spread out across our little table and a tall milky glass of Café Bustelo waiting for me on the kitchen counter, sweetened to syrup just the way I liked it.

I croaked out my thanks before raising the sacred vessel to my lips with both hands and chugging half of it down.

"Want dibs on the shower, Bunny?"

I shook my head. "I'm late for work."

He put a hand on my shoulder. "Are you okay?"

"Fine," I lied.

The narrow lane before me whipped and curved through bare black woods framed stark against that just-before-dawn gray light, everything to the east brushed with a faint anticipatory pink.

This early, mine was the sole car on the road, which in my seemingly perpetual lateness was no bad thing. I turned up the tape-deck volume: the Sex Pistols' "God Save the Queen."

Coming out of the last hairpin bend before campus, I had to downshift and brake like crazy to keep from back-ending a rusty old Volvo wagon.

Volvos, Jesus. My nemesis.

I blew by it on the straightaway. Double yellow, but I didn't want to do a turn-in for showing up after the faculty meeting had gotten under way.

I raced between Santangelo's stone gate-posts at 6:27 a.m., hoping I'd luck out and discover someone had committed a grosser transgression than lateness in the last nine hours.

My right eyelid twitched from lack of sleep. I wasn't in the goddamn mood to ape

78

contrition, saying that my being late all the time was just totally fueled by passive-aggressive shit and I was so grateful to the community for helping me get committed to tackling the *real* work on my issues around punctuality.

I'd had my fill of seventies neuro-hooey from Dad. It wasn't until I'd washed up at Santangelo that I realized he'd armed me with native-speaker fluency — like, slap a set of headphones on me and I could've snagged a simultaneous-translation gig at the UN, psychobabble to English.

Why didn't I have the balls to stand up and say that I drove fast because I damn well felt like it, *and so fucking what?*

Because part of me still wanted to believe there was some point to this therapy crap.

Wiesner was right, after all. I was here for more than the paycheck. I wanted absolution.

Could be worse.

Could be Syracuse.

I cranked the Porsche's wheel toward the dining hall and parked in the second-to-last spot.

Opening the faculty-lounge door precipitated an extended hush of annoyance from the forty people already ensconced therein.

79

I dropped my gaze to the ratty carpet, slinking crouched toward a spot at Lulu's feet.

There were a dozen kids on the floor around me, most of them holding hands with the teachers seated behind them.

These were the responsible students. At another school, they might have been proctors or prefects. Here they were more like prison "trusties." Future Mindys. Future Geralds.

I drew my knees to my chest, penitent and hot-faced under the room's weight of disapproval. Someone coughed, and chairs creaked under their occupants' shifting weight.

I didn't look up until I'd sensed that all eyes had shifted back to the blackboard, just left of the doorway.

Dr. Santangelo glared at me from the center of the board's dusty expanse, his arms crossed.

His attendance at these meetings was exceedingly rare.

Bad bad day to be the last vulnerable arrival.

At least he'd left the cape at home this time.

"Nice of you to drop by," he said, staring me down as he stroked the beard that didn't quite hide his double chin.

I mumbled an apology, practically tugging my forelock.

He turned a half-step and pointed a chubby finger at Tim. "I believe you had a question?"

Tim nodded, a faint tinge of red rising to his cheeks. "I just . . . last night in the dorm . . . ?"

Santangelo smiled encouragement.

"I was on duty," Tim continued, "with Simon and Cammy? So during bed check, we found graffiti in the upstairs hallway, and we felt pretty sure we knew who'd done it, but I'm not real comfortable with how that was handled, you know?" He coughed and put his hand on his chest. Sookie's remedy gesture.

"What made you uncomfortable?" asked Santangelo.

"Well, even though it seemed pretty clear-cut that it was Forchetti, he didn't do a turn-in right when we first asked him about it, so we got him back out of bed and brought him downstairs to the living room."

Santangelo tilted his head to the side, listening, nodding.

"It was already pretty late," said Tim. "And he wouldn't own up to . . . wouldn't *own* doing it at all, so after about an hour,

Cammy told him to kneel on the floor with his hands behind his back. This is in North, you know? It's a stone floor? Like slate or something . . . so then it was after midnight, but we made him stay like that. On and on."

"How long?" asked Santangelo.

"Three hours." Tim's eyes brimmed. "He was, you know, crying. Shaking. Legs all cramped. I should have said something, but Cammy and Simon have been here so much longer."

Santangelo shot that chubby finger back out fast, straight at Tim. "How *dare* you!"

Everyone flinched at the bellowed words, and I don't think I was alone in expecting him to jump down Tim's throat for having allowed Forchetti to suffer.

"You little piece of *shit!*" Santangelo stomped around in a small circle, screaming. "How *dare* you question what we do here?"

Tim bowed his head.

Santangelo slammed a fist against the chalkboard, his legs apart. "*Look* at me."

Tim peeked up, tears gathering at the corners of his eyes.

"What's your name?"

Tim mumbled.

Santangelo cupped a hand to his ear. "Louder."

"Tim?"

Santangelo swept an arm around the room, his sleeve flapping. "If I was one of these kids, *Tim,* I'd shove your goddamn head right through this chalkboard."

Tim sobbed, a bubble of snot expanding at one nostril.

The good doctor sighed. "You're disgusting," he said. "You make me want to puke. You make *all* of us want to puke."

"I'm sorry, Dr. Santangelo."

"Doesn't he make us want to puke?" Santangelo looked at random people around the room — Cammy, Mindy, New Guy Pete — his eyes boring into them one by one until they blushed and nodded.

Tim absorbed each betrayal, caving into himself by degrees.

Santangelo turned back to him. "Stand up."

The accused rose to his feet, shivering.

Santangelo smiled. "I think we all agree that you should fire yourself, Tim."

"Yes, sir. I'd like to fire myself."

"I think we all agree that you're lucky to have found a community that *cares* enough about you to let you keep your job after such an appalling lapse in judgment."

Tim looked up at him, broken.

Santangelo nodded to himself. "Any other

school, doing the important work we do here . . . well, you'd be packing your bags, Tim. Out on the street."

"Yes, sir, Dr. Santangelo."

"You're a lucky man, Tim."

Tim nodded.

"You're a lucky man because we believe in forgiveness here at the Santangelo Academy. We believe in love, and we love *you,* Tim. All of us in this room, unconditionally. No holds barred."

The good doctor glanced around the room again, waiting for everyone to nod.

Tim pulled a cuff down over one hand, used it to wipe the ropes of snot from his upper lip. "Thank you," he said. "That means a lot to me."

Santangelo spread his arms wide, palms toward the ceiling, then flickered his fingers at the crowd until someone started to clap. He stood there like some storefront preacher as the applause caught and spread around the room.

He brought his hands closer together, directed at Tim. "Come here, son," he said. "Something tells me you could use a hug."

Under cover of the still-burgeoning ovation, Lulu leaned down until her chin grazed my shoulder.

"Get me the fuck out of here," she whispered, "before I really *do* puke."

"We've got half an hour before first period," said Lulu. "Want some real coffee?"

"I would worship you forever," I replied.

The two of us set off for her apartment at a caffeine-hungry trot.

Teachers lived across the road in a defunct motor court. Its Laundromat-Colonial façade sported tissue-thin brick face and a tilted horse 'n' carriage weather vane.

Lulu scraped her front door inward across a mauled arc of shag carpet. Santangelo had bought the place complete with fixtures and furniture: The toilet ran constantly, and you could still see where they'd unbolted the coin-op Magic Fingers unit from her Formica-swathed headboard.

"There's hazelnut or vanilla-raspberry," she said.

"The Harlequin Romance Line of caffeinated beverages."

"Don't be a whiny-hiney," she said, shaking a finger at me.

I collapsed into a splayfooted Jetson-esque armchair. "Hazelnut, please."

Lulu skipped around behind the kitchenette's jutting counter to fill her Mr. Coffee carafe at the sink, then dumped three scoops of perfumed grounds into the fluted sheaf of a paper filter.

"That Santangelo," she said. "I just can't stand it."

I sighed agreement.

"I mean, *really*, Madeline. I just sat there watching that man, thinking I could be back at the front desk of the Econo Lodge, joking around with decent people."

She reassembled Mr. Coffee and set him brewing.

"Makes me miss the old commercials for these things," she said.

She patted the top of the unit, then startled me by singing, " 'Where have you gone, Joe DiMaggio?' " in her clear, heartstring-plucking soprano. The notes lingered, sweetening the room.

"Don't stop," I said.

" 'Joltin' Joe has left and gone away.' " Spoken, not sung.

" 'Hey hey hey,' " I answered, disappointed.

"Maybe we should follow suit," she said, spanking her hands together. "I could load my car right now and be at Mother's farmhouse in half a day. Get back my old job at the Econo Lodge. They *liked* me there. I liked *them*."

"You'd have to leave the kids," I said. "Abandon them to the predations of Mindy and Santangelo."

"And Tim, that abject pitiful worm."

She started rubbing her knuckles across her hair in frustration. "Please give me a goddamn cigarette."

I did.

"Those tiny little minds, Madeline. Colorless, narrow, and utterly lacking in joy." Lulu started to pace, trailing Bette Davis wreaths of smoke. Fuming, literally. "I am not willing to admit defeat. Someone has to stand up for *joy.*"

"You do," I said. "You are."

The room had begun to smell like hot, sweet air freshener. When the drizzle of coffee slowed, she pulled flowered mugs from a high cupboard.

"That first week we were here," I said, "when they were breaking us in —"

"All those *meetings!*"

Lulu handed over my mug, and I consumed a candied swallow.

"I had hope for Santangelo," I said. "He seemed to have a spark. He said some intriguing things."

"We both wanted to believe him. Believe *in* him."

I savored another drag of Camel, another sip of coffee.

During one of those early meetings, Santangelo had explained why he'd banned both vices on campus. "We used to let the kids smoke," he'd said, "if they were of age and had their parents' permission. Not in their dorm rooms, just in a couple of designated areas outdoors."

It had been hot that day. Late summer.

He walked along a row of French doors in the Mansion's library, all of them open to let in any longed-for afternoon breeze.

"The thing is," he said, "whenever these kids run away, they go looking for a means of defiance — first thing, every time. A lot of them are here because they'd become addicts. Kid hits the road, right away he'll go score."

Santangelo paused to lean back against a column between doors. "We lost a boy who'd been with us for three months — took off and hitchhiked home to Boston. Six hours after he left campus, he OD'd on heroin. The police found him dead in a park."

We were all leaning forward, perched on the edge of our chairs and sofas.

He crossed his arms, pausing to gaze deep into the eyes of one person after another, around the room. "Another boy broke into an old shed in Stockbridge. His thing was huffing, anything with fumes enough to get him off and dull the pain he was in. He found a quart of paint thinner and some rags — sucked down the vapors until he passed out, holding a lit cigarette. The shed caught fire, but they got him out in time."

Santangelo turned to look out over the broad expanse of lawn. Everything shimmered in the summer heat.

"The thing is," he said, "what we're asking these kids to do, the kind of work this place is about — well, it's damn hard. We force them to confront the most painful experiences they've ever had: molestation, beatings, rape . . . instances of cruelty that will break your heart and spirit, just hearing about them after the fact."

Old hands around the room nodded at this.

"It's no wonder the kids want to run away," he continued, "when we're pushing them to feel the impact of those horrors honestly. The damage . . ."

He shook his head sadly, then turned to face us again. "I can tell when a kid is ready to bolt. It's always when our work here first starts to become truly meaningful. They want to shut down, to escape from having to relive the worst of it, and from having to see *themselves* honestly, without the comforting filter of denial."

Santangelo started sauntering along the row of windows again, backlit, with his hands clasped at the small of his back. "Perfectly natural response. One we in fact expect, even strive for. We just don't want to lose the child in the process of trying to save him."

Someone coughed behind me.

"I realized," Santangelo continued, "that the best way to protect them was to set the boundaries close — give them avenues for rebellion that could satisfy their appetite for defiance but wouldn't kill them."

Tim raised his hand. "Can you tell us what those were?"

"Caffeine and nicotine," said Santangelo. "I made those the forbidden fruit. Kid hits the road now, I guarantee you his first impulse won't be to score smack. He'll feel compelled to get his hands on a pack of smokes and a black coffee."

Tim smiled. I wondered whether the female students rated a mention.

"Works like a charm," said Santangelo. "Half the time these days, they don't even make it to the Mass Pike. We'll get a call from the night cashier at some gas station mini-mart. Kid will still be standing outside when the school van pulls up — big Styrofoam cup of bad joe in one hand, Marlboro in the other."

Tim waved his hand again. "So you ask *us* to give up coffee and everything for, like, solidarity?"

Santangelo nodded. "You have to be doing the same kind of work on yourself as the kids are. If you don't have as much at stake as they do, you can't ask for their respect, and we can't help them."

Tim beamed in response to that. "That's so true, Dr. Santangelo."

Santangelo beamed right back.

Even then, captivated as I was by the man's charisma, I figured there was more to it.

For one thing, I'd caught a back-window glimpse of the honking big brass-and-copper espresso machine that glittered at the center of the man's kitchen counter.

And as the semester progressed, I began to suspect that the thousands of petty rules he expected his employees to comply with — not to mention the fear and exhaustion that doing so engendered — were designed to keep us off balance, to break us down. Like, say, boot camp in the Marine Corps, or not being allowed to go to the bathroom during EST seminars back in the day.

He wanted us on edge. Vulnerable. Hankering for a cool chalice sip of Flavor Aid after he'd run us ragged on the Long March.

Good for the program.

Good for the disease.

Good, most of all, for Santangelo.

Lulu barged into my musings. "Want a refill?"

"Bet your sweet ass," I said, lighting myself another Camel before I tossed her the pack.

If nothing else, this place had gotten me well in touch with my inner sixteen-year-old boy.

He was pissed.

9

By the time lunch rolled around, I was actually hungry. I loaded my plate with salad and a hunk of lasagna, joining the other teachers at a corner table.

Lulu patted the empty chair next to her, then resumed her conversation with Pete.

I'd barely peeled off the top layer of dessicated pasta when Santangelo rose from his seat across the room.

The sight of him extinguished conversation table by table. He cleared his throat, and the last voice winked out midsentence.

"Today," he said, "I want to discuss something of vital importance to all of us as a community. Something that should stand as an emblem of our concern for one another — our mutual respect, our common courtesy."

His gaze roved across the room, pausing to narrow in on random offenders. "We all — every one of us — need to become more *aware* of the salad bar."

He rocked back on his heels, looking up as though petitioning the heavens for the strength to continue. "The level of *disrespect* . . . croutons in the Thousand Island . . . carrot shreds mixed with the chickpeas *and* the olives . . ."

Below the table, Lulu began to saw the blade of a butter knife slowly back and forth across her wrist.

"We cannot continue to operate in this state of confusion," Santangelo declaimed, shaking an indignant finger, "this passive-aggressive inattention to our surroundings."

"He is *so* right," said Mindy.

She maneuvered a wedge of fish stick into her prim mouth, then chewed while nodding and blinking in reverence.

"If we are to *survive* as a community," said Santangelo, "we cannot continue to indulge ourselves in such appalling displays of arrogance."

He looked around the room again. "I'd like you all to join me in a moment of reflection."

He walked over to the source of his consternation and laid a loving hand on the hazed Plexiglas of its sneeze guard, then bowed his head. So did the band of administrators and staff at his table.

Mindy closed her eyes and followed suit, still chewing.

Lulu made a sly choking noise. I leaned my shoulder against hers. If we laughed, we were dead meat. She pressed the knife's blunt tip into her thigh. I bit the inside of my cheek.

New Guy Pete looked over at me and raised an eyebrow. I wasn't sure if that was intended to convey commiseration or judgment.

Santangelo raised his head. "Thank you," he said. "I know you'll all take this conversation to heart, because each of you values the integrity of our community as deeply as I do."

The room stayed quiet while he walked back to his seat, then everyone slowly resumed the business of eating lunch.

Tim asked Pete if he could please pass the salt. Mindy turned to Gerald and picked up where she'd left off about lesson plans.

Lulu and I exhaled.

The lasagna sucked, but I wasn't about to go get more salad.

I sank into the middle of Sookie's love seat two minutes early, relishing my rare sole possession of the thing.

"Hi," I said. "How's your day going?"

95

It had gone gloomy outside, afternoon sky piled thick with gray-blue Brillo clouds.

Sookie turned on her desk lamp, then pulled up a chair within hand-holding distance. "Have you given more thought to what we discussed in our last session?"

"Things have been frenetic," I said. "You heard about Mooney punching out the window?"

She gave me a disappointed smile. "And you didn't feel your own issues merited consideration?"

"No offense, Sookie," I said, "but having failed to recognize the slightest connection between myself and the issues you ascribed to me, I didn't feel they had merit *to* consider."

"Then why are you here?"

"I wasn't aware I had any choice."

The radiator clanked on, sending up a yeasty and slightly burnt perfume, like cafeteria toast.

"Look," I said, "I have no idea what this is supposed to accomplish."

"This session?"

"This session. Therapy in general. I mean, do you really expect me to have some big epiphany about repressed memories of sexual abuse in the next hour?"

"I think it's worth pursuing," she said.

"Why, exactly?"

"Your resistance," she said.

"See, here's what I don't get about this whole process — how does my saying your hypothesis is bullshit deepen your conviction that it's valid?"

"That hostility tells me this idea resonates with you in a profound way. We resist what we can't face."

"So the only way you'd believe I wasn't molested is if I agreed that I *had* been?"

She cleared her throat and started fussing with her skirt, smoothing it out over her crossed knees.

"I mean, Sookie," I said, "why not throw me in a pond to see if I float like a witch?"

"If you're embarrassed to discuss your sexuality —"

"God, no," I said. "I'd be happy to regale you with anecdotes about my misspent youth. *That* might actually be interesting."

"So you were promiscuous?" She perked right up. "Another classic hallmark of childhood molestation."

"Sookie, give this shit a rest, okay?"

"I don't bring it up lightly."

"You brought it up because of my *posture*, for chrissake," I said. "What next, you'll analyze the color of my aura?"

"You meet all the criteria," she said.

"Discomfort with intimacy, aversion to physical contact —"

"Wait, I'm promiscuous *and* I can't stand physical contact?"

Sookie glared. "You dislike being touched whenever someone offers you a gesture of comfort during our sessions."

"Want me to sit in Mindy's lap and lick her forehead?"

She ignored that. "Then there's your insomnia, the perfectionism, the distrust of authority figures —"

"Figures such as yourself?"

"Not limited to me," she said. "Your attitude hasn't gone unnoticed by the administration."

"So the hallmark of an *un*molested childhood is blind faith in authority? I hate to break it to you, Sookie, but that's not mental health, that's Stalinism."

"Once again, I see I've struck a nerve."

"Struck a nerve? You're trying to convince me I'm non compos mentis because I have the gall to insist that my life experience differs from your cheesy movie-of-the-week presumptions about it."

"You'd characterize childhood sexual abuse as cheesy?"

"Don't be an idiot."

"So now I'm Stalin *and* an idiot." The

98

woman was actually pouting.

"Oh, for God's sake," I said.

She was plucking at her skirt again, avoiding my eyes.

"I don't deny having major gnarly fissures in my psyche, okay?" I said. "But you're trying to shoehorn me into some completely bogus *DSM-III* template, here."

She sniffled, and I wondered if I'd have to do a turn-in for making my therapist cry.

"Sookie?" I put my hand on her knee. "I'm sure you mean really well with all of this, and if it were true, you'd be doing a bang-up job and everything, you know? It's just that Lolita has left the building."

She stared into her lap, eyes all glittery with gathering moisture.

"Look," I said, trying to coax a smile out of her, "would it cheer you up if I swam out to the middle of a pond and sank, as proof of my good intentions?"

Her head snapped up. "Why are you so *hostile,* Madeline? What's behind your pathological need to belittle everyone you come in contact with?"

I yanked my hand back.

"This is a healing, supportive community," she went on, "and all you can do is snipe at us. Maybe I'm off base, concluding you were molested, but I just want to figure

99

out what kind of trauma could have produced someone so hell-bent on slapping away the hand of anyone offering the slightest kindness."

I crossed my arms. "This is kindness?"

She nodded. "Absolutely."

"And you've never questioned anything done here in the name of therapy?"

She flinched away from me, dropping her eyes again.

I leaned toward her. "Explain how dorm parents making a kid kneel on a stone floor until three a.m. is kindness, Sookie."

"I'm sure Dr. Santangelo would never countenance such a —"

"Dr. Santangelo spent half this morning's faculty meeting screaming at Tim because Tim had objected to it. The man was spewing all this corrosive shit about how the kids should shove poor Tim's head through a blackboard because he'd had the gall to speak up."

"That's not —"

"Not *what,* Sookie?" I asked. "Not 'healing and supportive'?"

She blanched.

"You're forgetting what I tried to discuss yesterday," I said. "How I'm terrified that I'm not doing my best to help these kids.

100

That wasn't worthy of your consideration, was it?"

"Madeline, you have to know that I'd never —"

"I watched a kid practically bleed to death when he punched his hand through a window yesterday. I watched his girlfriend eat a hunk of his flesh off the glass after they took him away in the ambulance."

Sookie winced.

"And all Santangelo can do is scream at a concerned teacher when some other boy gets tormented until dawn by his dorm parents?"

She didn't answer.

"You wonder why I'm hostile?" I said. "Get a kumba-fucking-ya *clue,* lady."

I stood up and walked over to the window.

"Goddamn joke to call this place a 'healing community,' " I said, taking in the sorry-ass view of campus. "Kids would stand a better chance if you guys broke out some leeches and gave them all a good bleeding."

Okay, so now she *was* crying.

I sighed and turned around.

Sookie tried to choke back a sob.

"Have some Kleenex," I said, grabbing a box off her desk and putting it in her lap.

She yanked out a half dozen sheets and blew her nose, then balled them up and made a wussy pitch at the wastepaper basket. It landed two feet short.

I leaned down to pick the wad off the carpet and tossed it home.

"I'm sorry," she said.

"So you throw like a girl." I shrugged. "There are worse things."

"No," she said, "I mean —"

Her hands fluttered, and she got all choked up again.

"I went back to school for this," she said. "I worked my ass off to get a degree because I want to *help* people . . . the kids . . ."

"What'd you do before?"

"Wall Street."

Perfect, my very own shrink-broker.

All the same, I felt shitty for making her cry.

"Look," I said, "you want to do therapy, let's do some goddamn *real* therapy."

She nodded, taking a shaky breath.

I sat on the love seat and took a shaky breath of my own.

"Last year," I said, "someone I cared about a great deal tried to kill me."

"My God, Madeline! How did you cope with that?"

"I shot him."

She reached for my hand. I let her take it.

"Are you worried he'll come after you

again?" she asked.

"No," I said.

"You're sure?" she asked. "Depending on his pattern of behavior —"

"I emptied both barrels of a shotgun into the man's neck from so close it practically took his head off."

She didn't say a word in response to that, just held my gaze and reached for my other hand. The two of us were so quiet I could hear the rumble of a man's voice from behind some closed door down the hall, then the hesitant clatter of a hunt-and-peck typist.

"Someone you cared about," she said at last.

I closed my eyes.

"A great deal," she said.

"Yeah." Such a tiny word, with so very much freight behind it.

I pulled both hands free of hers. Covered my face.

"Madeline, I have no doubt you did the only thing you could have in that devastating situation."

I opened my eyes. Drew my knees up to my chest and wrapped my arms around them.

Sookie was tearing up again. "I'm proud of you. You chose to survive."

"The hard part," I said, "is learning to live with that decision."

"You've taken the first step, telling me about it."

Not first step. More like last resort.

The warning bell rang for the day's final class. I stood up.

"Will you come back to see me on Monday?" she asked. "I'd like to hear more."

"Glutton for punishment," I said. "Same bat time?"

"Same bat channel."

10

The Brillo sky was spitting down cold rain, so I sprinted out of the Mansion with my jacket pulled over my head.

Sitzman and Wiesner were already in the classroom by the time I skidded down the hallway. It was just the three of us for the day, what with Mooney and Forchetti being down on the Farm.

We got through a good bit of the late forties and early fifties, polished off the Korean War (with a fast-forward to Eisenhower's Military-Industrial Complex speech in '61), even worked in a bit of McCarthy intro before the bell rang.

I was expecting the pair of them to bolt on the dot of three o'clock, but they didn't budge. Maybe it was the rain.

"Are you going to make us talk more about this Red Scare shit on Monday?" asked Wiesner.

I tilted my chair back. "What kind of shit

would you prefer?"

"I don't know," he said. "Something that doesn't revolve around, like, totally boring dead guys."

"It's a history class, Wiesner," I said. "History tends to revolve around totally boring dead guys."

"Maybe you could skip the boring part just for a day? There must be a couple of interesting dead guys."

"Pick one," I said. "Doesn't have to be a guy."

"Oh yeah, like dead *chicks* are interesting," said Wiesner. "Betsy goddamn Ross. Give me a break."

"Amelia Earhart," said Sitzman. "She was cool."

"Bitch might still be alive if she wasn't such a sucky pilot," said Wiesner.

Sitzman laughed. "She was not sucky, Wiesner — she had a drunk navigator."

"Yeah, *and?*" Wiesner threw up his hands. "You want to impress me, Sitzman, try landing your plane someplace that's not the middle of the Pacific Ocean. I mean, Amelia couldn't have just said, 'Yo, navigation dude, I know you're all drunk and shit, but that's totally *water* down there . . . drop the tequila and find us a damn island already'?"

"She still kicks major Betsy Ross ass," said

Sitzman.

"Oh, like I actually picked Betsy Ross."

"So pick someone else already, Wiesner," I said.

Wiesner looked down at his desk. "Judy Garland."

"What're you, gay?" asked Sitzman.

"Suck my dick," said Wiesner. "She was really good in *The Wizard of Oz.* Especially if you do bong hits and watch it with Pink Floyd going."

Sitzman wasn't buying it. "What, like, 'Another Yellow Brick Road in the Wall'?"

"*Dark Side of the Moon,*" said Wiesner. "You start the CD right when the MGM lion roars the second time. Then all this stuff happens that matches the lyrics . . . like it goes to color at exactly the start of 'Money,' and then Glinda the Good Witch floats up in her bubble right when they say, 'Don't give me that do-goody-good bullshit.' "

"You have to start it at the end of the *third* roar, Wiesner," I said.

They turned to stare at me, slack-jawed.

"Oh, please," I said. "My *parents* did more bong hits than you guys."

"Huh," said Wiesner, "no wonder you've got such a shaky sense of boundaries."

"Make up your mind," I said. "Yesterday

you told me I had issues around authority."

"Six of one . . ."

"Whatever," I said.

"Who've you got for therapy?" asked Sitzman.

"Sookie," I said. "And I just made her cry."

"Big deal." Wiesner snorted. "Bitch is a total lightweight."

"She's your first shrink?" asked Sitzman.

"Fourth or something," I said, "since high school. Never had one burst into tears on me before."

"Progress," said Wiesner. "I made this chick at Lake Haven slap me once."

"He grabbed the poor woman's ass," Sitzman explained.

"Out of pity," said Wiesner.

"Pity?" said Sitzman. "She was a grad student. With an ear piercing shriek, I might add."

"But so damn ugly," said Wiesner. "I figured it would cheer her up, you know?"

Sitzman looked skeptical. "And what about that guy last year?"

I wondered if he meant Gerald.

"Which guy?" asked Wiesner.

"What's-his-face from Ireland," said Sitzman. "The one who quit halfway through his first session with you."

"Declan," said Wiesner. "The guy had serious issues."

"Dude, you lit him on *fire*."

"Wiesner," I said, "you torched a shrink?"

"Accidentally," he said.

"Um, yeah," said Sitzman, "except for the part where you chased him down the hall, flicking that lighter and yelling, 'Freebird.' "

"At which time I seem to remember *you* standing in a doorway behind us," Wiesner shot back, "laughing your ass off."

Sitzman raised both hands in concession. "Still," he said, "poor Declan just kept going, straight to the parking lot. We never saw him again."

"You guys didn't even try to put out the fire?"

"It's not like he was consumed in flames or anything," said Wiesner. "I, like, barely singed his sleeve."

"Accidentally," I said.

He dropped his head to beam me a picture-of-innocence look through those thick lashes, guilty grin making his dimples crease.

I was unmoved. "You're a piece of work, Wiesner."

"And you made Sookie cry," he said. "How'd you manage that?"

"Nothing to do with lighters," I said. "The

rest of it stays between me and her. I'm not entirely boundary-free."

"No fair," he said. "I told *you.*"

"Not everything, though, right?"

Sitzman laughed, and Wiesner gave him a little punch to the shoulder. With affection, but still.

I was about to say they should cut the shit when they went quiet, heads swiveling toward the doorway.

Wiesner said, "Hi, Dr. Santangelo," just as I turned to see who it was.

The man was in his cape and a fresh Jefferson shirt, having added a beret to the ensemble. "Nice to see the two of you spending time with a teacher after class."

"Madeline's cool," said Wiesner. "She's even making me kind of enjoy history."

"We all appreciate the fine work she's doing," said Santangelo, giving me a nod. "You boys mind letting us have a moment alone?"

Wiesner and Sitzman booked out of the room so fast I could practically hear the whistle of backdraft.

Santangelo smiled and swung the door half-shut behind them.

Crappe diem.

11

Santangelo took off his beret and sat down on the corner of my desk.

"We haven't had any one-on-one conversations, Madeline," he said, "for which I apologize. I thought it was high time I checked in to see how everything's going."

"It's, uh . . ." I suddenly felt like there was a chunk of dust on my uvula.

I coughed, then sputtered, "Fine. Things are fine."

"I'm making you nervous," he said. "That's the trouble with running a school. I can't spend as much time with everyone as I'd like, so when I do show up — well, I can't blame you for being a little tense."

"So you're not here to discuss my lack of appreciation for the salad bar?"

He let out a bark of laughter and slapped the desk. "What a crock of shit, eh?"

"Sir?"

"Not a trick question," he said. "My

performance was *intended* as farce. Making a complete ass of myself seemed to be the order of the day."

"In that case, Dr. Santangelo, congratulations on a job well done."

"It served a purpose," he said. "You're familiar with the broken windows theory?"

"Fixing the small things," I said. "Attention to detail as a way to prevent larger-scale anarchy."

"Exactly," he said. "In this case, substitute the salad bar for windows. I launch into a goofy rant, and the kids know we're paying attention. They feel cared for. I'm willing to look like a buffoon for that."

Wiesner's pen lay next to my hand. I started rolling it back and forth across the desk.

"What about screaming at Tim this morning?" I asked. "Was that intended as farce?"

"You were shocked."

"I was. Yes."

"In fact, you thought I was a raging asshole."

I gave the pen another roll.

He laughed again. "That's the appropriate response."

I looked up at him.

"I was hoping to hell it was the one I'd get out of Tim," he said. "You honestly believe I'd condone what happened in that dorm last night?"

"You seemed to," I said. "I mean, threatening to shove his head through the blackboard, all that."

"Tim should've challenged the other dorm parents. He should've challenged *me.* Instead, he caved. That's goddamn dangerous."

"I admit to some remaining skepticism," I said, "as to your methodology."

"Tim is terrified of his own passion," said Santangelo. "I wanted to push him until he pushed back."

"Does he know that? Poor guy's probably in the dining hall right now, waving incense over the damn chickpeas."

Santangelo winked at me. "Might be the best use for him."

He crossed his chubby forearms and leaned forward. "Let me tell you something. When I looked around that meeting this morning, I was appalled. There were only two people in the room who didn't suck down my line of shit and applaud it."

"And I was one of them."

"Yes, you were one of them," he said. "Your friend Lulu was the other."

"Did that come as a surprise?"

"No," he said. "Especially considering

how the two of you responded to the situation with Mooney and Fay. You think Tim would've handled that as well as you two did?"

I didn't say anything, but my answer had to be pretty obvious. Tim would've puked and fainted. Not necessarily in that order.

"I'm not after setting up a cult of personality," said Santangelo. "This school can't succeed if it's staffed with Tims."

"Okay," I said.

"If we're going to make a difference for these kids, we've *got* to have people here with personality of their own. Not to mention courage."

He made a fist and tapped the table with it.

Once. Twice.

"Madeline," he said, "do you have any idea how rare those people are?"

"In my experience? Right up there with hen's teeth."

"I'm here in this room because we need all the hen's teeth we can get."

"I . . . um . . ."

"That's a compliment, Madeline."

"Okay," I said. "Thank you."

"Dhumavati and I talked about you earlier today, and I felt it was important to let you know how much we appreciate everything

114

you're doing here."

That sure didn't sound like Sookie's take on their opinion of me. I wondered who was lying.

Santangelo gave me a smile. "Obviously, the kids see the same qualities in you that we do. Your students this afternoon . . . Fay and Mooney yesterday . . ." He picked up his beret. "We'll be giving you a raise, and we may have some changes in staffing soon. I'd like you to consider taking on a little more responsibility. On a trial basis at first, but we could make your new position permanent."

"What kind of position did you have in mind?" I asked.

There was a tap at the door, and Dhumavati poked her head inside.

"Great timing," said Santangelo. "I was just telling Madeline what you and I discussed this morning."

"I'm not interrupting?" she asked.

"Of course not," he said. "Come on in."

Dhumavati walked to the desk and put a hand on my shoulder. "You did a wonderful job yesterday. We're very grateful."

Santangelo stood up. "I've explained that we're going to bump up her pay. Can you fill her in on the rest? I've got a dozen calls to make."

"My pleasure," she said.

Santangelo settled the beret on his head and left us to it.

"I have to run Mooney's homework down to the Farm," I said.

She smiled at me. "Why don't I walk you there? We can talk on the way."

I opened a desk drawer and took out two assignment sheets. "What's the date today?"

"November seventeenth," she said.

I jotted that down on each page — one for history, one for English — then didn't know what else to write.

"Is this the first time one of your kids has been sent to the Farm?" asked Dhumavati.

"Yeah," I said. I wrote: "Finish reading *I Know Why the Caged Bird Sings*," on the top sheet, then looked up page numbers for the next three history book chapters.

Whatever.

"Okay," I said. "I'm all set here, unless he needs textbooks."

"His dorm parents took care of that."

We started for the door.

"Usually, the kids pack up what they need by themselves," she said, "but we didn't want him to have to carry anything. They gave him fifteen stitches yesterday."

She held the door for me, and we walked across the lobby.

"Poor guy," I said. "Can someone help him with his notes and stuff?"

"I'm sure Fay will want to pitch in."

I shouldered my way through the outer door. "She's allowed to go down there?"

"You haven't heard?" she asked, following me outside.

"Heard what?"

"Fay got sent to the Farm this morning."

"For what happened last night?"

"No, not for that."

I felt my stomach clench, and worried that Fay had done a turn-in about her pregnancy, given Mooney's predicted outcome of any such confession.

Dhumavati sighed. "One of the kids found her in the dorm bathroom this morning, cutting herself."

I stopped walking and looked at her. "Is she all right?"

"It wasn't severe. Just ritualistic. Some of the girls do it. It's rarer with boys."

"Ritualistic?"

"It's considered an effort to communicate distress that they're unable to voice," she said. "I've been told it's soothing when the girl is overwhelmed by a mood state she can't cope with. Pain lowers the level of arousal almost immediately — makes it tolerable. It can become addictive."

117

"She's done it before?"

"For a long time." Dhumavati touched my back and got us walking again. "Not within the last year, however. She's made remarkable progress here. I'm deeply concerned that it's started up again."

"Understandably," I said.

"Did she say anything to you last night that might indicate what's behind it?"

I struggled with how to answer that. I wanted to believe that these people actually had the kids' best interests at heart, but Santangelo's freak-outs du jour still didn't sit right with me, despite his effort at schmoozing. The idea of a raise made me even more uptight about it.

"She was . . . upset," I said. "I don't know the specifics beyond that."

"She seems to feel comfortable with you," said Dhumavati. "I'd like you to talk with her, if you're willing."

"Of course."

"And if anything were to come up?"

"You'd be the first to know," I said.

The rain clouds were scudding away. In the stronger light, Dhumavati looked pale and tired, ten years older than she had the previous day.

She misjudged the height of a curb, catching her toe. She stumbled slightly and grabbed my arm to steady herself.

I braced her for a second until she got her balance back. "Are you all right?"

"I'll be fine," she said.

"You look exhausted."

"I had trouble sleeping last night. I'm concerned about Mooney and Fay. Fay especially."

"She seems so fragile," I said.

We were walking on grass now, a shortcut to the path that would take us into the woods and down toward the Farm.

"She's survived a great deal," said Dhumavati. "Horrible family life."

"Mooney hinted at that," I said. "He's very protective of her."

"Fay brings that out in people, I've found."

"Yes," I said.

"I found her very compelling from the moment she came to us. She has great depths of compassion, especially for a child who's been through such trauma. I think she's tremendously brave."

We reached the trees and soon hit a rough patch of trail.

"You're limping," I said. "Lean on me, if you'd like."

"I'm fine."

"Really, it's no trouble."

Dhumavati smiled at me and put her arm across my shoulders. "Fay reminds me of my daughter. Similar-looking, but really, it's that sweetness."

We walked on in silence, her weight shifting onto me slightly whenever she took a step on the tender ankle. We came to a break in the trees, the Farm below us, alongside the large vegetable garden the kids were put to work in while they were doing time in the low-slung building.

"Where is she now, your daughter?" I asked. "Don't tell me you have a kid in college. I can't believe you're old enough." That was a lie — she looked ancient in the slant of light filtering through the surrounding trees. I just wanted to cheer her up.

A brief grimace of pain crossed her face. "I'm sure she would have been. Allegra died when she was eight years old."

"Oh, Dhumavati," I said.

"That was the hard time I told you about when we first met."

"I'm so sorry."

She slowed as we approached the garden's white fence — nothing much inside this time of year. Pumpkins. Spent stalks of corn that had faded from green to gold with the season.

"Allegra loved to be around growing

things," said Dhumavati. "Gardens. This one was my idea. In her memory."

The hand-painted rectangle nailed to the gate read: GREETINGS. EVERYTHING GROWS WELL IN THIS PLACE, ESPECIALLY THE CHILDREN.

"Did you make that sign?" I asked.

Dhumavati nodded. She'd painted a colorful border of flowers and butterflies around the words.

"Lovely," I said. "And that saying seems so familiar."

"Not original to me," she said, "by any means. But I was always fond of the sentiment."

"You do a lot to make it true around here."

We'd drawn abreast of an old wooden bench set in a ring of white stones just off the path.

Dhumavati eased herself down on it. "Would you mind if we rested up for a bit here? I'd like to catch my breath before we head in." I sat next to her. "You look tired yourself, Madeline," she said.

"Not a lot of sleep lately. And today was a little intense."

"David's thing this morning?"

David. Dr. Santangelo.

"Partly that," I said. "Partly some stuff I brought up with Sookie after lunch."

121

"And last night's drama with Mooney and Fay."

"Sure," I said. "That too."

"This is a very hard place to be. Especially for people like the two of us, who care so very much about the kids."

The two of us but not Santangelo?

She sighed. "I knew it wouldn't be any easier for you than it is for me. I recognized that about you when we did your interview for this job."

"I think I'm flailing most of the time."

"You're there for these kids in a way few people have the courage to be."

I crossed my arms. "They matter to me."

"Yes."

"I'm not always sure how it all —"

"You mean David?" she asked.

I didn't answer.

"He and I don't always walk in lockstep," she said. "But I've found over the years that I can trust him. He's tremendously committed, and he's got an astonishing depth of insight even when his methods seem counterproductive. I hope you'll be with us long enough to know the truth of that for yourself."

"You're worried I'm going to leave?"

"I've seen dozens of teachers come and go. I know the signs. This is grueling work,

122

in every sense of the word. And I'll tell you, in confidence, that many of the people who stay here the longest are the ones least suited to the job."

I snapped my head toward her.

She laughed. "We aren't stupid."

"*You're* not," I said.

"I have seen miracles happen here," she said. "And I want you to know that I believe you can be part of that, even become one yourself."

"I'm honored."

"I know you'd probably like nothing better than to go home tonight and never see this place again."

True enough.

"I want you to try toughing it out," she said. "We need you. And I think you need us."

"I'd like to believe that."

Kind of.

She looked away from me, out toward the garden. "David told you we're considering changes around staffing?"

"Nothing specific."

"I may be taking time off after the winter break." She turned back to me. "David thinks you're the best candidate to fill in while I'm gone. We both do."

"Dhumavati, you've got to be freaking kidding —"

She held up a hand to cut me off. "I want you to think about it."

"I don't *have* to think about it. That's the most harebrained idea I've ever heard. I can't even remember to bring pens to my classes. There's no goddamn way I could handle your job."

"My job doesn't require perfection," she said.

"Dhumavati —"

"It requires compassion. That's why David wants you." She got to her feet, wincing a little.

There was a small bronze plaque screwed to the back of the bench, right where she'd been sitting. BELOVED ALLEGRA, it read, APRIL 3, 1970–NOVEMBER 18, 1978.

And I'd just written November 17 on Mooney's homework sheets.

Dhumavati kissed her fingertips, then pressed them against the raised letters of her daughter's name.

I took her hand. "Tomorrow?"

"The eleventh anniversary," she said. "Yes."

"And Santangelo picked today to discuss replacing you?"

"Madeline," she said, "*I* picked today to tell him I need replacing."

Something in her voice made me doubt that. I pointed at the plaque. "And does he realize?"

"David had this bench made for me."

I wasn't sure the gesture could be considered evidence of kindness.

"I'm exhausted," she said. "I want a couple of months to myself. Three at the most. David has a house in Mexico — San Miguel de Allende. If you'll cover for me, he's willing to let me go down there. You'd only have to take the reins temporarily."

I wondered if she'd overheard him mention the possibility of making my reassignment permanent.

"You'd be doing me a tremendous favor," she said. "Promise me you'll think about it?"

"I think it's a mistake."

"It's not," she said, turning to limp toward the front door of the Farm.

12

They had a woodstove cranked up inside, flames jumping red-orange behind the isinglass in its doors. The air was roasted so dry that breathing made my septum ache.

The kids were expected to chop all necessary wood. No furnace in this place.

Pete took Mooney's assignment sheets from me, adding them to a pile on a long table at the center of the room. Beside that were two clipboards and a dented cardboard carton filled with Walkmans, each tagged with the name of the kid who owned it.

I asked Dhumavati what they were for.

"The kids can listen to music for study period if they've finished their quota of chores. David decided there had to be some tangible reward at the end of the day, something to anticipate."

Pete picked up a clipboard and started reading off names. One by one, the kids took homework sheets off the pile, then lined up single file by a door at the back of the room. No one spoke.

"Textbooks are kept on their bunks during the day," Dhumavati explained. "Could you help Mooney carry his?"

I got in line behind him. Pete opened the door to the bunkroom hallway. We shuffled past him, silent.

There was a girls' room and a boys' room, both doorless, as were the pair of singles for overnight supervisors. The air was cold away from the stove, with a sharp edge of mildew.

I followed Mooney into the boys' room. The bunks were triples, made up quarter-bounce tight with army blankets and coarse sheets. He'd rated a bottom-tier bed because of the stitches.

I reached for the pile of books at its foot, whispering, "You guys warm enough at night? Those blankets look pretty damn thin."

"This time of year," he whispered back, "you gotta bring a hat."

He lifted the pillow to show me a knitted watch cap. "Can you give this to Fay? I don't know if she remembered."

I snatched it up and hid it between two textbooks.

Back in the main room, the kids dropped their piles to claim scattered armchairs and sofas, then lined up at the table.

Dhumavati read a list of names off the second clipboard, and Pete distributed Walkman swag to every kid but Fay and Mooney.

"Two hours," said Dhumavati. "Let's all do a good job and keep it quiet."

She followed Pete into the kitchen, pausing beside its swinging door to hang the clipboards on their respective hooks.

I was still holding Mooney's stuff, so I lowered it onto the table.

"Sorry to make you miss out on the comfy spots," I said.

He shrugged, watching Fay pull out a straight-backed chair. She didn't look up at him, just placed her books on the wooden seat, dragging the load away from us toward a windowed corner across the room.

Mooney moved around to the other side of the table so he could keep an eye on her.

Fay pushed her books off the chair, then turned it so her knees shoved into the corner when she sat down. She slumped over toward the window, her cheekbone and temple coming to rest against its glass.

"Why's Fay over there?" I asked. "Did you guys have a fight?"

Mooney shook his head. "She's cornered."

"Explain 'cornered.' "

He picked at the mitt of gauze enveloping his injured hand. "Unless she's doing chores, she has to sit in a corner with her back to everyone."

I could hear the tinny whine of the other kids' music, the crackle of the woodstove, Dhumavati and Pete murmuring in the kitchen. Against all that, Fay started humming a tuneless riff, soft and throaty, like Astrud Gilberto.

No-Hope Samba.

"Us kids aren't allowed to talk to her," Mooney said. "That's why I want you to give her my hat."

"Does she have to eat there?" I asked.

"Everything. From now until lights-out."

"What if she needs to go to the bathroom?"

"She'll raise her hand, wait for a teacher."

I straightened his pile of textbooks. "It's too much. She's already on the Farm."

"They don't do both at the same time a lot. Santangelo got all freaked out when he found out she was cutting again."

I shook my head. "Even so."

"They should have made her be handheld."

"What the hell is that?"

"Someone holds your hand all day. Comes to classes with you and stuff."

I didn't want to ask him again about the toileting logistics. "Another kid?"

"Yeah," he said. "They wouldn't've picked me, but it's still better. At least you can talk."

"They ever do that to you?"

"A bunch of times," he said. "I actually think it helps, you know? You can't just wallow in your own shit. It makes you want to not be a total suckbag, for the person who's gotta hang on to you."

"I guess I can see that."

"It's kind of comforting once you get used to it," he said. "That's what they should've done for Fay. Not cornering."

"How long will it last?"

"If she does all her work, they'll probably let her stop over the weekend."

"How about your work?" I said. "You could finish reading *I Know Why the Caged Bird Sings.*"

He didn't answer.

"Want me to crack the spine," I asked, "so it stays open?"

My question skittered across his attention, weightless as a flat stone whipped sidearm along the surface of a pond.

I slipped the novel free. He didn't take his eyes off Fay.

She was swaying a little now, one shoulder

rocking slowly forward and back along a slender arc, keeping time as she continued to hum.

"It's my fault," said Mooney.

"Mooney," I said, "you can't take it all on yourself."

He checked the room to make sure no one was listening to us. "*I* got her pregnant. She'd be okay if it wasn't for that."

"How did it happen?"

He looked away, shifting in his seat.

"Madeline," he said, "if you don't know, I'm not sure I should be the one to explain it to you."

"No. I mean, did a condom break or something?"

"Right," he said, "like we're allowed to have condoms."

Of course they weren't. And the kids had no access to a drugstore unless they ran away.

Add another item to Santangelo's "first things kids want to score on the road" list: coffee, Marlboros, pack of Trojans.

"I just —" He paused, picking at the corner of his math book. "I pulled out. I guess it wasn't soon enough."

"Mooney, pulling out doesn't *work*," I whispered. "There is no 'soon enough.' Didn't they teach you that in sex ed?"

131

He didn't say anything.

Of course they didn't teach him that in sex ed, Madeline, because there wasn't any sex ed at the hospitals they'd both been in before this place, and there sure as shit wasn't any here.

"Fay keeps saying it's her fault," he said. "How can I make her understand that it's mine?"

"First of all, you guys have to stop thinking of it as *fault,*" I said. "I mean, we're all programmed to reproduce, you know? The decks are stacked in that direction. Believe me, I've done some really stupid shit —"

"I don't just mean that," he said. "It's everything else, too. Like how I freaked out and punched the window . . . I scared her. Fay only cuts herself when she's scared."

He poked at the math book again. "If I'd been able to keep it together, she wouldn't have done that. And we wouldn't be down here."

"You guys love each other, Mooney. You're both scared."

"You know they upped her meds after this morning? Tranqued her until it's like she's not even in her body anymore."

"Jesus," I said.

"I just hope they let her celebrate her

birthday. She needs something good to happen."

"Will they do that on the Farm?"

"Usually, you get a cake when you turn eighteen. Probably so they can sucker you into staying."

"I'll talk to Dhumavati about it," I said. "I promise."

"Listen, can you give her my hat before those two come back out of the kitchen? I don't want to get busted."

"If you start your homework, okay? Let's get you out of this place as soon as possible."

He took the paperback from me after I bent its spine wide at the page he'd dog-eared last.

I grabbed his hat and stood up.

"Tell her everything will be okay," he said. "Tell her she has to remember I love her to pieces. That's what the necklace is for."

I told her.

Fay didn't open her eyes, didn't stop humming — just raised her right hand to touch the silver moon at her throat.

The motion made her shirt cuff slip, revealing a glimpse of the tape-anchored white gauze around her wrist. She pinched the sleeve's fabric and twitched it back up an inch, exactly enough to cover the bandage.

A practiced gesture. She didn't even have to lift her cheek from the window to look.

There was no dressing on her left wrist. I wondered if Dhumavati's interpretation took into account the fact that Fay had damaged herself on the same side that Mooney had.

I stayed crouched beside her, watching her breath fog the glass. "Anything you want me to tell Mooney?"

She pressed her fingertip against a point of the crescent charm. "Tell him I'll never take this off."

I did, and Mooney looked so happy I thought he was going to cry.

"You'll get through this," I said. "Both of you."

He squirmed again, tensing his jaw to tamp down the advent of tears.

"First I have to get through tomorrow morning," he said. "I can't chop wood so they've got me on rat duty."

"Rat duty?"

"Tons of them in this place, gnawing on the walls all night."

"Nasty," I said.

"I have to help spread poison around at lights-out. Then I get to wake up early and scrape up the suckers that ate it."

I looked at his bandage. "One-handed?"

"There's this scoop thing. Opens up when you step on it, then you kick the bodies in."

"Pretend they're Santangelo," I said.

"Or maybe Pete."

"Aw, come on, the guy seems pretty decent."

"Guess ol' Wiesner called it right, then."

"Called what right?"

"How Pete's got you all over weak and swoony for those blond curls," Mooney said.

"Wiesner's an idiot."

"Poor boy's jealous." Mooney popped a cheek with the tip of his tongue, grinning.

"Oh, *great.*"

"Still and all, you might wanna watch out for Goldilocks," he said. "Word is, him and Santangelo are all buddy-buddy — like from back in college and shit."

"No way they're the same age," I said. "College?"

The kitchen door started swinging outward.

Mooney snatched up *Caged Bird* before Dhumavati had so much as a toe across the threshold. He looked for all the world like he couldn't get enough of Maya Angelou's deathless prose.

I felt his knee nudge mine under the table.

"Might wanna watch out for Wiesner while you're at it," he sotto-voced.

Dhumavati was eyeing us, so I poked a finger at some random paragraph in his book.

"Who was Joe Louis?" I said, loud enough for her to hear. "A famous boxer. They called him the Brown Bomber."

"Just keep wearing those big sweaters," Mooney mumbled. "Wiesner'd get nasty with a dead goat if he found it alone in the showers."

Dhumavati looked at Pete. "What've we got for time?"

He checked his watch. "Ten after five already."

"Who's on night shift?" she asked.

"Gerald and Cammy. Guess they're running a little late."

She smiled at him. "Why don't you and Madeline go on ahead, start enjoying the weekend? I'll cover until they get here."

Mooney coughed into his bandaged hand as I stood up, and I could've sworn it sounded like "look out."

Dhumavati walked me and Pete to the front door and shooed us outside.

I let him go first, then paused in the doorway, turning back to her. "I hope tomorrow goes okay."

"Thank you," she said.

I remembered my promise to Mooney. "I

have a favor to ask."

"Fire away."

I dropped my voice. "It's Fay's birthday on Tuesday. I'm hoping we could bring her a cake?"

"Of course," she said. "You see? That's exactly the kind of compassion I've been talking about."

Pete and I started trudging back up toward campus.

"Long day," he said. "Lulu asked me over for coffee. Want to join us?"

"I've gotta get home, but tell her hey for me."

"I hear she's got a clandestine stash of caffeinated."

"High-test," I said, a little worried that she'd let him in on the secret, given Mooney's warning.

"Can't beat that with a stick." Pete rubbed his hands together, flashing me a grin of anticipation. "I'm sick of drinking David's crappy decaf."

"Aren't you fancy with the schmancy, calling him David already," I said. "How long have you been here, a week?"

"That's what he asked me to call him when he interviewed me."

"So how'd you end up at this place?" I asked.

"A friend told me about what David was doing here. He said this might be a good place for me at the moment. I figured it was worth a shot."

"Had you met Santangelo beforehand?"

"We all went to the same college. David graduated a few years before I showed up there."

"Only a few? How old *are* you?"

"Okay, maybe he graduated ten years before I got there," he said. "I don't really know. And I turned forty last September."

"You're fourteen years older than me?"

Pete smiled a little, vain about it. Still, it meant he and Santangelo hadn't been frat brothers or anything.

I was just starting to feel relieved when he added, "I think David's doing a remarkable job with these kids, you know? He's absolutely amazing."

"Oh yeah," I said, fighting to keep the sarcasm out of my voice. "I find myself *constantly* amazed."

"His whole thing this morning, calling that guy Tim on his shit? I thought David was just incredible, the way he handled that."

"Sure," I said. "Incredible."

"You and I need to work on Lulu, then. She's got a lot of doubts."

"Ya think?"

"I've been talking to David about it. He's hoping I can bring her around."

"You know," I said, "I really *could* use a cup of coffee."

"Did you bring your cigarettes?" he asked. "Lulu told me she always bums them from you, and I'm dying for a smoke."

I felt a little sick. "You gonna talk to David about that, too?"

He laughed. "Not if you share."

"You sure this guy's cool?" I asked Lulu after Pete had asked to use her bathroom.

She gave me impatience: crossed arms with a tapping foot. "Don't be an idiot, Madeline."

I tossed the Camels onto her countertop. "Get us busted. See if I care. But I will seriously hurt you if you tell him about Fay."

"For chrissake." Lulu rolled her eyes and handed me a mug of coffee.

"I'm not kidding," I said. "He's been chatting you up with Santangelo, promising to bring you into the fold."

"And I think we can keep him *out* of it," she said. "He's a decent guy. We can't let him end up bald in some airport with a fist-

139

ful of carnations."

"Why the hell not?"

"Madeline, you know you wouldn't wish that on a fucking dog."

"Depends on the fucking dog," I said. "He's one of *us.*"

"How do you know?"

"I just do," she said. "You have to trust me."

"But can I trust *him,* Lulu? We barely know this guy."

"Worst-case scenario, we've got dirt on him already. Coffee and smoking."

"Yeah, that's putting my mind at ease."

"When you find out what happened to him . . . why he ended up here . . ."

"I have to go home."

"Give me fifteen more minutes. You'll know I'm right."

"Come for dinner Sunday," I said. "Tell me then."

"I'll bring Pete."

"Why?"

"You are going to feel like such an asshole when you realize how wrong you are about him."

"Jesus," I said, "I hope so."

He came back out of the bathroom and shook a Camel from my pack.

"Madeline's gotta take off," said Lulu,

"but we're both invited to dinner at her house Sunday night."

"Sounds great," he said, holding a flame to his cigarette and squinting against the smoke. "What can we bring?"

A signed-in-blood loyalty oath?

"We've got it covered," I said. "How 'bout seven o'clock?"

And when you both wake up scalped at LaGuardia, don't come crying to me.

Dean greeted me with a hug and a cold beer back home. I clinked my bottle against his and drank off a third of it.

"Hard day, Bunny?"

"Complicated," I said. "How about you?"

He didn't answer that, just said, "You look exhausted."

"Pretty much."

"That place is going to suck you dry."

"Already has," I said.

He walked me toward the sofa, depositing my beer on the brown oval surface of our butler's-tray table. "Take off your coat and stay awhile."

"Listen," I said. "Something came up today about work."

"For me, too," he said, grinning.

"Good news?"

"That temp place called back. They have

a gig for me. I don't even have to piss in a cup."

"That is so *great!*" I said.

He shrugged. "It's just a few weeks — something with computers up at GE. Most of the place is shut down, but even so, they said it might lead to more work."

I jumped up to hug him. "I'm so damn happy for you."

He kissed the top of my head. "So what's your news?"

I pulled free of our clinch. "That will definitely require more beer."

"Please tell me you quit."

"Not exactly," I said.

"So what happened?"

"I think maybe you should sit down."

"Just tell me."

"Well, first off, I got a raise," I said.

He decided to sit down after all. "And?"

"And they want me to be dean of students after Christmas."

"Holy shit," he said. "I should've bought a keg."

■ ■ ■ ■

PART II

■ ■ ■ ■

Your life is in some bizarre state when priests are throwing abuse at you on the street.

— Ken Bruen
The Magdalen Martyrs

13

Late Sunday afternoon, Dean and I parked outside the Big Y.

"The Existential Grocery Store," he said. "What's for dinner?"

I grabbed a cart. "Bustelo and Nothingness."

"I could go for some Ham-Burger Hesse," he said, "but I'm a little tired of that Ramen de Beauvoir."

I bagged a couple of heads of butter lettuce and threw them into the cart's kiddie-seat basket. Right then this fat cockroach scuttled behind the Frito-Lay endcap.

"Kafka-Roni," he said, "the Sad-and-Dismal Treat . . ."

"Dude, seriously, I need to figure out what the hell we're cooking for Lulu and Pete."

"How about a little coq au vin? Maybe with couscous?"

"Perfect," I said, heading for the poultry section.

"On the way home, can you drop me at the Shop-n-Rob?"

"For what?" I asked.

"I'm out of rolling papers."

"Dean, they're showing up in twenty minutes."

"If you think we're too tight on time, I can run up there now and meet you back home."

"Grab me some smokes?"

"Dueling vices," he said, then took off.

Dean got to the apartment well after Lulu and Pete. She was sautéing bacon while I washed the chicken. Pete was in the living room perusing our pile of CDs.

"It's damn cold out there," said Dean, his cheeks offering chill-flushed proof.

I handed him a glass of wine. "Glad you could make it. What took you so long?"

"I had to make a second stop," he said. "The old lady at the first place got all pissy when I asked for Zig-Zags."

He dropped a Cumberland Farms bag on the counter and fished out my Camels.

"Thank you," I said. "Looks like you stocked up for winter."

"Well, when she went off on her 'we don't sell that filth' rant," he said, "I snapped back, 'So get me a box of condoms, *extra-*

large, *extra*-strong.' "

Pete guffawed from the living room, and Lulu said, "No way!"

Dean grinned, whipping out what had to be the world's biggest box of Trojans. "You should've seen her face. I thought she was going to keel over."

"And what are we going to do with all those?" I said, crowding pieces of chicken into Lulu's skillet. "Get hammered and throw water balloons at cars in the rotary?"

"Sounds like a blast," said Pete, cueing up some Vivaldi.

Lulu looked thoughtful. "Maybe we should bring them down to school, pass 'em out to the kids?"

"Yeah, that'd go over big with Santangelo," I said.

"What," said Dean, "he's got something against jimmy hats with a reservoir tip?"

Pete came into the kitchen doorway. "David thinks a commitment to abstinence is an important step for the kids to take."

"I'd be more comfortable with that if the kids had better information," I said. "It's high school, no matter what else. Not talking about sex doesn't mean it won't happen."

"There's no prohibition against talking about it," said Pete. "I think there's a great deal of openness on campus, compared to any other high school I'm familiar with."

"But there's no official provision to make sure they're equipped with a reasonable facsimile of the facts of life, either," I said. "Not so much as a basic health and hygiene class, much less sex ed, you know?"

"I have heard a lot of dumbass things about this Santangelo," said Dean, "but that's gotta be the dumbass-iest."

Pete shrugged, heading for the front-door coat hooks to grab more wine out of his knapsack.

"It's part of the school's overall philosophy," he said, holding up the bottle. "Are we up for some Valpolicella?"

"I still think that's just sheer idiocy," said Dean, handing him a corkscrew. "I mean, you want philosophy, you're better off watching the Stooges."

Pete tackled the cork. "I can see David's point. He's trying to foster self-respect, steer the kids away from masking pain with addictive behavior, from using sex as a means to act out —"

"Keep them from enjoying *anything*," said Dean. "It's still high school, no matter what else. I say you toss them a damn bone."

"So to speak," said Lulu, making us all

smile as she held out her glass to Pete for a refill.

"It's not Riverdale High down there," said Pete. "We aren't dealing with Archie and Betty and Veronica wondering what to wear to the prom. A lot of these kids are getting over heroin addiction or years spent shooting coke."

"So you guys are on the front lines with a bunch of randy teenagers who may have a history of IV drug use," countered Dean. "I'd think that's all the more reason they should have access to condoms."

I handed Dean the lettuce. "Can you wash this for the salad?"

He started ripping up leaves and tossing them into the spinner. "Seriously, Pete, these days? Standing on that kind of principle might mean you're giving some kid a death sentence."

"I know David struggles with that possibility," said Pete. "But it's a tough call either way. How do you keep kids safe without making them think you're condoning promiscuity?"

I started flipping the pieces of chicken, now nicely browned.

"He might try *talking* to them about it," I said, "instead of pretending it's not going on. The stuff I hear my students say in class?

They have no idea what's at stake. I swear to God, Jughead was better equipped to navigate this stuff. How can David countenance that? How can he not even trust them enough to provide some kind of sex education?"

Lulu caught my eye, and I knew we were both thinking about Fay and Mooney.

"He's a devout Catholic," said Pete. "So are a lot of the parents. This is what they want."

"And how about what the kids want?" I said. "How about giving *them* a say in their own destiny?"

"Madeline," Pete said, "they're underage."

Lulu shook her head. "Not all of them. Some of the kids stay at Santangelo until they're twenty-one."

"Voluntarily," said Pete, "after they turn eighteen."

"So what happens if a kid gets pregnant?" asked Dean.

"I don't think they've had to deal with that, at least recently." Pete looked at me and Lulu. "Has it ever come up for you guys?"

I didn't answer and tried willing Lulu to follow my example without any overt signal.

"Not directly, no," she said.

"Indirectly?" asked Pete.

"Can I have some of that wine for the chicken, Pete?" I interrupted before she could reply.

He gave me the bottle, and I poured a healthy pint or so into the skillet.

"Let's go hang on the sofa," I said, "until that's done."

"Anybody up for a joint?" asked Dean as we filed out of the kitchen.

14

The change of room helped, and I have to say I was relieved when Pete took a hit after Dean passed him the joint.

Lulu and I declined to partake, so Dean put it out.

Pete had made me nervous, backing up Santangelo's whole "save yourself for marriage" program. But I figured he couldn't turn us in for disagreeing, since David was even more adamantly opposed to pot smoking. We were all supposed to obey every law on the books, in and out of school — from speed limits to pointing out the discrepancy if anyone ever gave us too much change at a cash register. Not that the latter was exactly a law or anything.

I wanted to get Pete off the topic of kids recently knocked up on campus.

"So how's it going after your first week?" I asked him. "You seem pretty positive about the program vis-à-vis the kids."

"It's a good place for me to be, I think."

"You said you heard about it from a friend of Santangelo's?"

"Yeah. I was going through a pretty rough time. He thought I could use the support."

I took a sip of wine. "What were you doing before?"

"I was in an orchestra, playing the cello, up until six months ago."

"And you gave it up for this?" I asked.

"Madeline, geez," said Lulu.

Pete shrugged. "I didn't have much choice. I was in a car accident and messed up a few vertebrae. The nerve damage knocked out the strength in my right hand. I can only play for a few minutes before I get too shaky."

"I'm sorry," I said, feeling like a complete asshole.

"It's okay," he said. "I just . . . Well, I didn't have a damn clue what to do next, you know?"

He gave us a game little smile. "I was drinking a lot, to the extent that my friends were worried. Rightly so."

"I hope it helps," I said, "being here."

"So far so good," he said. "I drove straight up as soon as David told me he had a job open. Figured it couldn't be worse than the alternative I was considering."

153

He stared at the window for a moment, looking so broken that it seemed pretty clear what the alternative was.

He turned back toward us. "I did make one detour on the way to campus."

"Where to?" asked Dean.

"The sheriff's department," Pete said. "I asked them if they'd hang on to my gun, since I was hoping I wouldn't be tempted to use it."

Lulu put an arm around his shoulders. "We'll make sure you aren't."

"Lulu," he said, "I think tonight is the first time I honestly haven't found the idea appealing. That's a remarkable thing, you know? Feeling like there's a point to sticking around — finding a place I want to be and people I want to be with."

"I'm glad," I said, and meant it.

"I'm not batting a thousand yet," he said. "But I think I'll get there. Just learning about the kind of stuff the kids have been through . . . I feel damn lucky, and I think we can all help each other heal. That's what gives me faith that David is on the right track."

"If you think it's working for you," said Dean, "I'll give the place some credit."

"I know you guys are more cynical about it," Pete said. "And don't get me wrong, a year ago I would've thought David's whole shtick was bullshit."

He looked down at his wineglass, then put it on the table in front of him without taking another sip. "It's just that I got to a place where I felt like cynicism was on the verge of killing me — and I mean that literally. So I figured I had to give something else a chance. Hope, maybe, or trust."

"You can trust us," said Lulu.

I was moved by what Pete had said, but I still wasn't sure the two of us could trust him.

Pete turned to me. "I know that David is ready to trust you," he said. "Have you made a decision about his offer?"

"What offer?" asked Lulu.

He looked surprised. "Madeline hasn't told you?"

"Told me what?"

"David wants her to take over for Dhumavati," he said, "starting in January."

Lulu laughed. "And would you like to share with the group how that made you feel, Madeline?"

"I feel like it's ridiculous. Obviously."

"Are you going to take him up on it?" she asked.

"You should," said Pete. "You'd be great."

"And Dhumavati's on board with this?"

155

asked Lulu.

"She wants some time off," I said. "It would only be for a couple of months. But I still think they're nuts."

Pete shook his head. "David's serious about it. I know he is. And it may very well turn out to be a long-term thing. I think he's tending toward that."

"Which is even more ridiculous," I said. "I mean, come on, Lulu, can you see me trying to be Santangelo's permanent mouth-piece?"

"It would liven things up," she said. "And I'd sure as shit like to see a little of that."

"Do you think she should take the job?" Pete asked Dean.

Dean pulled his roach out of the ashtray and sparked it up.

"No offense, but I think she'd do better as a Hare Krishna," he said through clenched teeth after taking a hit. "At least they don't make you pay for the uniform."

I stood up. "Chicken's probably done. You guys ready to eat?"

"Let me help," said Lulu, following me back to the kitchen.

Dean and Pete kept talking. Lulu turned on the taps at the sink and then pulled me into a corner, away from their line of sight.

"Are you really thinking about stepping in

for Dhumavati?" she asked.

"Look," I said, "I guess it's flattering to be asked, and it would mean more money, but I would suck at that job — just from the standpoint of keeping the paperwork organized, not to mention the whole ideology angle."

"I'd rather see you do it than anyone else on campus," she said. "I mean, can you imagine Mindy at the helm? I'd be out of there faster than a greased bat."

"A greased bat on *fire,*" I said, "totally."

"That alone might be enough reason to do it."

"If I didn't need the money, I'd rather just quit," I said. "Dean has some work lined up."

"You'd leave me there alone, with Mindy in charge?"

"We don't know it would be Mindy. Maybe they'd pick you."

"If I'd been in the running, I'm pretty sure Pete would have said something."

"You think he's that close with Santangelo?" I asked. "Close enough that he'd have been let in on who made the short list?"

"I don't know," she said. "But if my name had come up, I don't think he'd keep it to himself. You said they'd talked about me, right?"

Yes, and not in a good way.

"And what have you talked about with Pete? Please reassure me that he doesn't know about Fay and Mooney," I said.

"Of course not," she said. "I gave you my word, and I wouldn't say anything without asking you. But if we *were* to tell anyone else, Pete strikes me as the right person to start with."

"Lulu, I like the guy, and you're right about him having a good reason to buy in to Santangelo's trip, but it doesn't mean I trust him enough to betray that confidence."

"Just think about it," she said. "That's all I'm asking. I know he's only been here for a week, but I knew I could trust you before I'd known you even that long. And we didn't write off Santangelo right away, either."

"It's just that Pete is way more gung ho on the come-to-Jesus program than we were, even our first week. I worry about that."

"Maybe he needs something better to be gung ho about."

"Such as?"

"Such as us. The guy needs to know he has somebody looking out for him. Somebody who's not Santangelo," Lulu said. "I think he's worth the risk."

"Let's wait and see if he gets us busted for smoking first. That's about all the risk I can handle right now."

"You're going to feel really stupid when it turns out I'm right about him."

"That's a stupidity I'd welcome."

"You mean it?"

"Sure," I said. "I *want* him to prove me wrong by turning out to be a decent guy. But just in case he doesn't, don't let's give him any more turn-ins than we have already, okay? Especially not about the kids. Pete needs a little more seasoning before we teach him the secret handshake."

"You're right," she said, "but I wish you weren't."

"Are you sweet on this guy?" I asked.

"A little," she said. "Sure."

"A little?" I said. "Hey, can you smell that?"

"Smell what?"

"The smoke," I said, "from your pants being on fire."

"Shut *up!*" She grabbed a dish towel to thwack me with, but I'd made her blush.

"Let me get the plates out," I said. "I think food would help at this point."

We walked them down to our building's parking lot around ten, me and Dean.

"So check out Lulu's car, it's totally Methodist Blue," I said, that being Dean's nickname for the powdery shade his own farming parents always chose.

"Little bit paler than you'd see around Syracuse," Dean said to Lulu. "You sure you're not one of those Presbyterians?" He opened the driver's door for her, and I walked Pete to the other side.

"Madeline," he said, "I just want you to know that was the best night I've had in months." He gave me a hug, adding, "You and Dean are friends I hope to spend a lot more time with."

"It would be our pleasure," I said.

Lulu started up the Methodist-mobile and cruised out of the lot onto North Street. Dean and I waved our final goodbyes after them and started back inside.

While we waited for the elevator, he turned to me and said, "That guy Pete? Talk about a candyass."

"I felt bad for him, didn't you?"

"Sure," he said. "But I still wouldn't trust him for half a heartbeat. He's Santangelo's lapdog, ready to drop everything at a moment's notice on the off chance he'll get to hump the man's leg."

"Lulu seems to think we can do a little deprogramming."

160

"No way in hell," he said. "It's a goddamn miracle he didn't show up tonight in saffron robes, waving a tambourine."

The elevator dinged, and the doors peeled wide in front of us.

"Hare Krishna," said Dean, climbing aboard.

"He's not *that* bad."

"He's Hare freakin' *Rama* bad, Bunny. Mark my words."

■ ■ ■ ■

Part III

■ ■ ■ ■

I almost think we're all of us Ghosts. . . .
It's not only what we have invited from our
father and mother that walks in us. It's all
sorts of dead ideas, and lifeless old beliefs,
and so forth. They have no vitality, but they
cling to us all the same, and we can't get
rid of them. . . . There must be Ghosts all
the country over, as thick as the sand of
the sea. And then we are, one and all, so
pitifully afraid of the light.

— Henrik Ibsen, *Ghosts*

15

Monday we had parent-teacher conferences, as promised.

All classes were canceled, and lunch was far more edible than usual — roast beef and au gratin potatoes and green beans that had been harvested sometime after the Korean War for a change. They even trotted out real coffee in rented urns, looking all shiny and spiffy atop the rented table linens.

Meds, meanwhile, were distributed off-stage.

It wasn't a happy occasion for anyone. I'd say only half the families showed up, if that. I wanted to believe they were too strapped for cash to venture across the country, in light of Santangelo's hefty tuition.

I spent most of the day in my classroom, staring out the window while ticking off the no-shows with the passage of each fifteen-minute chunk.

Wiesner's people gave it a miss. So did

Forchetti's and Sitzman's.

Fay's parents wandered in, confused —
her impeccably blonded mother in head-to-
toe size-four Chanel, her father sporting
bespoke duds up the wazoo. I redirected
them to Lulu, next door.

Mr. and Mrs. Gonzaga, parents of chair-
tossing Patti, cowered in the doorway until
I stood up to welcome them in. They
seemed so tired and sad, clutching each
other's hands on the other side of my desk,
that I didn't have the heart to say anything
true about their little girl.

"Patti's awfully shy, as I'm sure you
know," I said, smiling at them. "But she's
sweet as can be all the same. A consistent
pleasure to have in class."

They wanted to believe me, but it was a
stretch for all of us.

"Is she," said her mother, "is she keeping
up with her studies?"

"Oh, yes," I assured her. "And she contrib-
utes especially fine work whenever we have
free writing."

Patti's entire free-writing output consisted
of five crumpled binder-paper sheets, one
for each week since the start of the term —
the words "THIS SCHOOL SUCKS! THIS
SCHOOL SUCKS! THIS SCHOOL
SUCKS!" scrawled thick and black down

all of them, both sides, with respect to neither margin nor rule.

"And she hasn't," said her father, "thrown anything?" He coughed.

"Thrown anything?" I asked, picture of innocence.

"At you?" murmured Mrs. Gonzaga.

"Patti?" I said. "Oh my goodness, no!"

Her father coughed again. "It's just that we . . . sometimes . . ."

"Chairs, you know," said her mother, "at us . . ."

"The occasional plate or bowl," he added.

"Well, then, she's made tremendous improvement," I said, hoping I wouldn't be struck by lightning on account of that blatant falsehood. Hoping, too, that they wouldn't credit Santangelo — who probably remembered their daughter's existence only when he had occasion to cash their checks.

Mr. Gonzaga shook my hand when the bell rang. His wife was about to do the same but then stepped closer, to hug me instead.

I knew they hadn't believed a word.

They shuffled to the door, and I heard Mrs. Gonzaga break down out in the hallway.

"There, there, my dear," her husband murmured. "It won't be long until we have

167

our sweet girl home again."

Patti's mother didn't answer, but she managed to cry more quietly until they got to the doors at the end of the hall.

Just about killed me, hearing that, so I was relieved that Mooney's parents showed up ten minutes late.

Mr. and Mrs. LeChance wanted to be anywhere but in that classroom. They were good-looking people, tanned and fit. If they'd been birds, a naturalist would have noted the female's brighter plumage.

"Mooney's turned in all his work on time this term," I told them. "We're just finishing up our unit on the Second World War, and he's made a real contribution to the classroom discussion."

Mrs. LeChance was fidgety.

"Your son is just terrific," I said, catching her eye.

"Oh, honey," she said, "he's not mine."

Mr. LeChance had the decency to blush at that. "My first wife died several years ago. Beebe is Mooney's stepmother."

She patted her husband's knee, making damn sure he got an eyeful of trophy cleavage. "Poor ol' Sally. Such a tragic loss — and then the lawsuit dragged on, of course."

"I'm so very sorry," I said.

"That Mooney's been out of control ever

since," she said, tossing a hand to wave away my concern. "Spoiled rotten, what with all the money we got for the settlement."

Beebe stroked her husband's knee again. "Isn't that right, honey?"

She turned back to me, swinging her crossed leg to make the diamonds in her ankle bracelet flash against that golden tan. "Place like this is the very best thing for him. Thank the Lord we're well enough off to afford it."

Mr. LeChance cleared his throat.

She leaned over to straighten his collar.

"We best be going now," she said. "Wouldn't want to miss our flight."

Mr. LeChance looked at his watch. "I just want to catch a few minutes with my son before we leave."

"We're not allowed, remember?" she chided. "Seeing as how Mooney's got himself in trouble. Again."

Beebe stood up, turning toward her husband. She pushed her hair back, and I was overjoyed to spot the scars from her facelift.

"Get a move on, Bucky-boy," she said, clapping her hands. "Antigua waits for no man."

She turned to wink at me when they reached the door. "Y'all keep up the good work, now, hear?"

Wiesner and Sitzman wandered in moments later, interrupting my prayers that a sudden loss of cabin pressure over the Caribbean would make Beebe's implants blow up.

As such, the sharp crack of a small but definite actual explosion made me jump about three feet.

It had gone off somewhere in the building — not enough concussion to damage the windows, but my eardrums ached.

"What the hell was that?" I asked.

Sitzman looked at Wiesner.

Wiesner shook his head in denial, then sniffed the air.

I followed suit and caught an acrid hit of nail polish remover.

"Peroxyacetone," Wiesner said. "Made by some total amateur."

"Yeah, right," said Sitzman, "with absolutely no help from you."

"Dude, I've been with you all morning," Wiesner replied.

"Whatever," said Sitzman. "I still totally know you did it."

"I wouldn't cook a batch of that shit if you paid me," insisted Wiesner.

Sitzman and I traded doubting smirks.

"Seriously," said Wiesner. "This friend of

mine, Stevie, put a few grams in his front pocket a couple of years ago, and then he stood up too fast at the end of French class." He bowed his head with great sadness. "Now we call him One-Nut."

16

Tuesday afternoon it was cold as shit out-side, wind pushing bits of everything around under a low brow of sky.

Forchetti was back in class, freed from the Farm, so that made four of us — him, me, Wiesner, and Sitzman.

"You guys really want to talk about the sixties?" I asked.

"Like out of the textbook or real stuff?" asked Wiesner.

"We could do real stuff," I said. "With maybe some pictures out of the textbook."

"I want to hear about what it was like for you," said Sitzman.

Forchetti snorted. "She was a little kid back then. What the hell does she know about it?"

"I was born in '63, Forchetti," I said, "but I remember the last few years pretty well. And a lot of what you guys think of as the sixties kind of leaked into the first chunk of the seventies — at least until the war was over."

"What," said Forchetti, "like tie-dye and all that shit?"

"Tie-dye was the least of it," I said.

"Ooooo," he said, his head wobbling as he made peace signs with both hands. "Flower power with granola on top. Let's all go pick daisies and talk about *love*."

"Shut *up,* Foreskin," said Wiesner. "You wanna sit here listening to crap about that McCarthy guy? At least maybe this won't be totally boring."

"Fine," whined Forchetti. He slumped down in his chair like he knew full well I could bore him to sleep even if Godzilla suddenly bashed through the wall with a truckload of free tequila and strippers.

"Well," I said, "I remember the time somebody sent us two keys of dope from Maui in this welded-shut mailbox. I think that was around when we were hiding the guy who went AWOL right before he was supposed to ship out for Vietnam. We used to dress him up in my mom's clothes and put sunglasses and this big Afro wig on him to take him grocery shopping if he got bored of hanging around the house."

"What happened to him?" asked Wiesner.

"Somebody drove him to Canada, I think.

173

Nice guy. I got the grown-ups to do the Stoned Balloon on his last night, for good luck."

Forchetti asked, "What's a Stoned Balloon?" before he could cover up the fact that I'd gotten him interested.

"You take a dry-cleaning bag and twist it up into a rope until it doubles back on itself, then you put it on a wire hanger and hook it on a chandelier or whatever and light the end of it on fire."

"Why?" he asked.

"Well, it just looks cool, you know?" I said. "You have to turn off all the lights and put a big bowl of water under it. And then these chunks of burning plastic drip off the bottom slowly. They make this zip noise, and there's a streak of blue flame until they hit the water. It goes faster and faster near the end — zip-zip-zip-zip, with the blue streak getting so bright it just glows solid — and then the last one hesitates, balanced on the hanger, until it tips off and kind of pops and whines down and sizzles out in the water, and there's just total darkness and silence. The grown-ups thought it was cool that we could get into it, even though we weren't high."

"What would you do after that?" asked Wiesner.

"Listen to Hendrix or Donovan and bitch about Nixon, mostly," I said, "while passing around a bowl of Screaming Yellow Zonkers. By then it was usually my bedtime."

"Just you and your parents and this army guy?" asked Forchetti.

"My mom and my stepfather, three of us kids," I said. "But there were always lots of people around."

"Like who?" asked Forchetti.

"Like maybe we'd pick up a couple of kids hitchhiking down the coast, and they'd crash in the living room for a night, or Black Panthers would come from Berkeley for the weekend. These guys Chet and Paul lived in the backyard in a really funky orange van for a while, in exchange for carpentry. Sometimes Joe the Woodchopper came up from Big Sur to cook potato latkes. Eldridge Cleaver was supposed to stay with us, but he went to Algeria."

"Who's Eldridge Cleaver?" asked Sitzman.

"This guy who escaped from prison," I said. "I think it was for having a shoot-out with the cops in Oakland."

"Who else?" asked Sitzman.

"Ken and Ginny sometimes. I think Ken could play thirty-two instruments. He'd mess around with my flute and stuff —

totally cool guy."

"So it was like a commune?" asked Forchetti.

"Just our house. But people were welcome to hang out."

"Hitchhikers, though? That seems really dangerous," said Sitzman.

"They were young, most of them," I said. "We found a lot of cool babysitters that way."

"Babysitters?" sputtered Forchetti. "Just strangers off the street?"

"It was different then," I said. "I mean, you can make fun of flower power and granola in retrospect, but for a while there it actually worked."

"Sounds like you miss it," said Wiesner.

"You have no idea how much," I said. "I mean, I was a little kid, so I'm sure I have a skewed perspective, but there was something about it that was kind of . . . *splendid.*"

"How do you mean?" asked Wiesner.

"You always knew who the good guys were, and it seemed like we were really going to win out at long last. Shit would get better, you know? All we had to do was more peace marches until it sank in."

"Peace marches?" said Forchetti. "What the hell for?"

I picked up my copy of *We the People* and

176

flipped to the closing chapters. "Check out the picture on page four-oh-seven," I said.

They opened their own textbooks.

"See the girl in the middle, running down the road?" I asked.

"The naked one," said Forchetti.

"Her name is Phan Thi Kim Phúc," I said. "This was taken right after her village got napalmed by accident. She's naked because it burned her clothes off."

"What's napalm?" asked Forchetti.

"Jellied gasoline," said Wiesner. "Pretty much the same shit that's in Molotov cocktails, except not homemade."

"You know how to make Molotov cocktails?" asked Forchetti, impressed.

"You mix the gas with dish soap. Stick it in a Coke bottle or something, with a rag in the neck to stop it up. Light the rag and toss it. Not exactly rocket science."

"The soap makes it stick to whatever it lands on," I said. "Fabric, wood, flesh — it keeps burning. Just like napalm."

"That's disgusting," said Forchetti.

"It was all disgusting," I said. "The whole war."

He looked back down at the picture. "How old was she?"

"Nine," I said. "Not much older than I was."

"Did she die?"

"No. But she wasn't expected to survive. I think she was in a hospital for about fourteen months." I flipped back to the previous page. "Check out the picture on four-oh-five," I said. "That was taken the year I was born."

"What the hell is it?" asked Forchetti.

"Read the damn caption," said Wiesner. "It's a Buddhist monk who set himself on fire in Saigon to protest the war."

"Why do those cops in the next picture have dogs?" asked Forchetti. "They look like they're about to eat that kid's face off."

"You never heard of Martin Luther King, Forchetti?" asked Wiesner. "What the hell is wrong with you?"

Forchetti slammed his book shut. "Just because I don't sit up all night reading this shit like you do, Wiesner — trying to get in Madeline's pants."

"At least I *can* read," said Wiesner.

"I can totally fucking read," said Forchetti.

"Then try shutting up for five seconds, you ignorant piece of shit," said Wiesner. "You might actually learn something."

"Lighten up, you guys," I said, "or I'm going to start talking about McCarthyism."

"I want to hear more about this," said Sitzman. "You said you used to go on peace marches and stuff. What was that like?"

"It was cool," I said.

I glanced out the window, watching all those bare black branches tossing in the wind. "When I was a little kid, it really seemed like everybody would just keep linking arms in the streets, marching and singing, until the war stopped and people didn't have to get hurt or messed up anymore."

"You actually believed that?" asked Wiesner.

I looked back at him. "I miss the hell out of believing that."

"So what happened?" he asked. "I mean, here you are at Santangelo, all dressed in black, making fun of shit all the time. Total cynic."

"It just stopped," I said. "It was like one day we all woke up and went about our business, as though none of it had ever happened. No more hitchhikers, no more Stoned Balloons."

"Because the war was over?" asked Sitzman.

"More than that. Maybe everybody grew up or something. Watergate happened. People started looking inward instead of to each other when they felt like they needed help."

When they didn't lay down cash on the bar-

relhead for reassurance from EST or Arica or primal therapy.

"After that," I said, "it was pretty much selfish bullshit. Disco. Chardonnay. Consciousness-raising."

"You ever get the feeling the sixties stuff could happen again?" asked Forchetti, looking like he'd give anything for me to say yes.

"Sometimes it feels like there's a glimmer of it around the edges," I said. "But I don't think it ever lasts."

I leaned my chair back. "Remember the picture of that one guy standing in front of a tank in Tiananmen Square?"

Wiesner and Sitzman nodded. Forchetti just crossed his arms.

"I remember the first time I saw it," I said. "I felt like I totally knew what he was thinking: that all he had to do was stand there, because it was so obvious the stupid bad shit had to stop, and that he wasn't alone. Like, even the guys driving the tank knew he was right, so there was no reason for him to be afraid of getting run down."

I looked down at my desk. "It was the saddest damn picture I think I've ever seen."

"Why?" asked Wiesner. "The tank stopped. He was right."

"Yeah, but he was wrong about everything

180

else," I said, "because the stupid bad shit *never* stops — he just didn't understand that yet, and I knew how much it was going to suck when he figured it out."

Forchetti smirked. "So are you gonna let us go early today?"

"No," I said. "I'm going to make you sit here and listen to 'Alice's Restaurant.' "

The bell rang just as Arlo was wrapping up the last round of "You can get anything you want . . ."

Lulu peeked in the doorway after the kids took off. "You remember we've got a faculty meeting?"

I groaned.

"Next to the dining hall," she said. "I'll walk you over."

We trudged off, hearts heavy.

"Don't we have to make Fay's birthday cake?" I asked.

"Already baked," she said. "Two layers of devil's food. I just need to frost it."

Dhumavati opened with a list of announcements: The student soccer game against guests at a yoga center up the road on Wednesday. The week's dorm-parent duty roster down at the Farm. An entreaty to

181

search our classrooms for unreturned library books.

She looked up from her notes. "That's it for official business, so I thought we'd make tonight an open session."

There was a sharp and universal intake of breath around the room. In the absence of a concrete agenda, meetings were never canceled or brought to an early conclusion. They were automatically transformed into windows of therapeutic opportunity, meaning we'd spend the next two hell-or-high-water hours rending the flesh of a random victim.

Mindy, Lulu, me . . . it didn't matter. Truth was immaterial, the object was fear.

Blue eyes or brown eyes, fellow traveler or counter-revolutionary capitalist roader, dirty *Juden* or dirty *Boche* — you never knew who'd ride in the tumbrel next.

Pick a card, any card.

Someone in the room was already guilty. Someone would prove to have a scapegoat-able flaw.

Santangelo was the last holdout of Mao's Cultural Revolution. We had the "Self-Criticism" sessions down pat. All we needed were a dozen or so copies of the Little Red Book to wave around while we performed the loyalty dance.

The idea of Mindy in a dumpy green Chinese suit made me want to refuse Dhumavati's job, raise or no raise.

"Who'd like to open tonight's discussion?" Dhumavati asked.

No takers, not surprisingly.

We all tried not to fidget, because the slightest tic of sound or motion — throat cleared, knuckles cracked, fingers unwittingly drummed against taut thigh — would bring the group down on your ass like some frenzy of sharks snapping at a slick of rancid chum.

I caught Mindy staring at me, her lips pursed in a mean little simper. Figuring I might as well beat her to the punch, I raised my hand.

"Madeline, you have something you'd like to share with the group?" asked Dhumavati.

"Yes," I said. "I'd like to appreciate Mindy."

Dhumavati's eyes widened, a flicker of surprise. "And what would you like to appreciate Mindy for?"

"I need to let Mindy know that I'm feeling gratitude for how she's always really *being* there for me in our therapy sessions with Sookie."

"Tell us more about that," said Dhumavati.

"She totally calls me on my shit," I said, "which is just so important to the process, you know?"

"Let's all join Madeline in appreciating Mindy for her help with that piece," said Dhumavati, raising her hands to lead us in a round of applause.

When the clapping died down, all eyes remained on the object of my appreciation.

"Mindy, do you have anything to share with us about how being appreciated by Madeline made you feel just now?" asked Dhumavati.

"I, um . . ." Mindy faltered, looking like she was about to hack up a fuzzy pink hairball.

Not above a little simper of my own, I blinked at her. Twice.

Gerald put a hand on her shoulder. "Just go with what you're feeling right now."

"Surprise?" Mindy said.

"Why does being appreciated by Madeline surprise you?" asked Pete.

Tim leaned forward, resting his elbows on his knees. "Maybe because Mindy knows she doesn't call Madeline on her shit to be helpful?"

"That's a very interesting observation, Tim," said Dhumavati. "Can you tell us why you think Mindy does call Madeline on her shit?"

"Because she feels threatened?"

"Nuh-uh!" blurted Mindy.

Dhumavati turned toward her. "Do you think there's any truth to what Tim's saying about your feelings toward Madeline?"

Mindy looked at the floor and shook her head.

"I think she does," said Tim. "I think she *totally* does."

Mindy's hands were now clasped in her lap. I watched a fat tear plop down onto her thumb.

"Nuh-uh," she said, sniffling.

Gerald got up to fetch her a box of Kleenex.

"Mindy," said Dhumavati, "I'm feeling some truth in what Tim is trying to tell you. Can you hear that?"

Mindy was silent, hugging the Kleenex box to her belly.

"I think you do feel threatened by Madeline," Dhumavati continued. "So much so that you can't take in how much she cares for you."

"Dhumavati?" I said.

She ignored me. "Can you let us know what you're feeling now, Mindy?"

Mindy shook her head again.

"Dhumavati," I said, "this is ridiculous."

"What do you mean?" she asked.

Everyone looked at me.

"I mean that I don't particularly care about Mindy."

Mindy blew her nose at that, more tears plopping into her lap.

"I mean, I care about her right now," I said, "because she's so bummed out, but I didn't do the appreciation thing because I care about her generally."

"We can learn from people we don't care about, Madeline," said Dhumavati. "I think that was your point in appreciating her."

"Look, what I'm trying to say is that I *don't* actually appreciate her."

"Be that as it may, you're still grateful to Mindy for keeping you honest in your therapy sessions. That's what counts."

"Dhumavati, I'm not grateful to Mindy for that. In fact, whenever we have to do therapy together, she's an annoying bitch."

"But you appreciated her!" said Tim.

"So I lied."

He went white. "Why would you do that?"

"Because she was gunning for me," I said. "Right, Mindy?"

"Pretty much," she admitted.

I looked back at Tim. "Last time we had group together, you poked Mindy in the arm and told her to shut up, right?"

"Well, yeah." He crossed his arms.

"So I'm not alone in thinking she's an annoying bitch, at least occasionally."

Tim shrugged. "You still lied."

"I know."

"Why would you do that?" he asked.

"Because," I said, "I didn't want to get eviscerated all night over some pointless bullshit. Mindy was going to set me up, so I did it first. She and I don't like each other — I'm sure she'd characterize *me* as an annoying bitch."

Mindy nodded.

"But here's the thing, Tim," I said. "I feel like shit now because you guys went for her throat with such astonishing gusto. And she didn't deserve that, even if she would've enjoyed the hell out of watching it happen to me."

Nobody said a word.

I shrugged. "Okay, so I just felt like it was important to be honest for once. Mindy and I can keep on hating each other, and you guys can go right ahead and take out whoever you want for the rest of the session."

Dhumavati cleared her throat. "Mindy, would you like to share with the group how you feel about what Madeline just said?"

Mindy simpered at me again, then she

said, "I feel like Madeline needs to fire herself."

"Oh, shut *up*," said Lulu.

"Lulu, I'm feeling some hostility from you," said Dhumavati.

"I'm feeling some hostility from me, too," said Lulu. "I mean, for God's sake, Dhumavati, Madeline's right. What the hell is the point of sitting around tearing into each other like this?"

"Even if Madeline's original intention tonight was dishonest, I certainly feel as though we're clearing the air now. Don't you think that's worth doing?"

"If viciousness is the only thing we'll accept as authentic emotion," said Lulu. "But I refuse to concede that's all there is. I think it's just what we've allowed ourselves to settle for."

"We have a perfectly authentic way to express our positive feelings. That's the whole point of appreciating one another," said Dhumavati.

Lulu sighed.

"I'd like to appreciate you for reminding us how important that is, Lulu," said Dhumavati. "I agree with you that these meetings can all too often degenerate into accusation and shame-mongering. In fact, I'd like to see our time together put to more generous and compassionate use. But it's not up to me. That's why we call it an open session — the agenda is yours, not mine."

Pete raised his hand.

"What would you like to add to the discussion?" asked Dhumavati. "I value your input on what's been said so far tonight."

"I'd like to appreciate Lulu and Madeline," he said. "They've made me feel incredibly welcome here, and I value our new friendship a great deal."

Lulu was soothed by that, I could tell.

"Thank you, Pete," said Dhumavati. "I'm grateful to you for demonstrating what I was just trying to say."

"My pleasure," he said. "And I'd also like to do a turn-in."

Lulu was suddenly looking a whole lot less soothed. I tucked my hands under my legs so no one could see how hard I was gripping the sides of my chair's plastic seat.

"Good for you," said Dhumavati. "And what would you like to do a turn-in for?"

"Smoking cigarettes," he said.

My stomach threatened to give dinner an encore appearance right onto the carpet.

"On campus?" she asked.

"Friday afternoon," he said. "But a couple of times off campus over the weekend."

"Anything else you'd like us to know?"

asked Dhumavati.

"That's it," he said. "I was feeling stressed. Now I regret the decision to cover that up with smoking."

"How do you feel now that you've done your turn-in?" she asked.

"Better. It feels like it will be easier to resist the temptation now that I've admitted it."

"That's the whole point," she said. "You have a fresh start."

Pete smiled at her. "Thank you for that. I appreciate it."

"Is there anything else you'd like to share?"

I held my breath. *Oh yeah, and I was with Lulu and Madeline, who were smoking right along with me, and then I smoked pot at Madeline's house, and we've all been slamming down as much coffee as we can get our hands on.*

"No," he said, "I think that's about it."

"Let's let Pete know how much we appreciate his candor, shall we?" said Dhumavati, starting to clap again.

We all joined in, Lulu and I somewhat more tepidly than the rest of the crew. Lulu caught my eye, the corner of her mouth twitching up in relief. Or maybe dismay.

I wondered what the point of him doing a

190

turn-in was if he was going to lie about it. Was it meant to show what a good little lap-dog he was? Or — to give him the benefit of the doubt — was he was trying to come to my aid by deflecting the conversation?

But then I wondered if he'd been hoping Dhumavati would ask him whether he'd been with Lulu and me at the time of his transgressions, given how quickly he'd tacked that turn-in on to his purported appreciation of us.

Pretty damn candyass, no matter how you sliced it. I just hoped Lulu would get that before she was tempted to open up to him any further. I sure as hell wasn't about to waste any more Camels on the guy, even if he begged.

"Let's go home early for a change," said Dhumavati. "I think we could all use a break."

People bolted out of the room like she'd fired a starting pistol.

I figured I'd wait, so as to avoid getting trampled. Lulu was of the same mind, apparently. She didn't budge from her chair, just hummed "Goodnight, Irene" under her breath.

Dhumavati stood up and started gathering her papers. "Are we all set for Fay's birthday?"

"I baked a cake," said Lulu. "It should have cooled enough for me to get the frosting on by now."

"I'll bring ice cream and paper plates and party hats," said Dhumavati.

"I bought a box of candles," I said, pulling them out of my jacket pocket.

Dhumavati laughed. "You got off easy."

"I have a feeling Lulu is way better at baking," I told her. "And thank you for letting us go early."

"Madeline," she said, "you may not believe it, but I'm as sick of these meetings as you are. The human capacity for pointless sniping never ceases to amaze me."

"I admit to being shocked," I said.

"If you think you had me fooled for a moment," she said. "Appreciating Mindy? That woman's about as appreciate-able as head lice."

"And here I thought you were a true believer," I said, "waving your Little Red Book."

"It's not that bad," she said. "Sometimes the tension makes people bring up topics that actually matter. In Synanon, they called it the Game."

"You were in Synanon?" I asked.

"Close enough," she said. "Why don't you two go frost that cake?"

192

Lulu and I stood up.

"And for God's sake," said Dhumavati, "get yourselves some better mouthwash. I can't stand smoker's breath."

Lulu and I just stood there, stunned, as she walked out of the room.

"Did somebody put acid in my coffee this morning?" Lulu asked me.

"Looks that way."

"Luckily," she said, "it was good acid."

It was dark in the woods about an hour after we'd finished supper in the dining hall. Lulu and I were toting the cake down to the Farm. She'd frosted it creamy white and written Fay's name across the top in pale blue script, with little candy pearls.

"Should've brought my flashlight," I said.

"We're almost there. You've got a lighter?"

"Always," I said. "You want me to hold it up so we can see?"

"I'm fine," she said. "Just wanted to make sure we had something to light the cake."

"Right here in my jacket." I fingered the Bic and the box of tiny pink candles in my pocket.

"I'm a little surprised Dhumavati's letting us do this," Lulu said.

"After that meeting?"

"Well, maybe not as surprised as I might

formerly have been," she admitted.

"I think she feels bad for Fay, you know?"

"It gives me hope for this place — the kids *should* have a little celebration on their birthdays."

We came out of the trees. The windows of the building below were lit up — rectangles of welcoming yellow light.

"What'd Sookie have to say yesterday?" asked Lulu, picking her way carefully down the hillside. "Anything useful? I forgot to ask you."

"She wasn't in her office. Her kids have the flu or something."

"There's a nasty bug going around," she said. "The whole second floor in New Boys was down for the count over the weekend. We'll probably get it, what with being shut up in all these damn meetings, breathing each other's fumes."

"Something else to look forward to."

"At this point I'd pretty much welcome it. I could hole up in my bed for a couple of days with mugs of tea and some crappy novels."

"Looking forward to the flu," I said. "That's just sad."

"Tell me about it," she said. "Pitiful."

We reached the bottom of the hill and trudged toward the garden fence.

"Well, I'll be dipped," said Lulu.

"What?"

"First snow of the year. Check it out."

She was right — I could see the onset of gentle flakes drifting down across the building's windows.

I stopped walking. "Makes it seem like it will be all cozy inside."

"I doubt it," she said. "Have you decided what we should do about Fay and Mooney?"

"No."

"I've been thinking we should talk to Dhumavati."

"What?"

"Tonight," she said. "After the party."

I shivered but didn't take another step forward.

"Madeline," she said, stopping beside me, "I don't know what else we can do. They're kids. If they went on the road and anything happened? I can't stomach that responsibility."

"But can we live with what will happen if they don't go?"

"Maybe there's a third option if we come clean with Dhumavati. She seems like their best bet. And ours."

"Telling her is the same thing as telling Santangelo," I said. "We know that."

"Do we?" she asked. "I've been wondering whether it's that black and white anymore — especially after today's meeting."

I thought about that. Deep down, I knew the only reason I'd agreed to keep Fay and Mooney's secret was that I had no fucking idea what to do about it — how to help them, how to be the grown-up who could make it all okay. And Lulu was right, I couldn't imagine the pair of them surviving on their own. They were children. Damaged children.

But wouldn't Santangelo just compound that damage?

"Madeline," Lulu continued, "why does Dhumavati want to take this leave of absence in the first place? I think it's pretty obvious the woman's wrestling with some rather profound doubts of her own."

"I'm not sure the leave was Dhumavati's idea. I get the feeling it's more about Santangelo doubting her. Especially given his hints that she won't be coming back."

"So let's ask her. We'll start there. If she's honest about that, maybe she really is a viable third option for Fay and Mooney."

"What can she do about it, even if she wants to run interference with Santangelo?"

"More than we can," said Lulu.

"Maybe," I said.

"Madeline, come on. The idea of those

two kids out on their own? No meds, no skills, no jobs — what the hell are they going to do? You can't hide them in your apartment."

"They trusted me," I said. "I promised them I'd help. I just don't know how."

"Maybe they wanted you to tell someone. Maybe that's the only kind of help you can give."

"You believe that?"

"I don't know what to believe. I just don't think we can handle it alone, any more than they can. With Fay pregnant —"

"What if she wasn't?" I asked.

"She is."

"Lulu, there must be a Planned Parenthood somewhere nearby. We could get her there."

"And then what?"

"We bring her back."

"What good does that do?"

"The main thing is she wouldn't be sent home. From what Mooney told me, she's better off here than with her parents. That's why the two of them want to run away — to keep Santangelo and her family from forcing her to have the baby."

"I don't know," said Lulu.

"It's a real third option," I said. "If we work it right, no one else has to know."

"They'd know she left campus."

"So she'd get sent back to the Farm for a while. They'd corner her again. Whatever."

"And the baby?"

"Given the meds Fay's on, would it stand a chance of being born healthy? Especially since they've upped her dosage."

"I still think we should tell Dhumavati."

"We have to talk it over with Fay and Mooney first. Ask them what they want to do. If they agree to have us tell her, I'm all for it, but it's gotta be their decision."

"Madeline —"

"You're going to say they're just kids."

"Because they are."

"They're both eighteen, Lulu. As of today they're adults."

She looked down at the cake in her hands. "In name only."

"What else is there?"

"I wish to hell I knew," she said. "But all right. Talk it over with them before we make any decisions."

"Let's get inside," I said, starting toward the door of the Farm. "I'm freezing my ass off."

"You should've worn pants."

"I should've done a lot of things."

The living room seemed bright and hot after

our walk through the woods. There were ten kids on the Farm, with Tim and Gerald on duty to complete the party. I tossed my jacket on a chair by the kitchen door as Dhumavati led us inside to light the candles.

"All set?" asked Gerald as I held my lighter to that last tiny wick.

"Good to go," I said. "Why don't you dim the lights?"

Dhumavati held the door for him, and I headed forward with the blazing confection once he'd finished the task. She started singing "Happy Birthday," and everyone joined in from the next room.

I walked carefully, trying to keep the candles lit. Lulu followed, holding the cake knife Dhumavati had brought down — along with ice cream and little hats for everyone to wear, printed with confetti-throwing teddy bears to match the paper plates.

Fay was at the head of the table, her head slightly bowed. I put the cake down in front of her.

"Make a wish, Fay!" someone called out from the back of the crowd.

She didn't move, so I crouched down beside her.

"What do I wish for?" she asked me.

"Whatever would make you happy," I said.

Fay closed her eyes and nodded, then blew so gently on the candles that the flames barely shifted. I added a gust of my own, keeping it up until the last one flickered and died.

"You did it," I said, hoping she'd open her eyes to check. She didn't.

Gerald snapped the lights back on, and Lulu stepped in with the cake knife as kids jostled into line, gripping their paper plates.

"We'll serve the ice cream and punch in the kitchen," said Dhumavati. "Come back there when you've gotten your cake."

Mooney put two plates on the table next to Lulu — one for himself, one for Fay. "What kind of ice cream do you want?" he asked Fay. "Chocolate or vanilla?"

"Doesn't matter," she said.

"I'll get you both, then."

Lulu put a slice of cake on each plate and then looked at his bandage. "You can't carry two of those in one hand without getting them all mushy, Mooney," she said. "Let me help."

She passed me the knife and picked up both plates.

"We need to talk," I whispered to Mooney before he followed Lulu away from the table. I couldn't tell if he'd heard me.

Forchetti dropped his plate next to me.

There was already frosting smeared on it.

"You're getting seconds before everyone's had firsts?" I asked.

"Give me a decent slice this time. Lulu was all stingy."

"Go get some ice cream," I said. "The birthday girl hasn't even had cake yet."

"Give him mine," said Fay. "I don't want it."

"You heard her," said Forchetti. "She doesn't care."

"*I* care," I said.

Forchetti flicked his plate closer to the cake. "Why are you always such a bitch?"

"Why are you always such an asshole?" I said. "You could at least try saying please."

"Please," he whined, like he was auditioning for the part of Postnasal Drip in a really bad school play.

"And why are you back down here, anyway?" I asked. "You just got de-Farmed yesterday, didn't you?"

"I got in a fight. What's the big deal?"

"Nothing," I said.

I pinched the edge of his plate before slapping a thin slice of cake onto it, knowing he'd try to yank this ill-gotten bounty away.

I locked eyes with him and didn't let go of the plate. "I'd like to hear a thank-you, Forchetti."

He mumbled a buck's worth of nasty in lieu of the word "thank." I let him take the damn cake anyway. I served the last three kids in line much fatter slices than I'd given Forchetti, just out of spite.

Everyone else in the room was distracted, finally — eating cake, chatting, horsing around.

I pulled up a chair next to Fay. "We need to talk."

"I know," she said, "but this doesn't seem like a good time."

She seemed more alert now that no one was watching us.

"Maybe it's the best time," I said. "Nobody's paying any attention."

"Mooney has some stuff he wants to say, too, though. We were thinking maybe tomorrow, if you could come down during study hours again?"

I looked around the room. "Promise me you guys aren't planning to take off?"

"Not now," she said. "Don't worry. We have something to ask you."

"And I have an idea I want to run by both of you. I just want to make sure you're okay about sitting tight until then."

Fay glanced over my shoulder. "Dhumavati's coming."

I spoke a little louder. "How's your homework going?"

"I'm almost caught up," she said, acting all zoned out again. "I've been working really hard."

Dhumavati pulled up a chair across the table from me. "Fay's really been applying herself down here. I'm proud of her," she said.

Fay touched Dhumavati's hand. "That's so nice of you to say."

Lulu and Mooney came back. He put a plate down gently in front of Fay. "Here you go, a little bit of chocolate and vanilla."

They sat down, and Lulu handed him his own plate.

She looked at me. "Aren't you having any?"

I put the knife down on the cake plate next to the remaining wedge of frosted goodness. "That woodstove's really hot," I said. "I just want something to drink."

The roaring fire had made the air so dry that Gerald had to keep ladling watery fruit punch from a faceted plastic bowl in the kitchen. I lost my cup twice. Kept setting it down only to have it disappear in the general chaos.

The conversational volume went up and up, everyone buzzed on sugar and the rare break from routine.

I went back to Gerald for a third serving of bug juice, asking him to load it with extra ice. He took my cup.

The cafeteria vats of chocolate and vanilla Frozen Treat were getting soupy.

"Why don't I put these in the freezer?" I said.

"Great idea."

When I returned, he handed me my cup. "I think I'm going to make this self-serve from now on. I don't want to miss the party."

Another thirsty gang of kids shoved one another through the doorway.

"Nick of time," I said.

Outside the kitchen, Lulu was lining up chairs in the middle of the room. Dhumavati put a boom box on the table and plugged it in to a wall socket.

"Ready for the games portion?" she asked me and Gerald.

"I'd like to bow out," I said, "at least for the first round."

The air felt stuffy and close. I set my punch down on the arm of a sofa at a seemingly safe distance from the jollity, then started pulling off my sweater. As I was yanking it past my head, I heard someone step up next to me.

It was Mooney.

"Good thing Wiesner's not around," he said. "You with no sweater on."

"We need to talk, okay?" I said. "Fay told me I should come down tomorrow, when you guys are doing homework."

"Sounds good. You can pretend you're going over some stuff from class with me. I'll make sure Fay and I are both sitting at the big table."

"And you're not going to leave before then, right?" I asked.

"No way. Not unless you've told anyone else."

I shook my head. "I haven't."

Time enough to ask them about Dhumavati tomorrow, when I came back.

"Cool," he said. "And thank you for making sure Fay got to have such a nice birthday. You really made her happy, you and Lulu."

Dhumavati started jollying the kids into a game of musical chairs. At first they were reluctant, but when she recruited Gerald into the action, the competition picked up. Tim landed in Gerald's lap in the race for the final seat, and even the stragglers started to laugh and get into the spirit of the thing.

"First one knocked out has to be the DJ," Dhumavati said, putting Tim in charge of the music.

Lulu bustled around the room, picking up sticky abandoned plates and forks to throw in a garbage bag she was dragging around.

Tim punched the stop button on the boom box, and the group surged for available chairs. Forchetti stumbled over Gerald and almost landed on the sofa next to me. I was too close to the game and the wood-stove.

Standing up made me dizzy, and I'd broken out in a sweat from the heat of the fire. I reached to grab my sweater so I could blot my forehead with it.

Tim punched "play" while my face was covered, and the crowd shoved into me. I could've sworn there were a hundred people in the room. I dropped the sweater and turned back to get a sip of punch, but my cup was gone again.

Lulu was sliding her garbage bag around behind the sofa.

"Hey, did you take my juice?" I asked.

She picked up a brimming red cup from the little side table next to my sofa. Not where I thought I'd seen my cup last. "This it?"

"Must be," I said, taking it from her so I could knock back the cold sugary liquid in one go, ice cubes bumping against my lip.

"Are you okay?" she asked. "You're really

flushed."

"It's just so hot." I reached for my wadded-up sweater again, mopping my face and neck with it.

Lulu pressed her wrist to my cheek. It felt cool and lovely.

"I need some air," I said, standing up again. My chest felt tight, and everything looked all wobbly.

"Don't go without your jacket," said Lulu. "You'll catch your death."

"Just for a minute," I said.

"Wait until I get this stuff in the garbage," she said. "I'll go with you."

She started walking toward the kitchen, obviously thinking I'd stay put, but I had to get out right then. I couldn't catch my breath, and my jaw felt sore and tight. I lurched for the door, making my way through the spinning crowd, all of them jostling again for too few chairs.

The music stopped, and I could hear them all laughing and shoving behind me as I burst outside into the blessed cold, panting with relief. The buzz of noise died away as the door swung shut behind me.

There was a moon rising up over the trees, and the ground's dusting of snow looked all blue-white and sparkly in the watery light.

"Pretty," I said, watching more flakes

dance down.

I walked away from the building and turned my face up, closing my eyes in the hope that the snow would cool my still-burning cheeks, but the motion only made me dizzier.

I opened my eyes and took another step forward. The ground felt like it was moving. I swayed and then fell, landing hard on my hands and knees.

I stayed like that for a while, panting. The idea of getting back up off the ground seemed overwhelmingly difficult. I was tempted to lie down and press my face against the snow.

"Get *up,*" I said, but I couldn't convince my body to make the effort. My voice sounded like it was coming from ten yards away.

I crawled toward the garden fence, hoping to pull myself back to my feet. Halfway there, I felt my stomach heave, and I started vomiting up an acrid-sweet mess of punch and cake and ice cream — hot and pink all over the ground — droplets melting the thin cover of snow with a hiss wherever they touched down.

I fought against the next wave of nausea to no avail. It just kept groaning up more, again and again, until I was emptied down to my boots.

I wanted to lie down but not in my own mess, so I kept crawling, making it almost all the way to the fence before I collapsed.

The snow felt good. Soft and velvety. Cool but warm.

I wanted to stay there forever.

After what seemed like a stretch of days, I raised my head a few inches — only then realizing that the ground wasn't covered with snow at all but was instead teeming with millions of tiny white spiders. They were glassy and feral in the moonlight, and every moment saw more of them drifting down to earth through the night sky, plummeting faster and faster until they were piled so thick that everything went black.

I woke up in bed in the dark, curled into a ball with the covers half thrown off me, aching all over like I'd asked too much from each muscle in my body.

Everything hurt: neck, scalp, forearms, the arches of my feet. My face felt sticky, my mouth sour and raw. I turned my head, but all I could see was a line of light spilling inward from between a set of drawn curtains. Morning?

But that's not where the window is in our bedroom. And we don't have curtains.

I was cold, too. I reached for the covers, letting out a little yelp when the movement made everything hurt even more.

"Madeline?" said Lulu in the darkness. "Are you awake?"

"Think so," I said, my voice all raspy.

She turned on a light, and I squinted against the glare.

"Hurts," I said.

"The light?"

"Mmm."

I tried opening my eyes. Lulu was wrapped in a blanket, sitting in a chair beside the window.

"Where?" I asked.

"Dhumavati's guest room," she said. "We carried you here last night." She turned off the light but opened the curtains, revealing a window seat piled with a funky jumble of Moroccan-looking pillows. The mattress jiggled when she came over to sit on the edge of the bed.

"Ow," I said. "Time is it?"

Lulu consulted her watch. "Just before eight. Dhumavati told me to keep you here, make sure you were okay."

I took in the room's contents: mismatched armchairs, a framed art nouveau poster of some buxom chick on a bicycle, a dark bureau topped by a ripply oval mirror, spent crumbs of incense on the paisley-shawled table beneath a large tanka portrait of Ganesh.

But for the lack of peacock feathers and my view of bare trees against November-sullen Berkshire sky, I could've sworn I'd woken up circa 1970, somewhere in the Haight.

"Try drinking a little water," Lulu said, reaching for a glass on the bedside table. "You couldn't keep anything down last night."

My lips were so dry it hurt to clamp them onto the edge of the glass. She tipped it up. More water spilled down my chin than got into my mouth, and she pulled the glass away.

The tiny sip made me feel thirstier. "More?"

"See if that stays down. I can make you some tea if you like."

My head was too heavy to hold up, so I let it fall back to the pillow.

"I'm going to go put the kettle on," she said.

I dozed off while she was gone, waking up when she sat down and made the mattress jiggle again.

She gave me another small sip of water. I kept it all in my mouth this time.

"You had a rough night," she said.

I swallowed. "What happened?"

"I thought you'd gone back to Pittsfield at first," she said. "Figured you'd ditched me because you didn't feel well."

"No."

"I know, it seemed pretty strange. I started walking home alone when the party was over."

She brushed a strand of hair off my forehead. "But on the way, I saw your car. So I got Pete, and we started looking for you. We finally found you mumbling to yourself out behind the vegetable patch, down by the Farm. You'd been sick. You kept talking about spiders."

"The snow," I said. "It looked like spiders."

"You were delirious." She gave me more water.

"How long was I out there?" I asked.

"They'd all gone to sleep down at the Farm."

The kettle started whistling.

"Peppermint tea okay?" she asked, standing up.

The idea was repulsive. "Just water."

"The mint will soothe your stomach. I'll put some honey in it."

The whistling got shriller. Lulu stood up

and left the room. After a minute I could hear her opening and shutting cabinet doors. She returned, bearing a hand-thrown clay mug, steam rising up off it with the smell of mint.

The scent made my stomach ripple, and I felt my mouth filling with spit.

She put it down on the bedside table. "I'll let that cool off."

"Yeah," I said. "I don't think I'm quite up for it."

"Give it a minute."

"Tell me what happened first," I said, shutting my eyes again.

"It was tough getting you here. We were going to take you to my apartment, but we didn't think you'd make it that far. You were so sick. This was closer."

"I'm sorry." I cringed, picturing her and Pete carrying me uphill from the Farm while I was covered in puke.

"Whose nightgown is this?" I asked, plucking at the unfamiliar sleeve on my arm.

"Dhumavati's. Your clothes were pretty nasty. I washed everything last night, but we had to put you in something." Lulu pointed to a pile of folded stuff on a small wing chair near the door. My jacket was hanging on the back.

"You didn't have to," I said.

"Well . . . I really did. Either that or throw it all out."

"Oh," I said.

"Plus, everything was wet from the snow."

"You guys must all be exhausted," I said. "I'm grateful."

"I'm just glad we found you."

"So am I."

"Have some tea," she said.

She held the mug to my lips, and I took a big swallow. It felt like it was going to stay down all right. I took it from her, drinking more, slowly.

She closed her eyes, leaning against the headboard next to me.

"Dean knows I'm here?" I asked.

"We called him after we got you cleaned up. He wanted to come down, but we told him he might as well let you sleep."

"Why don't you lie down all the way, get a little rest yourself?" I said.

"Feels good just like this, after that chair."

I heard the front door open in the next room. A breath of cold air washed over us.

Pete appeared in the doorway. "She's awake?"

"We both are," said Lulu.

"Hey," I said, slowly sitting up, "thank you for everything. Both of you."

"Are you feeling a little better?" he asked.

"Better," I said. "Not exactly great."

The two of them were silent for a bit too long.

"Have you told her?" Pete asked Lulu.

"Told me what?"

The phone rang out in the living room.

"I'll get it," he said, looking relieved.

"Told me what?" I asked Lulu.

"Shhh," she said.

He mumbled a few things, then got quiet. Finally, he said, "I'll let them know."

I heard him exhale before he fumbled the phone back in place.

He came into the doorway again and looked at Lulu. "That was Tim," he said. "Everything's canceled for the day . . . classes . . ."

I looked at him. "We got a snow day?"

Pete shook his head. Started to say something and then stopped.

"Pete?" I said.

He cleared his throat. "The police are here."

I tried to catch his eye. "Why?"

He walked over toward us. Took a seat at the foot of the bed. "They want to talk to everyone about last night."

"About what, last night?"

"Mooney and Fay."

"They ran away?" I asked.

He shook his head.

"What?"

Pete stood up again.

"Come on," I said, "what happened?"

He wouldn't look at me, couldn't stand still.

"So it's true?" asked Lulu.

"Yeah," he said.

I turned toward her. "What the hell's going on?"

"Last night," she said, "Mooney and Fay committed suicide."

"But they were just . . ."

"Oh, honey, I know." She put an arm around my shoulders to draw me close, tears running down her face.

I couldn't even cry, I was too numb. "How do you know for sure?"

"Dhumavati got a call this morning," she said.

"Why didn't you tell me?"

"She asked me to wait. We wanted to make sure you were okay first."

I looked up at Pete. "Who found them?"

"Gerald," he said. "Early this morning. Up in the loft."

"What loft?"

"Above the living room at the Farm. He wondered why the ceiling hatch to it wasn't closed all the way."

"How do you know they . . ." I couldn't finish the question.

"They drank something," said Pete. "Nothing up there with them but two half-empty cups of punch, and Gerald said there was some —"

He stopped.

"Some what?" I asked.

He shook his head.

I pulled away from Lulu. "Some *what,* Pete?"

He grimaced.

"Tell me," I said.

"Gerald said there was foam. Around their mouths. And that the cops were talking about poison."

I pushed the covers off my legs.

"Madeline, what the hell do you think you're doing?" asked Lulu.

I didn't answer, just crawled away from her and started to climb out the other side of Dhumavati's guest bed.

I felt horrible when I stood up — pounding headache, still sore all over. Weak and shaky. I caught sight of my reflection in an old mirror hanging over Dhumavati's bureau. I looked so horrible I closed my eyes. "This wasn't suicide."

"How do you know?" asked Pete.

I opened my eyes and stared at him in the

mirror. "I just do."

"Madeline," said Lulu, "come lie down before you fall over. I told Dhumavati I'd keep you in bed."

"I can't." I walked over to the bureau and braced myself, one hand against the top drawer.

"Don't be ridiculous," she said.

I turned toward Pete. "Where is everyone, in the dining hall?"

Lulu stood up. "You're sick as a damn dog."

"No," I said. "I'm not."

"Oh, please," she said. "You puked all over yourself in the snow. Couldn't even walk without us holding you up. I've never seen anyone get hit that hard with the flu."

"Look, Madeline," said Pete, "if the cops want to talk to you, they'll come down here."

"Dhumavati told me to let you rest," said Lulu. "Half the school's down with this bug."

I walked back to the bed so I was standing in front of her.

I took her hand. "Feel my forehead."

She reached up, laying her palm against my skin.

"No fever, right?" I asked. "And I didn't have any fever the first time you touched my face this morning, did I?"

She pursed her mouth, unswayed.

"And I haven't puked since you guys found me out there last night."

"Once," she said. "We had to change the sheets."

I turned to Pete. "Was that the last time, after you guys put me to bed?"

"We're not going to argue about this. You need rest," he said.

I walked over to the chair that held my folded clothes. "I need to get up there."

Lulu said, "You don't."

Pete stepped into the doorway, blocking my way out and looking all concerned.

He put a hand on my shoulder. "Lulu's right. You shouldn't go out in the cold. You're just gonna make yourself worse."

"Trust me," I said, "right now there's nothing I'd rather do than go home and lie down, preferably through Thanksgiving."

He pulled my shoulder gently, trying to turn me away from the door.

I shrugged his hand off. "Look, you guys — I don't *have* the flu. Somebody fucking dosed me."

17

"That's why I have to talk to the cops," I said. "Ask them to find out what the hell I threw up out in the snow — see if it's the same shit Fay and Mooney drank."

Lulu considered that. "You don't think it was suicide?"

"Was there a note?" I asked.

"I don't know," she said. "I'm not sure the police would discuss that with us."

"Gerald would've," I said. "And I can tell you right now he didn't find one."

I picked up my clothes off the chair. "I talked with Fay and Mooney last night. There's no way they were planning to kill themselves."

She nodded, but Pete looked like he wasn't about to give up blocking the doorway.

"If the police think they *did*," I said, "they're not going to look at anything else. Because then it's just a couple of crazy kids up at that crazy school. That's not what happened. They have to know."

"But Fay cutting herself," said Pete. "And the idea that anyone here would —"

"Maybe I'm wrong," I said. "I hope to hell I am."

"But maybe you're not," said Lulu.

She stood up and walked over to Pete.

"Go wait in the living room. Let Madeline get dressed."

She closed the door behind him, then turned back toward me. "You're sure about this?"

"Fay and Mooney wanted me to come back down to the Farm this afternoon so we could talk. They promised me they weren't taking off before then." I tossed Dhumavati's nightie onto the bed and started getting my clothes on.

"Okay," she said.

I sat down and reached for my boots. "Did you tell anyone about the rest of it?"

"No."

"You're sure?"

"Want me to spit into my palm so we can shake on it?"

"I'm sorry," I said. "I had to ask."

I stood up and checked myself out in the bureau's mirror again. There was a crocheted panel of lace laid out beneath it, with a few small mementos and framed photographs scattered across its surface. "You're just the only person I can trust," I added.

"Same here," she said. "Do you think there's any way this *was* suicide?"

"I told them I had an idea about something we could do," I said.

"Did you tell them what?"

"No," I said. "But I know they wanted to find out. Mooney's the one who told me to come back today."

I picked up a tin ashtray that held a white shell button and couple of bobby pins. Somebody's dented souvenir from Fisherman's Wharf. "I mean, I could believe they decided to blow me off and run away, but even that would've surprised the hell out of me."

"And where would they have found anything to do it with on their own?" Lulu asked.

Her question brought me up short. Because the first time I went down to the Farm, Mooney had told me about laying out the poison for rat duty.

If he and Fay *had* wanted to die, Mooney knew exactly what to spike the punch with.

But wouldn't rat poison be locked away? We weren't allowed to keep bottles of Wite-Out in our desks. Too many kids wanted to huff the fumes.

And Fay and Mooney had been so much less morose the night of the party. He'd even given me shit about keeping my sweater on around Wiesner.

I tilted the photos so I could see them better. One of young, dark-haired Dhumavati with a pretty little girl on her lap, the pair of them sitting on a picnic blanket in front of a spindly pagoda. One of Dhumavati alone, holding up a GET OUT THE VOTE! sign in a crowd of cheering people.

"When was the last time you were on overnight duty at the Farm?" I asked Lulu.

"Couple of weeks ago," she said. "Why?"

"Did you have to do anything about the rats?"

"We set out traps at night. I didn't think it was working too well."

"It wasn't," I said. "They'd started using poison."

"Would Mooney have known that?"

"He had to help spread it around at lights-out," I said. "But I can't believe anybody would leave shit like that sitting on the kitchen counter till morning, can you?"

"Of course not," she said. "There's a locked cabinet. Everything questionable goes in there — right down to the dish soap."

"Padlock or key?"

"A key. When you're on duty you have to wear it around your neck, even in bed."

"Are there any spare copies?"

"Probably," she said. "But Madeline, would it matter?"

"What do you mean?"

"Well, there was still poison on the floor, wasn't there? Whatever got put out for the actual rats . . ."

"And Mooney would know where those little piles were," I said.

"That's not how it works," she said. "We had a ton of rats in our barn back home. They don't just walk up to a pile of straight poison and lick it."

"So what do you do, spread it on cheese?"

"Mashed it up with peanut butter, in the old days. But now you're more likely to buy it premixed in little cardboard containers. The tops are perforated, and you rip them open when you want to use them."

"Did you see any in the cabinet?"

"No," she said. "Just the traps. But ask Pete. He was there last week, right?"

"I will," I said, "and thank you again for taking such good care of me last night."

"You can repay me by going up there to kick some ass on behalf of Fay and Mooney. I'll call Dean."

I put on my jacket, hugged her, and opened the bedroom door.

Lulu told Pete to drive me up to the dining hall, assuring us she'd stay to wait for Dean.

"You go in there with her, Pete," she said. "Call me if you need anything. I can leave a note for Dean, worst case."

She took a woolly hat and a scarf from the coatrack by the front door and bundled me up in them.

"Flu or no flu," she said, "you've been through a ton of shit, and it's goddamn cold out there."

She hugged me again, hard, then pushed us out the door.

Pete had an ancient hatchback, and it took a minute for the engine to turn over.

"There we go," he said when it finally caught and came to life. He gave the accelerator another pump to make sure, then put it in reverse and threw his arm around my seat, looking over his shoulder to back out.

"She's a good friend, Lulu," he said.

"She is," I replied.

We were going five miles an hour across campus. I couldn't see the dining hall yet.

"Listen," I said, "can I ask you something?"

"Sure."

"Mooney was on rat duty last week, when you had overnight at the Farm."

"He was," said Pete. "Do you think that's how they . . ."

"I don't know," I said. "But I wondered what kind of poison you guys were using. Lulu said it's usually these little cardboard things you rip open."

"Exactly," he said. "There's a gross of them, locked up in the kitchen."

"But some are left out at night, right?"

He nodded. Then he hit the brakes.

"This was my fault. I'm the one who put Mooney on rat duty."

"Pete, I still don't believe this was suicide."

"You don't know that."

"Even if I'm wrong, it wasn't your idea to use poison in the first place, was it? I mean, we're all told how dangerous Wite-Out is, but somebody thought it was okay to leave a bunch of little boxes of strychnine lying around?"

"Arsenic," he said. "At least that's what's printed on the box."

"Arsenic," I said. "That's just brilliant."

"I should've realized. Should've said something."

"Sure," I said. "Me, too. And Gerald and Cammy and anyone else who's been on duty since they stopped using traps down there. If anyone's responsible for that negligence, we all are."

"I'm still the one who chose Mooney," he said.

"But you're not the one who mixed it into his cup of punch," I said. "Or Fay's."

"I might as well have."

"Pete, you're forgetting that somebody put it into mine. And I sure as shit wasn't planning to kill myself last night."

"You're right," he said, lifting his foot off the brake pedal. "You've got me convinced. I think this was murder."

"What changed your mind?"

"Two things," he said. "First, if you had the same flu that's going around New Boys, you'd still be feverish and throwing up. You're not."

"Second?"

"I can believe Fay and Mooney might commit suicide, but there's no way they wanted to take you with them."

"And if I got dosed at the party, they couldn't have," I said. "The poison was still locked up, right?"

"Absolutely," he said. "And we only put out six a night. They got counted in the morning, so Mooney couldn't have kept one back for himself. Even if they killed themselves, it wasn't until after you left the building last night that he had access to any poison."

We'd reached the dining hall. Pete pulled up in front and turned off the ignition.

"When we go inside," I said, "you should explain all of that to the cops. I'll tell them what happened to me."

"Sounds like a plan," he said.

But we didn't get out of the car. We just sat there staring at the building in silence for a minute.

"Can we find out who was wearing the key to that cabinet last night?" I asked.

"It doesn't matter," he said. "There are spares to everything down at David's house — dorm keys, fire alarms, meds cabinets . . ."

"Who has access to those?"

Just David?

"Too many people to narrow it down," he said. "Everybody on staff, pretty much. I had to borrow a spare master for New Boys one afternoon last week, after I locked mine in the car. Not to mention there's probably more than one set of copies on campus: maintenance, Dhumavati, security . . . David wouldn't want to be woken up every time somebody got locked out in the middle of the night."

"Great," I said.

And then we just sat there staring at the dining hall some more.

Pete pulled his keys out of the ignition and held them up. There had to be more than a dozen of them hanging off the carabiner he used for a chain.

"I hate to admit it," he said, "but I wish this were 'just' suicide. Hard to say whether it's worse thinking any one of us could have killed two kids, or finding out which one."

"Going in there is gonna suck, isn't it?" I said. "Even more than everything already does."

"Big-time."

"Okay, then," I said, reaching for the door handle.

Dhumavati walked over to us the minute we got inside the building.

"Madeline," she said, "I just can't . . ." Then she broke down and wept.

"I know," I said.

She stepped forward and went slack against me. She didn't even have the strength to raise her arms to my waist — her hands just fell limp against my hips.

I snaked an arm tight around her upper back, worried she'd slide to the ground if I let her go, then reached up to cradle her head on my shoulder. We stayed like that for a long time.

"Have you talked to the police yet?" I asked her.

She pulled back. "I just finished."

"Then go home," I said. "You need sleep."

"Madeline's right," said Pete.

"I can't sleep," she said. "There's too much to do."

"Then at least take fifteen minutes," I said. "Let Lulu make you some tea."

She agreed to that, and Pete and I stepped through the inner doors into the dining hall.

The first thing the cops did was separate us. They'd spread out at various points around the room, taking preliminary statements from everyone who'd been at the Farm the night before. There was a young woman in uniform standing in the foyer, sorting everyone out. She'd already dispatched Gerald, Tim, and the kids who'd been on the Farm to separate tables. Pete and I were promptly assigned to distant chairs.

I waited for a couple of minutes but then got nervous about how much area they were protecting around the ostensible suicide scene down at the Farm. I got up from my solo table and walked back across the room toward the clipboard woman.

She glanced at me but was busy speaking into a handheld radio. I didn't want to interrupt her but finally worked up the nerve to say, "Hi?"

"Ma'am," she said, "please remain at your table. We'll take your initial information as soon as we can, okay?"

"I don't know if you're the right person to ask this, Officer" — I looked at her name tag — "Officer Baker, but I have a question about how much of the area you've cordoned off down at the scene."

"Ma'am, if you could just —"

"I know this sounds kind of out there, but I think you guys may be looking at a homicide here, and I was hoping to, um, run something by whoever is in charge of evidence collection?"

"Ma'am?"

"I was at the birthday party last night, and I think something was slipped into my punch. I was . . . I threw up outside the dorm and was really disoriented for a number of hours afterward, and . . ." I was sounding like a complete lunatic, even to myself. I half expected her to send me back to my quarantine table, but she held up a "don't move" index finger instead, while bringing the radio back up to her mouth. After a burst of static, she told the guy on

the other end to find Cartwright, ASAP. I
thanked her, and she motioned to another
uniformed guy across the hallway.

He grinned at her as he walked over.
"Whatcha need, Kas?"

Baker ignored him. "This is *Officer* Hoyt,"
she said to me. "He's going to take your
information."

Hoyt walked me back into the dining hall.
We sat down at a corner table, and he got
set with a clipboard and pen. He was maybe
a few years older than me. Wiry guy. Pleasant and polite.

All his questions were general, open-
ended. He started out with the basics: my
name, my address, how long I'd worked at
Santangelo.

I told him what I'd told Baker, but he
didn't bring the conversation back around
to any of that at first. Didn't interrupt me
at all — just let me talk until I was emptied
of words, after a question — giving space
and time for each of my answers to play
itself out.

I told him where I thought I'd gotten sick,
near the fence of the Farm's garden, and
told him why I thought it might be important.

"Do you want me to show someone where,
exactly?" I asked.

"I'll let them know. We want to keep people out of the scene as much as possible, ma'am."

"The guy I came in here with," I said, "Pete?"

I looked for him across the room. "Blond hair. Wearing a blue sweater, over there by the salad bar."

"Yes, ma'am, with Officer Stinson." He looked down at his clipboard to jot another note.

"Pete and another teacher — Lulu Costigan — found me down there in the snow last night, unconscious. I know where I started to throw up, but it sounds like I crawled farther afterward, and I don't know where to, exactly. You might want to ask Pete."

"I'll double-check, make sure we get that information."

"Thank you," I said. "I'm not sure it matters, but just in case."

"Better too much information than too little, ma'am," he said.

I nodded.

Hoyt looked up at me, pen at rest again. "So you think there was opportunity to slip something into your drink?"

"I kept losing track of my cup," I said. "I went back for a new one twice. It was hot,

233

with the woodstove going. I was really thirsty. Gerald didn't mind."

"Gerald?"

"Another teacher," I said. "The guy who found Fay and Mooney this morning. He was serving the punch, but it could have been anyone."

"We'd like you to go down to the station, Ms. Dare — do some follow-up on your preliminary statement. I'm sure Detective Cartwright will want to ask you some further questions once he reads my notes. He might like to get your fingerprints as well, see if we can match them with the cups you drank out of."

"Certainly," I said, trying not to look unsettled by that idea.

"Our crime lab's in Sudbury. They can analyze the punch, let us know if there's anything of concern."

"My husband's on his way down from Pittsfield," I said. "Lulu told him I'd be waiting at Dhumavati's apartment, across campus. In fact, he may be here already. Could I let him know before I leave?"

"We'll make sure he's brought up to speed," said Hoyt. "Would you like him to meet you at the station?"

"Yes, thank you," I said. "And thank you for taking my concerns seriously. I may be absolutely wrong. I don't want to think anyone here could have done something like this, but if it wasn't suicide . . . I just wanted you to know there might be another way of looking at what happened last night."

"Suspicious deaths are investigated as homicides at the outset," he said. "We don't make any presumptions. No way to have a handle on what's important until we've had a chance to reflect on everything."

A dark panel van drove slowly past the front windows of the dining hall. There was an official-looking seal painted on its door.

Maybe the coroner's. Maybe Fay and Mooney were inside.

It was snowing again. Bleak and gray.

"Officer Hoyt?" I said.

"Yes, ma'am?"

"I know this place must have a strange reputation. I mean, it's not the first time the police have had occasion to come up here."

His expression didn't betray any opinion on that.

"It's just . . ." My throat got all tight, and I could feel tears coming up at the corners of my eyes. An ache, a soreness.

I stopped for a minute, wanting to get the words out right without breaking down.

"Sir?" I said finally. "They were *good* kids,

Fay and Mooney. I want you guys to know that."

Then I lost it. I coughed up sobs and covered my face with my hands and felt the loss of them cut through me, hard and sad and awful.

I lowered my hands, wanting to tell him more, thinking, *Fuck it if my face is covered with snot.* I held my breath for a minute, trying to make my chest stop shuddering.

Hoyt touched my shoulder.

"Please," I said. "Whatever happened last night, Fay and Mooney deserved better. They *mattered.*"

"I know they did, Ms. Dare. And please let us know if there's anything you need down at the station."

I hunched down in the patrol car's backseat as it pulled out of the gates, headed for Stockbridge. My hands were cold, and I shoved them deep in my jacket pockets. I touched the half-empty box of birthday candles, surprised when something sharp poked into my fingertip. I scooped my hand under the contents of my pocket and pulled everything out slowly.

Four objects rested at the center of my palm: the candles, my lighter and cigarettes, and the silver crescent moon of Fay's necklace.

Its clasp was fastened tight, but the chain was busted — tiny links twisted open at the break as though it had been snatched off her neck in a hurry.

18

We didn't stop in Stockbridge, just kept on driving.

"Be going to the state police barracks in Lee, ma'am," the guy at the wheel explained. "Something like this, Stockbridge calls us in. Our branch of Troop B patrols sixteen towns locally. Five hundred fifty square miles."

I thought of Arlo Guthrie singing about how Stockbridge had "three stop signs, two police officers, and one police car."

Kid, have you rehabilitated yourself?

Cartwright was sure to appreciate me singing half a bar of "Alice's Restaurant" once they had me sitting on the Group W bench there.

Especially after they ran my fingerprints.

Especially once I told them I had Fay's necklace in my pocket.

I touched the point of that silver moon again, rocking it back and forth under the pad of my thumb while I wondered how the hell it had gotten there in the first place.

I remembered Lulu telling me not to go outside without my jacket on the night before, and I remembered ignoring her admonition.

For a second I wondered if Fay had tucked the necklace into my pocket herself, to say goodbye. Maybe she and Mooney really had committed suicide?

Except Fay would have unhooked the clasp, not broken the chain. Or asked Mooney to unhook it for her.

Someone else took it off her neck. Not gently — the chain was slender but well made.

And now I'd touched the pendant, probably ruined any chance of finding out who that someone was.

I pulled my hand away, too late. Nothing on the surface of Fay's moon now but my own fingerprints.

Prints that were on file at a police station in upstate New York — enshrined in some little folder, a study in black-and-white — because I'd been the first person to arrive at the scene of another murder the year before.

I shifted in my seat.

Looked at the back of the young cop's

239

close-cropped head.

Wondered whether I should show him the necklace right then and there.

He eased the car off Route 20 and onto Laurel Street. The state police barrack was a solid old brick building at the corner. Tall narrow windows marked each of its two stories, with a dormered third row jutting out from the low-pitched white roof.

My driver walked me inside before handing me off. I filled a crimped-foil ashtray with the stubs of my remaining Camels, waiting for Cartwright in a small back room. It contained two metal chairs and a scarred table but had no windows — just an overhead fluorescent panel, the kind I always blamed for the minor chord of despair in cut-rate department-store dressing rooms.

One of the fixture's tubes had developed an arrhythmic tic, its flicker and buzz compounding my bridle of headache. After cursing the damn thing for twenty minutes, I considered climbing onto a chair to yank it out.

The young guy who'd driven me down stuck his head in the door just before I actually stood up to attempt it.

"Can I get you anything?" he asked. "Coffee?"

I begged him for aspirin, and he took off to find some.

When he returned with a bottle of Bayer and a white cone of water from the office cooler, I asked, "Is my husband here yet? Tall blond guy?"

"He's out front, ma'am. We've told him it might be a while."

I could see a wall clock over the cop's shoulder. I'd been here close to an hour. "Can I talk to him, tell him I'm okay?"

The guy hesitated; he obviously didn't know what to say but wasn't about to let Dean come back and hang out with me.

"If he'd like to go home," I said, "please tell him I can call when we're done with everything."

He gave a clipped nod in answer to that, then left me alone again.

I pulled Fay's necklace out of my pocket and placed it at the center of the table. I didn't want to lose my nerve when it came to showing the thing to Cartwright, if he ever in fact arrived.

Not that I begrudged him the time, no matter how much I ached for sleep. The crime scene deserved his full attention, and cooling my heels at the station was the least I could do for Fay and Mooney.

I sparked up another Camel and pondered

the riddle of that necklace. Safe to presume Lulu had grabbed my jacket when she left the Farm. She was thoughtful that way.

But then how had the little moon landed in my pocket? Wouldn't Fay have noticed someone snatching it off her neck during the party? The idea of someone tiptoeing into Dhumavati's guest room to plant it on me in the middle of the night was ludicrous.

Nothing made sense.

I stubbed out my smoke and started kneading the tight thin flesh across my forehead, closing my eyes against the sickly flicker of light and willing the aspirin to kick in. Finally, I got up and flipped the switch by the door, feeling the way back to my seat in the dark.

I crossed my arms on the table and laid my head down. All I could think of was Fay and Mooney lying side by side in the back of that cold van.

I wept myself to sleep, haunted by the image of their faces, veiled beneath black bags that had been zipped unequivocally closed.

I startled awake, squinting, when the lights snapped back on.

A bulky guy stood in the doorway, gray-haired and bullnecked, wearing a sport coat that was tight across his shoulders and a touch short at the wrists.

"Sorry to keep you waiting here so long, Ms. Dare," he said.

"Not a problem, sir."

He stepped over to the table and stuck out his hand. I looked him in the eye and shook it.

"Detective Cartwright," he said.

"Please call me Madeline."

Cartwright pulled the second chair back from the table and lowered himself into it, thighs beefy enough that he sat with his legs angled a little apart. He wasn't fat, just former-fullback thick.

He butted a sheaf of papers and file folders against the table's surface to square them, then laid them flat in a crisp pile.

"Let's see what we've got so far," he said, opening the uppermost file to reveal Hoyt's notes.

He skimmed the first page while unbuttoning his jacket, then produced a ballpoint pen, clicked its top, and raised his eyes back to mine.

I pressed my fingers down against the tips of the necklace's broken chain and dragged it across the table to rest, centered, at the head of his paperwork.

"I thought you should see this, sir," I said. "It belonged to Fay."

"She gave it to you?"

I shook my head.

"How'd it come to be in your possession?" he asked.

"I found it in my jacket pocket," I said. "On the drive over here."

"And do you have any idea how it might have ended up there?"

"Not a one."

Cartwright exhaled through his nose, teasing the broken chain straight with the tip of his pen, then flipping over the little moon. There was engraving on the back.

"I touched it," I said. "I'm sorry. Didn't know what it was before I took it out of my pocket — just something sharp when I put my hand in there."

"You had that jacket with you last night?"

"I left it at the party. Felt so awful all of a sudden. I just wanted to get outside for some air, then I passed out."

I explained about Lulu and Pete taking me up to Dhumavati's apartment, and Lulu washing my clothes after they'd put me to bed.

"You probably know all that from Officer Hoyt's notes," I said, "but when he took my statement, I didn't know yet about the necklace."

"MDL," he said. "Are those the boy's

initials?"

"Mooney LeChance. I don't know his middle name."

"He gave her the necklace?"

"Yes," I said. "Fay told me she hadn't taken it off since."

I watched him move the ballpoint's tip away from the broken links of chain, tapping it thoughtfully against the table's edge.

"Doesn't seem as though she's the one who took it off this time," he said.

"No," I said, "it doesn't."

Cartwright looked up at me again. "When I spoke with Dr. Santangelo this morning, he expressed his profound remorse and grief that two students had chosen to end their lives while in his care."

I crossed my arms.

"He then added," Cartwright continued, "that while, of course, he and the entire staff of the Santangelo Academy were deeply saddened by this tragic outcome, he could not truthfully maintain that these two young people having committed suicide came as a complete surprise. Either to himself or to their respective therapists."

I didn't say anything.

"I gather, Ms. Dare, that Dr. Santangelo's last point is not one you agree with."

"You gather correctly, Detective Cartwright."

He smiled at that for a fraction of a second, though I bet he would've denied the hell out of having done so.

"All right, then," he said. "I'd like you to tell me why."

So I did.

19

They got me fingerprinted at the end of it all, and when I was dispatched from the back rooms of the building, I found Dean still waiting for me, not in the best of moods.

His neck was all cordy. When Dean is truly pissed off, his eyelids seem to open a little wider than normal, as though there's a buildup of something hot back there in his skull that wants to get out. A sharp hiss of steam, or sulphur, or maybe tear gas.

He looked not at me but up at the old black-rimmed clock on the station wall, its yellowed face over a foot wide.

"Three hours," he said, "and forty-seven minutes."

He kept staring at the clock.

"No shit," I said. "Could we please go home now?"

He didn't move. I started walking toward the front door. When I was almost there, I heard him stand up to follow me, the soles of his high-tops squeaking on the polished floor.

It was cold outside, and my jacket felt thin. The air rasped metallic on the intake, and the afternoon sky was low and dark — like some giant hand had clapped a stainless-steel bowl upside down over the surrounding hills.

Dean drew alongside me at the bottom of the concrete stairs. I couldn't see where he'd parked, so I slowed to follow his lead, uphill or down, just before the sidewalk bisected our path.

He cut across me to the right. I turned in his wake, jogging to catch up and then stutter-stepping to match his strides down the block. He threw off such a force field of bristle that the sidewalk wasn't wide enough for both of us.

I hustled beside him, off the concrete and along the front edge of a half dozen lawns. My boots punched through a thin crust of ice with each step, making the frosted spindles of grass beneath crackle and pop as I mashed them flat. Dean's rusted Mercedes sedan was another block down the street.

I wanted to ask him why he was being such a dick, but the cold sawed at my ravaged throat and I was getting dizzy.

I slowed down until I fell behind him, then stopped to rest against an old station wagon parked at the curb, hands cupped around my mouth to capture the warmth of my breath.

Dean turned around, walking backward. "Bunny, are you all right?"

I shook my head.

He stopped ten yards away.

I turned to brace myself against the car, then puked in the gutter, water and bile raining down on the exhaust-blackened chunks of snow at my feet. I heard Dean pounding back toward me, felt him lift my hair gently to get it out of the way. His other hand rested on my shoulder as I convulsed with dry heaves. He wrapped me in his coat when I'd finished.

"So tired," I said.

He put an arm around my waist to steady me down to the curb. "I'm going to get the car. Will you be okay here for a minute?"

"Mmm."

He pelted away up the street, and I wrapped my arms around my knees, shivering.

I woke up in the dark again but knew right away that I was home this time from the sound of cars hissing through slush in the rotary four stories below.

I shifted onto my side, saw Dean sitting cross-legged on top of the covers next to me, outlined against our bedroom windows by the soft glow of Pittsfield.

"Hey," I said, my voice ragged.

"How are you doing?"

"Shitty."

Talking made me cough, the effort hurting my belly and throat.

"Can I get you anything?" he asked. "Juice?"

"Please," I said, checking the clock when he got up. Ten-thirty.

He came back with a glass. Apple juice on ice. I took three gulps of it.

"Drink slowly," he said. "See if it stays down."

I set it on the bedside table after another two sips.

"I don't really remember getting into bed," I said. "Just the car."

"You were so wiped out I practically carried you. Thank God there's an elevator."

"How long have I been asleep?"

"Five hours."

"Anybody call?"

"Lulu did," he said. "Twice now."

"Did she tell you about Fay and Mooney?"

"Not a lot more than what she said this

morning when I got to the school."

"So if you already knew what happened, why were you being such a dick down at the cop station?" I started coughing again and reached for the juice to make it stop.

He waited until I could breathe, then said, "I was freaked out."

"*You* were freaked out?"

"They had you down there at cult central with two kids dead, and then you got whisked off by state troopers before I had a chance to see if you were all right, for chrissake."

"So you bitch me out the minute the cops cut me loose?"

He didn't answer.

"I mean, Dean," I said, "in case Lulu didn't fill you in, as far as I can tell, somebody tried to take *me* out last night, too. I could've died out in the goddamn snow."

"And I'm supposed to be all sunshine and flowers about that?"

"Touch of civility might've been appropriate, considering."

"I told you that place was fucked up *weeks* ago." Dean sat up straighter in the half dark. "What am I supposed to do, sit here with my thumb up my ass until Nurse Ratched belts you down for the shock treatments? I'm supposed to start this job next Monday.

251

What if it had been this week?"

He took my hand. "Look, it's just that you had me so worried."

"I'm sorry."

"I'm sorry, too, Bunny. I should've driven down there and brought you home the minute Lulu called last night."

The phone started ringing out in the living room.

"Jesus Christ," he said. "I'm about ready to yank that thing out of the wall."

"They'll call back."

He stood up. "Fuck it, I'll go see who it is. Maybe we've won the damn lottery."

He got it on the fourth ring.

I listened to his voice rumbling and pausing. He didn't sound happy with whoever was on the line.

I hauled myself upright and shoved out of bed, unsteady as hell.

"I don't care how important it is. It's after eleven at night," Dean said, "and Madeline's exhausted."

"Lulu?" I mouthed.

He shook his head, saying, "So she can call you back in the morning, then."

He listened to some argument against that. "Why not?"

I walked over to him. "Who is it?"

He shook his head, put a finger to his lips.

"Let me *talk*," I said.

"Fine," he said, "now you've gotten her up."

He shoved the phone toward me.

I took it and slumped into a chair, coughing again before I raised the receiver to my ear.

"Madeline?" A guy's voice.

"Speaking," I said. "Who's this?"

"Wiesner."

Great.

"Wiesner?" I said. "This has been a long and horrible day. Please reassure me that your calling me from school does not in any way involve that screwdriver out of my desk."

"I'm not exactly *at* school."

"Care to be more specific?"

"Well, I'm in Pittsfield."

"Pittsfield?" I covered my eyes with my free hand. "Jesus, Wiesner, how'd you get up here?"

"I hitched," he said, his shrug practically audible.

"Where are you now?"

"There's this Dunkin' Donuts, like, two blocks over from your apartment?"

I sighed. "Wiesner, this is really a bummer."

"Your husband sounded a little upset," he

said. "I thought you might like to come down, grab some coffee and a Boston cream?"

I figured I'd probably have to drive him back down to Santangelo, but didn't think I could walk across the living room again without passing out.

"We need to talk," he said. "It's important."

"I guess you should come over here," I said, knowing Dean was going to lose his shit the minute I told him.

"Cool," said Wiesner. "Any place I can score some Marlboros on the way?"

20

"You did *what?*" said Dean.

"Look," I said, "you'd prefer I met him for doughnuts? What the hell else was I supposed to do?"

"I'd prefer it if you called the damn school and had *them* drive up here to corral the kid."

"What if he got hit by a truck before someone got to him?" I said.

"So call the cops."

"Oh, for God's sake."

"Bunny — you're exhausted, you're sick . . ." Dean closed his eyes and jammed his fingertips against his temples. "I know these kids matter to you —"

"They do. A lot."

"I just . . . *You* matter more."

"Thank you," I said, thinking it was a bad time to mention how Wiesner had bashed out Gerald's front teeth the year before.

"You should be in bed. We're both tired

as shit," Dean said.

"I know."

"Please call the school," he said. "Have someone else deal with it for tonight. Lulu. Pete. Whoever."

"I will," I said, "but I want to talk to him first, find out what he had to hitchhike up here to tell me about in person."

"Your eyes look like two holes burned in a blanket."

"Feel like it, too."

"Go lie down on the sofa," he said.

He brought me an unscorched blanket and topped up my glass with juice.

When Wiesner's voice crackled over the intercom from the street lobby, Dean buzzed him up.

Wiesner sat in an armchair across from me. We were both smoking his Marlboros.

"You tell anyone I bummed this from you," I said, "and I will make your life suck forever."

He smiled. "Our little secret. Got any beer?"

"Don't push it," I said. "Just tell me why you're here."

He leaned back in the chair and crossed his legs. "Forchetti said you were down on the Farm last night."

I wondered how he'd managed a chat with Forchetti, then realized there was no way any kids would've been allowed to stay in the building once Gerald had found Fay and Mooney.

"I know you set the cops straight about what happened," he said, "but there's something else you should tell them."

"You know what I told them already?"

"That you think Fay and Mooney didn't off themselves. That you think someone dosed you with whatever killed them."

"How'd you hear that?" I asked.

"It's a small school."

"Not that small," I said.

"Someone was in the hallway outside Lulu's classroom when she was talking to Pete about it."

"Someone who?"

"Doesn't matter," he said, "if what you said is true."

"I don't know if it's true or not. I just wanted the cops to check out the possibility, in case."

"Bullshit," he said.

"Wiesner . . ."

"You are such a crappy liar, Madeline. And we both know there's no way those guys killed themselves."

Dean rattled some cups in the kitchen,

giving Wiesner a little hairy eyeball via the pass-through window.

"Let's hit the fast-forward here, kid," he said. "It's eleven-thirty, and we're beat to shit."

Wiesner looked cowed. It had obviously been a while since he'd found himself in a room with a guy bigger than he was.

He turned back to me. "You know about what happened to Gerald's teeth?"

"Yeah," I said.

"Do you know why I hit him?"

I shook my head.

"Last year me and Mooney and this guy Parker were roommates in New Boys."

He tapped his cigarette against the ashtray and took another drag.

"So this one night, when Gerald was doing bed check," he continued, "he grabbed Parker's dick."

"Gerald said you punched him when you were both in his classroom."

"Sure. That was a couple of days later."

"So what does this have to do with last night?"

"Gerald's court date is coming up," he said, "and Parker's family wanted Mooney to testify."

"Not you?"

"I was in the bathroom," he said. "Didn't

258

see it happen. And then, you know, the lawyers didn't like the whole thing about me knocking Gerald's teeth out."

"But you decked him because of Parker?" I asked, thinking better of Wiesner for that. Kind of.

"Parker was an asswipe from the get-go," he said. "Plus, his family took him home the minute they heard. I just didn't want Gerald pulling that crap on me."

Well, okay, so it was still better than his having belted the guy for fun.

"Why've they got you down there at Santangelo?" Dean asked him.

Wiesner shrugged. "Guess it's because I like to blow shit up."

I looked over at Dean.

"My best student," I said. "Tried to give him a gold star last week."

Wiesner grinned at me. "No shit?"

I felt sheepish. "Gerald kind of talked me out of it."

He laughed. "So Forchetti told me Gerald was down there, too, last night. Serving the punch."

I nodded.

"And he's the one who supposedly found Fay and Mooney this morning, right?"

I nodded again.

Wiesner tilted his head to the side. "You

getting more of an idea why I thought it was important to come up here?"

"Yeah, Wiesner, I am."

"You know that old joke? 'I may be crazy, but I'm not stupid . . .' "

He dropped his head and shot me a look through those long pretty lashes, tongue tip driving a sly bulge across the hollow of his left cheek — the side Dean couldn't see.

Wiesner left me three Marlboros.

Dean said he'd drive him back to school, joking that maybe they could compare notes about blowing shit up on the way.

Weisner paused in the doorway, then turned to look back at me. "Just promise you'll make sure the cops know about Gerald, if they don't already."

"Absolutely," I said.

I pulled the blanket up to my shoulders. The elevator dinged open out in the hallway. I could hear the two of them laughing until its doors slid back shut.

I figured I'd catch some sleep while Dean was gone, but he came back through our front door a few minutes later.

"Don't tell me you put Wiesner on a bus," I said.

"He took off the minute we got down to the parking lot."

"Did you go after him?"

"I didn't really see the point, especially since he was so damn fast."

Dean lowered himself onto the sofa next to my blanket-swaddled feet. "He did stop and look back at me after he got over that fence. Said he appreciated the offer of a ride, but there was no way in hell he was sleeping down there, at least until Gerald's arrested."

"Can't say I blame him," I said.

"No, but I wasn't about to let him crash here, either. He's not stupid — I'll give him that much — but he's still shithouse-rat crazy."

"Kind of charming, though, huh?"

"Sure," said Dean, "charm to spare, right up until he knifes you in your sleep."

"Or blows you up," I said.

"Six of one." He reached for my empty apple juice and carried it into the kitchen.

I hiked the blanket around my shoulders and climbed off the sofa.

"I should let Lulu know Wiesner was here," I said. "She can pass it on."

"Tell her the kid was last seen sprinting up North Street."

I dialed Lulu. Dean turned on the kitchen faucet and started rinsing out my glass. He snapped his fingers. "Hey, I nearly forgot —

Charm Boy wants you to know he still thinks you have a sweet ass."

"The little *shit*."

Lulu picked up, muttering a groggy "Hello?"

"Check it out," said my husband. "Bunny's blushing."

"What the hell was Wiesner doing in Pittsfield?" croaked Lulu after I'd related the most recent developments.

"He wanted me to know some shit about Gerald. Stuff that happened last year."

I could hear running water and clinking on her end of the line. "What're you, washing dishes?"

"Making coffee," she said. "It's after midnight and looking like I'm gonna be up awhile."

"Could you let Dhumavati know? Wiesner took off about ten minutes ago."

"I take it you'd like me to avoid mentioning this to Gerald?"

"Just call me back."

"Two shakes of a lamb's tail," she said.

I recradled the receiver.

"You've gotta get some sleep, Bunny," said Dean.

"Go on ahead. I'll be there in five minutes."

He yawned. "And I've got some prime swampland in Florida."

"I'll be quick as I can, okay?"

He started staggering bedward, mumbling, "Brooklyn Bridge" back over his shoulder at me.

I snapped up the phone on the first ring, pulling the cord taut to make it reach the sofa. "So?"

"Madeline?"

It wasn't Lulu. It was Dhumavati.

21

"I know you must be exhausted after today," said Dhumavati, "but I wish you'd kept Wiesner at your apartment until we could've sent someone to pick him up."

The phone line crackled a little. She didn't sound angry, just tired and concerned.

"My husband was going to drive him down to you," I said. "I'm so sorry. We never expected him to bolt from the parking lot like that."

"Wiesner's always been a bolter, but that's not your fault, Madeline. We've sent a couple of teachers up to look for him, and the police."

"You sound so tired," I said. "How are you?"

"Horrible," she said. "Devastated. When I called Fay's and Mooney's parents to tell them, I just —"

There was a catch in her voice.

"My heart goes out to them," I said.

"I'd've thought that breaking the news would fall to David?"

"You know how I cherished Fay," she said. "Mooney as well, but there was just something about that girl —"

Dhumavati started weeping, the inhalations between her sobs so jagged and heartrending that she got me crying again, right along with her.

"I should've done more, Madeline," she said at last. "I should have seen this coming."

I was on the verge of telling her that she couldn't have done anything to stop what had happened, if what I suspected proved to be the truth, but it seemed like too much to throw at her when she was already so shattered.

"Let's go to sleep," I said. "Let's just get to the end of this excruciating day, okay?"

"I've got to stay awake," she said, "in case there's any news about Wiesner."

"Let someone else wait up. Let David. It's so late, and you've been through far too much already."

She wasn't hard to convince, once she'd extracted a promise that I'd immediately go to bed myself.

I fully intended to call Lulu back but was

out cold on the sofa before I'd managed to dial.

Eight hours later, it was becoming increasingly evident that if I'd escaped the flu Tuesday night, I was now getting my ass kicked double for payback.

I lay on the bathroom floor, curved all fetal around the flared base of the toilet, wrapped in a blanket.

Dean plied me with ginger ale, since I'd already puked up the rest of the apple juice.

"Please don't make me drink any more," I said. "If I throw up anything else, my uvula's going to snap off and fall into this damn bowl."

"You didn't eat yesterday," he said. "You've got a fever of a hundred and three, and if you get any more dehydrated, I'm driving you down to the emergency room so they can put you on an IV."

My teeth started chattering. "Any way you could talk them into a little morphine? Maybe an *electric* blanket?"

"Just drink it," he said, waving the glass of bubbling beige at me.

"You talked to Lulu?"

"Yes, they know you're not coming in today."

"I have to call the detective. Cartwright."

"Ginger ale first," he said.

"If I drink that, I'm just gonna barf for another twenty minutes."

"Then he'll have to wait another twenty minutes."

"Cruel man," I said. "Why the hell did I marry you?"

He held the glass to my mouth, and I took three small swallows, front teeth rattling against the rim.

I started to salivate immediately, my stomach churning.

"Right back atcha," I said, leaning in to the bowl.

Dean crouched behind me, holding my hair back.

"Lulu said they haven't found Wiesner." His voice echoed off the porcelain. "Kid's probably halfway to Canada."

When I finally stopped long enough to inhale, I looked up at Dean.

"Call Cartwright. You've got to let him know what Wiesner told us about Gerald."

Then it all started up again.

"Go," I said, lifting my head during an all too brief intermission. "Call."

He didn't move.

"Please," I said.

He got to his feet, knees cracking. "You're sure?"

I flopped a weak hand at him, wanting privacy before I started to hurl again.

"Close the door," I said, so Cartwright wouldn't hear me in the background.

I heard the latch click shut.

The chills had passed. Now I was broiling, slick with toxic sweat and desperately thirsty. I ducked out of the blanket and slumped back down against the cool rim of the toilet.

I shut my eyes, but all I could see was the image of that coroner's van driving past the dining hall, shifting to an imagined tableau of Fay and Mooney, pale and still in each other's arms, drifts of foam spilling out of their mouths.

I blinked those pictures away and reached for the ginger ale — thirsty all over again, the Sisyphus of barf.

I spent the next couple of hours alternately sweating and shivering, drifting in and out of horrible sleep when I wasn't retching into a stockpot by the side of the bed. I heard a loud knock on our front door, and Dean answering it.

He came into the bedroom and touched my shoulder gently. "That Cartwright guy is here to see you," he said.

"See if he wants coffee, okay? Let me

brush my teeth."

When I came out into the living room, I saw Cartwright was accompanied by the young female officer, Kas Baker.

"We got results on those fingerprints back," said Cartwright.

Then he told Baker to cuff me and pulled out a Miranda card. "You have the right to remain silent —"

"What the hell is this about?" asked Dean.

Cartwright paused and looked up at him.

"This is about *whose* prints were on the cups found with those two kids," he said. "Theirs and your wife's."

He dropped his eyes back to the card and continued reading me my rights.

"Bunny," said Dean, "I'm calling your godfather, Alan Flynn. Then I'm coming right down to the station."

"Uncle" Alan, the Manhattan real estate attorney who'd said to Dean at our engagement party, "You two ever need something legal, I'm your beagle."

I was pretty sure this wasn't the kind of "something" he'd had in mind.

"She'll be in county lockup," said Baker, all terse, and Cartwright nodded.

On the bright side, I threw up all over the back of their squad car.

■ ■ ■ ■

PART IV

■ ■ ■ ■

Something did happen to me somewhere that robbed me of confidence and courage and left me with a positive dread of everything unknown that might occur.

— Joseph Heller
Something Happened

22

There were exactly two good things about my being in jail with the flu.

The first was that the upper bunk was empty. The second was I didn't have to worry about raising the seat on the cell's toilet when I had to puke, because the cell's toilet didn't have a seat.

Thoughtful decor, considering. Not to mention time-savingly ergonomic.

Otherwise, it sucked ass. No pillow, no sheet, no ginger ale — just a fire-resistant vinyl-covered mattress and one thin scratchy blanket and those cinder-block walls, ugly as my classroom at Santangelo.

My retching finally tailed off into a mere grainy crush of exhaustion. I crawled into the bunk and wadded a lump of blanket beneath my head, ravenous for sleep.

Not bloody likely.

Whenever I shut my eyes, this sad, crazy fever-Bosch slide show started cranking fast through my head:

Gerald grabbing some faceless kid's dick . . .

Wiesner bolting away from Dean for the dark streets of Pittsfield . . .

Santangelo bashing Tim's face against a blackboard over and over until his features gave way to a glistening mask of meat pulp and cartilage . . .

Fay and Mooney . . .

Fay and Mooney . . .

Bad sucker-punch pictures — snap crackle double-march pop.

My brain struggled to piece them all into a rickety construct of sense. All of it exhausting as trying to parse that old riddle about getting the goat and the wolf and the head of cabbage safely across some river in your too-small rowboat, only worse this time, because Kafka kept lighting the oars on fire and laughing his ass off.

Pictures again.

Click . . .

Click . . .

Fay and Mooney . . .

Sleep.

My attorney was one Markham D. Stuyvesant, according to his card.

In his thirties, maybe. Longish hair. Good

shoes. Suit courtesy of "the Brothers." An air of the young Winston, had Churchill grown up around Houston.

I liked him already. He'd told me to call him Markham, then had the guard give me a pack of cigarettes and a 7UP out of the soda machine.

Markham sat across from me behind a thick glass partition, each of us holding an old-fashioned black phone handset, so as to converse through the divide.

I took a sip of 7UP. "So how do you know Uncle Alan?"

"One of our senior partners played squash with him at Yale, I believe," he said.

Not a huge guy, Markham, but he had a big voice. Deep yet soft, with a bit of a drawl. Soothing. Good for radio.

"Small preppy world," I said.

He laughed at that, and I liked him even better.

"So," I said, "the squash partner sent you?"

"I'm their criminal guy."

"Lucky thing, seeing as how I'm the criminal."

"God forbid," he said.

"My sentiments exactly," I replied, "and yet here I am, sitting on the Group W bench."

Markham smiled. "Not for long."

"Define 'long.' "

"You haven't been charged," he said. "You and I are going to sit down with this Detective Cartwright and have a few words. Then you're out of here, lickety-split."

"Is your office here in Pittsfield?"

"Boston," he said.

It was still before noon. "How did you get out here so fast?"

"Made good time on the Pike, I guess. I'll be staying at the Red Lion. You can get ahold of me anytime, day or night."

A Boston lawyer with a fast car, working around the clock. Not cheap.

"I, um . . ." I coughed. "We should discuss your fees. Or whatever."

"That's all taken care of."

"Dude," I said, "you are shitting me."

"Madeline, I *never* shit my clients," he said right back, hand on heart before I'd even had the chance to blush at having said "shit" in front of some southern guy in a fancy suit whom I didn't actually know — one who happened to be my criminal-defense attorney, besides.

"Markham," I said, "please pardon my language. I am genuinely stunned."

"Understandably," he said, in that amiable drawl.

"Could you please explain how this miracle came to pass during my hour of darkest need?"

"Your godfather apparently feels," he said, "that he's been a tad remiss in the arena of celebratory checks on past occasions, including but not limited to birthdays and graduations."

I stared at him.

"I have been instructed," he continued, "to spare no expense when it comes to clearing up this little spot of misunderstanding."

"Uncle *Alan?*" I barely knew the man.

"I believe his exact words were 'That young lady's as good as they come, this whole thing is obviously a complete crock, and I expect you to get out there and start kicking some serious ass on her behalf.' "

I started to tear up, speechless.

Markham touched his hand to the glass. "Madeline, that 'small preppy world' thing? There are times when it doesn't suck. This would be one of them."

What with all the puking and fever and everything, it was only then that the enormity of my situation really *really* sank in.

All I knew from Cartwright was that my fingerprints had been found on the outside of Fay's and Mooney's cups. Which had to mean I'd been right on the money about there being a quantifiably mongo parts-per-million ratio of nasty-ass-toxic-shit to sticky-punch dregs *inside* those cups.

Unfortunately, it now struck me as pretty damn obvious that Cartwright had figured me for the one who'd put it there.

My prints on the cups.

My prints on Fay's necklace.

My prints on file in connection with those other murders back in Syracuse.

I wanted to believe that my having been the one to step forward and tell Cartwright that these two kids' deaths weren't suicides might serve as a mark in my favor.

Hard belief to maintain when you've just spent the last twenty-four hours puking your guts up in a six-by-ten cell, arrested on suspicion of having committed a double murder.

But still, you'd have to be insane to actively dissuade the cops from closing out their investigation on a pair of murders you'd actually committed.

Crazier still to make sure the police lab didn't miss out on the poison or the broken necklace in your pocket that had belonged to one of the victims.

I mean, who wouldn't want to get away with crimes like that, have them successfully written off as "tragic teenage suicides," case closed? Who wouldn't have just said, "Suicides. Yup. Those kids had been on the verge of offing themselves since, like, forever. We all knew it."

Who wouldn't have let sleeping dogs lie?

Nobody, for God's sake. You'd have to be certifiable.

Only maybe in Cartwright's mind, that's what I was.

I mean, he could perfectly well see me as a teacher from "that crazy school." Another whack job frolicking on the peak of Wifflehead Mountain, when she wasn't doing therapy up the 24/7 yin-yang.

Not to mention the daughter of a guy who thought ninjas were after him, when he wasn't worried about the goddamn KGB reading his goddamn mail.

No wonder Cartwright'd had Baker cuff me.

I was lucky they hadn't taken me down with a nice fat Marlin Perkins *Wild Kingdom* elephant dart of Thorazine in my own living room, just to be on the safe side.

"Markham?" I said. "I gotta tell you, I'm scared."

"Don't be," he said. "This is a fine mess, but I don't believe the two of us will have a lick of trouble getting you out of it."

He gave me a reassuringly Churchillian smile.

"Next time you see your godfather, however," he said, "you might want to kiss his ring."

23

Markham drove me home to Pittsfield.

"I didn't want to worry you before we got you sprung from the joint," he said once we'd climbed into his car, "but it seems you gave your husband the flu."

"A patient and long-suffering man, my husband."

"I'm sure he is, but I would all the same appreciate it if you tried not to breathe in my general direction, now that we are not separated by a wall of glass."

"I hope I'm not still contagious."

"It's not so much that I am fastidious about germs," he said, "but that I should perhaps have had the forethought to bring you a toothbrush."

I snapped a hand over my mouth. "Oh, *crap,* Markham," I mumbled. "I beg your pardon."

"May I offer you some chewing gum? I believe I may have a few sticks of Doublemint, there in the glove box."

He drove fast and well. Fancy-ass car, too. Big Beamer. It was like traveling aboard a large gazelle, one with excellent suspension. Made the previous twenty-four hours seem exceedingly unreal.

"Did all of that just actually happen?" I asked.

"You being in jail? Sadly, I believe it did. Now we must attend to making sure you don't ever have to return."

"I'd appreciate that a great deal," I said.

"Fine and dandy with me. It's always a pleasure to have the same goal as my clients, tell you what." He said that like "whut," and I could hear the H loud and clear.

"So what next?" I asked.

"We should go over what you know so far, starting with how you ended up at such a questionable establishment in the first place."

"The jail?"

"The *school,* honey lamb," he said. "How did a young lady like you end up in such an appalling excuse for an educational institution, not to mention at the mercy of the horrifically vulgar 'Dr.' Santangelo? 'Doctor' being an honorific that man should be ashamed to employ."

"He's not a doctor?"

"I believe he took a degree in comparative astrology," said Markham. "Since I doubt he was bright enough to tackle semiotics."

"No shit?"

"None whatsoever," he said. "More's the pity."

"Jesus," I said.

"Indeed."

"So you've done some research already?"

"Enough to know that the Commonwealth of Massachusetts should be run out of town on a proverbial rail for having allowed the Santangelo Academy to remain in business longer than a month, much less to have *ever* granted the place a license."

He started to rattle off a litany of horrors, year by year — the girl who'd been made to wait ninety minutes before an ambulance was called, after she'd swallowed razor blades. The overdoses of medication administered by untrained dorm parents at the behest of Santangelo's fly-by-night shrinks. The accusations of sexual abuse and harassment "allegedly" perpetrated by faculty and groundskeeping staff and administrators against the students and each other. The citations from fire and health and building and sanitation inspectors, going back decades.

The suicides.

"Markham," I said, overwhelmed, "I knew it was bad, but my *God* —"

"Considering where this odious charlatan has dredged up the majority of his senior staff, I'd say there should have been a good dozen people in line for handcuffs before they clapped any on you."

I slumped down into the passenger seat, closing my eyes. "Those poor kids. And their families. These are desperate, terrified people. They don't know where else to turn."

"It makes my blood boil, darlin'," he said, "outright, downright literally boil."

"Mine too."

"Now let us get down to some brass tacks about how you ended up there and what's happened since, starting from the moment you first ventured onto that nefarious campus," he said.

"I have this friend Ellis," I began. "She's the reason we moved to the Berkshires, and she suggested I apply for a job there when I couldn't get work at the newspaper. She did a stint running their computer lab last year. Said it paid all right and that the kids were decent."

"And what became of this Ellis, pray tell?"

"She left the Berkshires for Cincinnati and got married," I said. "I don't think we'd been here a week. I miss the hell out of that woman."

"It isn't as though she did you any favors, hooking you up with Santangelo."

"Ellis warned me . . . said it was a fucking snakepit, other than the students, but that the checks cleared all right."

I explained about Dean's rail grinders, about the earthquake in California leaving us stranded. "I *needed* checks that cleared, Markham. Small-preppy-world generosity doesn't extend to covering my rent and groceries."

I looked out the window. We were on the outskirts of Pittsfield already.

"So I came for the money," I said, "but stayed for the kids. I mean, how could I not? I wanted to pack them all up in my car and hide them in our apartment halfway through the first day."

" 'Nuff said. You're to be commended for sticking it out, but at this juncture, I must say I'm damn glad you've got me to take up arms on your behalf."

"Markham D. Stuyvesant, knight errant."

"Mais oui," he said.

We were half a block from the North Street rotary. "Tall building on the left is ours," I said, "the one with the bank on the ground floor."

"I believe we need to continue this discussion. May I come up?"

"You're more than welcome to," I said. "I just hope Dean doesn't puke on you."

"I will give the poor man a wide berth, in any case."

"Outstanding," I said. "Wouldn't want you to muck up that lovely suit."

"My sentiments exactly," answered Markham.

Lulu buzzed me and Markham into the apartment building. We found her stirring the contents of a ginormous stockpot on our stove. The whole apartment billowed with steam and the heady fragrance of chicken soup.

She dropped the spoon and ran over the minute she saw me, practically lifting me off my feet with a hug. "Jesus Christ, it's fine to see you," she said.

"Likewise, dear friend. I cannot begin to express —"

"Shhhh," she whispered. "Dean's finally asleep, poor thing. Nasty bug . . . hit him hard, and of course he's been devastated with worry about you on top of all that."

I thanked her for taking care of him, hugged her again, and introduced her to Markham. The two of them took one another's measure, obviously pleased with what they saw.

Lulu dished up a bowl of soup and handed it to me.

"Bring this in to Dean," she said. "Let him know you're all right. And take all the time you need to make sure he gets at least half of this down the hatch. Your attorney and I have a few things to discuss."

"Like what?"

"Like Gerald, for starters."

"You know about Gerald already?"

Lulu winked at me. "Let's just say a little bird told me during a late-night visit to my apartment while you were in the slammer. Well, not little — more like a tall, blond, and somewhat psychotic bird."

"Wiesner?"

"None other," she said.

"Kid gets around."

"Who doesn't these days? Now shoo," she said. "Dean's soup's getting cold."

The shades were all drawn in our bedroom, and Dean was huddled up under just about every blanket and duvet we had, wearing a woolly hat with earflaps on it, for good measure.

I put the soup down on his bedside table and kissed him.

He stirred awake, blinking up at me. "Bunny?"

"Dear thing," I said, sitting on the edge of the bed. "Talk about eyes like two holes burned in a blanket."

"Um," he said, "your breath could finish the job of combustion."

"Crap," I said. "I totally forgot. Poor Lulu!"

I snuck off to the bathroom for a thorough workout with Crest, then returned and started spoon-feeding him the soup.

"Think you can keep this down?" I asked.

"Broth of the gods." He was sweating now and started kicking off the blankets between swallows. "How the hell you survived this damn flu, locked up in a cell — I almost passed out when it hit me yesterday. Thank God I'd called your uncle Alan first. I was totally delirious."

"You should be better by Monday, when your job starts."

"I'm not leaving this apartment unless you're in the clear," he said.

"How long has Lulu been here?"

"She called up yesterday afternoon, wanted to talk to you about Wiesner and Gerald. I was lying on the bathroom floor — had to crawl to the phone. She drove up when she realized how sick I was."

I made him finish the soup, then told him to go back to sleep. He was out again before I closed the door behind me.

Back in the living room, Lulu and Markham were chatting up a storm, him taking furious notes all the while.

"What time is it?" I asked.

They both looked at their watches.

"Just past two," said Markham. "You should avail yourself of Miss Lulu's fabulous soup. I've just had a bowl and can recommend it quite highly."

"I'm so tired," I said. "I'm not sure I could eat."

Lulu wouldn't hear of that. She hustled me into a chair and set a bowl on the butler's table in front of me. I yawned over it.

"If you don't start eating it yourself, I'm not above feeding you," she said.

"Yes'm," I said, spooning up a swallow of golden elixir and blowing on it to cool it off.

Lulu turned to Markham, hands on her hips. "I think we should let them be for the rest of the day, Counselor. You're up to speed on the basics, here?"

He looked at me. "What've you got on tomorrow morning, Madeline?"

I swallowed my soup. "No idea," I said.

"You think I still have a job, Lulu?"

"Dhumavati says absolutely. Only you don't have to be there early."

"Why not?"

"They're having a Sitting Meeting."

"A what?" asked Markham.

"Someone kicked a hole in the side of the Xerox machine," explained Lulu. "Since no one confessed to the crime in the first twenty-four hours, the entire student body is now required to sit silently in a large circle inside the dining hall, with the teachers clumped on the floor in the middle."

"I take it Santangelo gets a chair?" asked Markham.

"Santangelo is too busy playing outside with his new helicopter," said Lulu. "He has an instructor working with him in four-hour shifts. Takeoffs and landings."

"You mean to tell me," said Markham, "that man has just had two students *murdered,* with one of his teachers in jail, and he's not only forced the entire school to play some punitive Quaker-meeting game over a broken copier, but he's hopping around the lawn in a whirlybird?"

"Pretty much," Lulu said.

"Oh, it's going to be a pleasure getting him in court," he said, rubbing his hands with glee. "In fact, I may have to do it several times. Pro bono."

Lulu gave him a conspiratorial smile. "Let's let these two get some rest in the meantime, shall we?"

"Madeline," said Markham, snapping his briefcase closed, "I will be back here early tomorrow with bells on."

He held out his arm to Lulu, and the two of them sashayed out the door.

■ ■ ■ ■

Part V

■ ■ ■ ■

When we remember our former selves,
there is always that little figure with its long
shadow stopping like an uncertain belated
visitor on a lighted threshold at the far end
of some impeccably narrowing corridor.
— Vladimir Nabokov
Ada

24

I spent that night trying to sneak up on the oasis of sleep, only to have it shimmer away, à la mirage, every time I thought I was about to reach the shade of its beckoning palm trees.

There was just too much moiling around in my skull — the likelihood of getting charged with murder, and how the hell I'd ever be able to repay my godfather for having dispatched Markham to the Berkshires in my darkest hour.

I got up around three and drank half a beer by the light of the icebox door, listening to Dean toss and mutter in the next room.

It didn't help, the beer, not that I'd believed it would.

Around five I slept for an hour. Dean came out of the bedroom at six-thirty, wrapped in a blanket and shivering.

"You should stay in bed," I said.

"Markham said he'd be back early. I want to hear the progress report." He lowered himself onto the sofa slowly, legs trembling.

"Can I get you anything?"

Dean pulled the blanket up around his head and closed his eyes.

"My skin hurts," he said.

"Do you think you could eat something?"

He didn't answer, just lay down on his side, one foot splayed across the floor.

I brought him dry toast with a cup of weak but heavily sugared tea. He looked at the stuff and emitted a creaky sigh.

"Just the tea," I said.

Dean drew the blanket closer around his head and pressed his lips together, looking for all the world like an old woman disappointed by the sight of Ellis Island after a month in steerage.

I put on some Strauss, hoping he'd find the schmaltzy magnificence of the "Blue Danube Waltz" soothing.

"Picture yourself frolicking through sundappled forests above Salzburg," I said.

Dean closed his eyes. "No frolicking. Even the thought."

"Okay, just picture trees."

"Can't," he said. "This music reminds me of the stewardess."

"What stewardess?"

"With the polyester lightbulb hat."

"I think maybe you need some Tylenol," I said. "You're getting delusional."

He didn't open his eyes. "Bunny, in *2001*. She cruises around wearing Velcro slippers so she can pass out Space Food Sticks without getting sucked into an air lock."

"Oh," I said. "That stewardess."

I made him take the Tylenol anyway.

Markham arrived an hour later, looking so exhausted that I immediately fired up a pot of Bustelo.

He opened his briefcase, lifting out files and fanning them out across our kitchen table. Then he leaned back in his chair and just stared at them.

"Markham, you okay?" I asked.

"Long night, honey lamb," he said. "For me and a number of the firm's die-hard young associates back in Boston."

"This is making me feel like Hunter S. Thompson," I said, "having an attorney."

" 'When the going gets weird, the weird turn pro,' " Markham said, looking up from his papers to give me a wink. "Just please bear in mind the caveat that I am not now, nor ever have been, Samoan."

"I'm fine with that." I poured a cup of coffee for my non-Samoan attorney. "Milk or sugar?"

"No, thank you. I believe I'm in need of all the uncut caffeine I can get this fine morning."

I handed it over. Markham took a healthy sip, let out a little whoop, and threw his shoulders back.

"That, my dear, has what I'd call a Twenty-Mule-Team kick," he said, raising his mug in my direction. "Much obliged."

"Least we can do," I replied.

He drank off a third of the brew, then placed its vessel carefully atop the kitchen pass-through's half wall, so as not to put his documents at risk.

"To business, then," he said. "Of which the first order is your fellow faculty member Gerald Jones."

"Who may actually have done it," I said.

"Who graduated ten years ago from Miami University in Oxford, Ohio," said Markham, "with a bachelor's degree from their Richard T. Farmer School of Business, where he was a member of the four-year undergraduate honors program — one of forty students in his freshman class to have made the cut. Graduated first among them, having completed a thesis on" — here he consulted a crisp sheaf of papers from the nearest file folder — "ah yes, 'Computer

Applications of the Mandelbrot Set in Today's Investment Banking Environment: Fractals and Financial Engineering,' with accompanying self-designed software. Special products, et cetera."

"Gerald?" I said. "Fractals?"

"Indeed," said Markham. "Good stuff, too. Seven companies tried to hire him before he'd quite finished writing the thing, not halfway through his junior year. He spent several years in the thick of it all. London, Tokyo, Manhattan."

"Seriously," I said. "Mousy, unprepossessing Gerald."

"Mousy, unprepossessing Gerald, whose personal net worth is estimated somewhere in the high eight figures," said Markham, "hard numbers being difficult to verify, what with the bulk of his fortune being divided between the Cayman and Channel islands."

"Markham," I said, "the man drives a Datsun. A really crappy Datsun. He's practically the poster boy for cheap shoes and Sansabelt slacks."

"And he gave up that rather astonishingly stellar career path for a job at the Santangelo Academy, when he could easily be teaching at Harvard. Or better. Not that he needs to work."

"So what happened?" Dean croaked from

the sofa.

"That," said Markham, "is exactly what my young associates back in Boston are even now attempting to determine."

"Nervous breakdown?" asked Dean.

"Fondness for smack?" I chimed in. "Imminent pedophilia conviction?"

"Nary a whiff of impropriety as yet," said Markham. "He serves on the board of directors for a number of charities. Active in the Society of St. Vincent de Paul. Supports scientific research with rather heavy donations to several universities."

"What sort of research?" I asked.

Markham again consulted his files. "An eye toward fostering advancements in neuroscience — more specifically, in the arena of psychopharmacology. He is apparently considering the endowment of a chair, to that end, at one of several prominent medical schools."

"While preparing for court dates," I said, "in the aftermath of having grabbed a Santangelo student's dick during bed check last year."

"In the aftermath of having *allegedly* done so," replied Markham, rather sternly, it seemed to me.

"There was a witness," I shot back.

"Who is now deceased."

"My point exactly."

"We can probably rule out the fondness for smack, then," said Dean.

"Markham," I said, "have you ever defended a pedophile?"

He shot his cuffs. "I have."

"To my knowledge," I said, "that's not exactly behavior tending to spring up unheralded. Out of the clear blue sky, as it were."

Markham nodded. "With rare exceptions."

"How much do you know about the circumstances in which Gerald made this career shift?" I asked.

"Circumstances in what sense?"

"Was he fired? Did he resign? Any dirt at all?"

"Gerald was not fired, that much we have ascertained," said Markham, "to my confident satisfaction."

He reached for his coffee and took a big swallow. "In fact," he continued, "our Mr. Jones resigned in the field . . . Japanese investment bank. Gave no notice, requested no severance, didn't even bother asking for his shares of equity in the company — shares that were literally weeks away from being vested."

"How many shares?" asked Dean.

"A chunk o' change worth pursuing,"

answered Markham. "Not least since it would certainly have been granted to him if he were, say, taking a leave of absence and had been on good terms with the company's officers."

"So you don't know what reason he gave for resigning?" I asked.

"We've been given to believe that he may have cited a family emergency," said Markham.

"Sure," I said, "but an emergency for whose family?"

"We should know more this afternoon. Tomorrow at the latest."

Dean sat up. "They work fast, your youthful associates."

Markham dipped his head in agreement, smiling.

I took a sip of my own coffee. "And in the meantime?"

"In the meantime, Ms. Dare," said my non-Samoan attorney, "you are to lay low."

"Cross my heart and hope to die," I said.

"Don't think I haven't turned my youthful associates loose with rakes to sift through your *own* background," he said, shaking a paternal finger at me.

"Bummer," I said.

"Shootings, suspicious deaths, family hunting compounds spontaneously combusting," he said, ticking these items off on that paternal finger and its cohorts one by one. "Not to mention Porsches suddenly inherited. I'm beginning to wonder if you didn't have a hand in the Watergate break-in."

I cleared my throat. "Now, listen, Markham . . ."

He cocked his head to one side and shot me a wicked grin.

"Watergate was Nixon's baby from the get-go," I said. "I barely even encouraged the man."

"And you listen to me for a moment, Madeline," he said. "I do not want you talking *to* or *about* this Gerald Jones — to anyone. Nor second-guessing the state troopers. Nor snooping around on your own. Nor answering a single question from anyone at that damn school, aside from admitting that you are enjoying the brisk November weather here in the Berkshires, before thanking the person asking *so* much for the gracious inquiry."

I nodded.

"We want you there," he said, "maintaining a clean record of employment, but I don't care how nicely anyone phrases the merest hint of wanting information from you — cop, student, teacher, whoever —

you refer the curious to me, your attorney, and politely inform them that you are not at liberty to discuss the case, on my advisement."

"Done," I said, hand raised in oath.

"And for God's sake," he added, "leave that shotgun of yours at home."

"You say that with a certain Samoan conviction," I said.

"Aloha," Markham replied.

"That's not Samoan," I said.

"Nor, as I warned you earlier, am I," he replied. "Shall I return around seven o'clock tonight?"

"I'd be honored," I said.

"We have a further meeting scheduled with Detective Cartwright. Ten a.m. tomorrow."

"I'll be there with bells on," I said.

"No bells," he said. "Bells make the police a trifle nervous."

25

On my journey to campus that morning, the Porsche got rode hard and put away wet. I blasted more Strauss with an Allman Brothers chaser, thinking about Markham's prohibitions.

No Gerald. No cop second-guessing. No chatting with anyone official at school.

Check.

Check.

Check.

Which left me Wiesner, in a letter-but-not-spirit-of-the-law kind of way, since the kid wasn't Gerald, a cop, an official, or even on campus, last I'd heard.

I parked near the dining hall, having passed Santangelo's completed helipad, on which sat a spanking new chopper. It was a little snub-nosed budgie-looking thing, white with two-tone-blue stripes swooshing along the undercarriage and up to the tail boom.

I wondered how many child-labor hours at the Farm "Dr." David had double-billed his students' families for, in order to swing the purchase, betting he would've hit up Gerald for a sweetheart loan had he known the guy's bank balance.

I climbed out of my car into the cold dry world, eyeballing the bulk of the school's population through the dining hall's picture window. Not a happy bunch.

The tables and salad bar had been shoved against a far wall, all the chairs pulled into a wide lumpy circle along the room's perimeter. The kids were seated in those, along with Dhumavati and some of the shrinks. As Lulu had explained to Markham, mere teachers got the floor — a clot of blank-eyed, cross-legged misery huddled on the threadbare carpet's center, like a band of early Christians resigned to their matinee-martyr fate.

I slogged into that shabby Coliseum and took my place among them, wondering whether to expect lions or gladiators. As if it mattered.

Nobody said a word when I grabbed a spot of carpet next to Lulu. Nobody said a word for the next hour, either. We all just sat there, looking at the ceiling or the floor or the windows, anything but each other.

Someone behind me had a bad cough. Mindy kept sniffling, then dabbing at her nose with the same soggy Kleenex.

Gerald picked at the carpet's weft, his pants riding up to reveal inches of thick white tube sock above each cheap wing tip.

There was a pair of galoshes lined up neatly beside his left hip — the short kind that slipped over your shoes only after a struggle, what we used to call "rubbers" before the advent of AIDS. Useless for warmth or protecting anything more than your shoes when the slush was deep. Anachronisms, like those thin plastic rain bonnets that folded up into little packets when they weren't protecting old-lady hairdos from rain and wind.

I wondered if Gerald had dressed this badly in Tokyo or London. Whether his prissy octogenarian fashion sense was the mark of tone deafness or subterfuge.

He started picking at his socks, stifling a yawn.

I tried to picture him as a ruthless pedophile and killer. Couldn't do it. Maybe the camouflage was doing its job.

If not him, who?

I glanced around the room, picking individual faces out of the silenced dozens in attendance.

Mindy with her chafed nostrils, pink enough to rival today's fluffy sweater.

Forchetti cracking his knuckles in a distant chair, grown-up black eyebrows clenched in that baby face.

Dhumavati checking her watch while trying to hide a yawn of her own.

Tim stretching out his legs, no doubt hoping to avoid their falling asleep, as mine were.

Lulu literally twiddling her thumbs, humming some snatch of Andrew Lloyd Webber under her breath.

Sitzman on the verge of sleep, snapping his head back up each time it started sinking toward his chest.

The usual suspects, none of them prime.

No Wiesner, no Santangelo. Skeleton half-crew for the adults, who did their Sitting in alternating duty-roster shifts, but kids had to suffer the full daily complement — two hours at a stretch, with half-hour meal and ten-minute toilet breaks.

Nobody could leave for the bathroom otherwise, which I supposed was some kind of homage-nod to Werner Erhard's early EST sessions on Santangelo's part. Or maybe he just figured full bladders might do more to speed a confession than straight guilt ever could.

Probably true, if you came right down to it. Not that that was any excuse. And fuck him for not being here in the room, too. Ever. Fuck him for setting up all these bullshit rules and "traditions" and torturous, meaningless crap in the name of therapy.

Fuck Freud.

Fuck Jung.

Fuck Werner Erhard, and his little dog too.

Santangelo was just the latest charlatan to wrap himself in their snake-oily mantle of overpriced navel-gazing hooey.

Who was it helping? How was it a good idea to cancel classes for kids who'd missed years of school already, locked down in wards and hospitals and sanitariums before they'd gotten "well" enough to end up here?

Maybe they didn't need to get crammed full of Yalta or Maya Angelou — maybe Wiesner was right, and that stuff wouldn't help, either — but they sure as hell deserved better than this.

Double-fuck Santangelo for his lip service to "solidarity with the kids" if he couldn't stomach it himself.

I pictured him lounging in his plush house with his stupid espresso machine, leering at his stupid fucking helicopter out on the lawn, licking the edge of his thumb before counting his piles of money again just for fun.

These kids weren't his patients/clients/charges, they were Santangelo's marks.

The shithead. The fat greasy weasel. The smug nasty pompous low-rent-lumpen Tennessee-Williams-Big-Daddy suckbag of a potentate.

O, the mendacity!

Patti Gonzaga stood up and started growling at everyone in the room. She picked up her chair and threw it at one of the windows.

I hadn't realized they were Plexiglas before the chair bounced right off.

Those nearest her started closing in for what was called a Limit Structure here at Santangelo, which consisted of all available hands piling on top of anyone who seriously lost his or her shit.

It took about ten people to pin her and a half hour before she ran out of steam.

Horrible thing to watch, and I kept thinking about her shy, exhausted parents, who only wanted to welcome their darling girl home.

The holders, teachers and students alike, waited to let her up until a good ten minutes after she'd stopped twisting around on the floor and screaming. Then they made her go pick up her chair and place it back in the circle.

She sat down in it, panting and flushed, tangled strands of hair sweat-plastered across her forehead and cheeks.

Sitzman started snoring.

Forchetti punched him awake.

I had to piss like a racehorse.

26

Lulu and I leaned against the outside of the dining hall, despite the cold.

"Oh my God," she said as Santangelo waddled across the snowy lawn toward his shiny new helicopter, flight instructor in tow.

We were on our ten-minute afternoon break from Sitting, not enough time to sneak off into the woods for a smoke.

Santangelo was wearing, for some reason, a hot-pink flight suit. His far svelter instructor wore one in a darkish alligatory green.

"Give them a couple of fountains to waltz around," I said, "and it would be that hippos-in-tutus number straight out of *Fantasia*."

The two men climbed into the cockpit.

"It looks like some giant bug," said Lulu, gripping her dining-hall mug of decaf. "What the hell would you even call that thing?"

Sitzman stood a few feet from us, clapping his hands and stomping against the cold.

"It's a Bell 206B-3," he said. "JetRanger III."

I smiled. "Any good?"

"The 206L-4's cooler," he said. "Seven-seater — the stretch model. Plus, it's got that whole Noda-Matic setup in the transmission to cut vibration."

Sitzman squinted as the engine started to whine, taching up. "Santangelo probably couldn't afford the upgrade."

The big rotors on top, still droopy, traced the outline of their first slow circles.

"So what did the basic model run him?" asked Lulu, taking a sip of decaf.

"A million bucks," said Sitzman, "give or take."

She did a Sanka spit take. I had to clap her on the back a couple times to stop the choking.

"A million *bucks?*" she said when she could breathe again.

Sitzman shrugged. "If you want to impress the chicks, buy a Sikorsky."

He stomped his feet again, turning toward the door.

"It's cold out here," he said. "Break's probably just about over."

"A million fucking dollars," muttered

Lulu, "and Santangelo won't even spring for decent coffee, the —"

And then the chopper got so loud I couldn't hear the last word she said, though I'm pretty sure it was "asshole."

Dhumavati stuck her head out the door and beckoned us both back for the next session.

Lulu and I trudged inside. The door closed behind us, and I could hear again.

"There's Gerald," she whispered.

"I can't talk to him anyway," I said, "on the advice of my attorney."

" 'My attorney.' " She chuckled a little. "Well, la-dee-dah."

"Oh please," I snapped, "who died and made *you* Annie Hall?"

"Get a good night's sleep, did we?"

"No," I said. "Sorry. *Really.* It's just . . ." I flopped my hands, useless. "Just . . . everything. Attorney. Jail. Fay and Mooney —"

"Sweetie?" she said, patting my shoulder. "Are *you* okay?"

"Oh, my dear friend . . . I am *so* not okay."

"Sweetie?" she said again, hand now steady on my shoulder.

An anchor.

A blessing.

I closed my eyes.

And then I started weeping, and Lulu

314

gathered me into her arms.

I heard a door close gently.

Felt someone else patting my back.

Looked up to find Dhumavati standing next to us, her face soft with concern.

"Let's go sit across the hall, Madeline," she said. "Just the two of us."

We were back in Santangelo's blackboard-tantrum room where I'd fake-appreciated Mindy. Same-old same-old, with the welcome addition of a saggy institutional sofa along one wall.

Dhumavati collapsed into it with a sigh.

I sat next to her. I didn't want to cry. I bit the inside of my lip to fight it back.

"Honey," said Dhumavati, "it's okay, just let it all out."

"Please," I said. "No."

I sat up straighter. Rigid. Shoulders back.

"Madeline," said Dhumavati, "you don't have to keep everything inside. There is room for you in the world. The couch will hold you up. Trust gravity."

It was halfway dark in the room, since the blinds were twisted almost shut. Dhumavati's voice was so gentle, so soft, and I was so goddamn tired.

"Why don't you just put your head down in my lap," she said, stroking my hair. "Talk

315

or don't talk, it doesn't matter. Whatever you want."

"I'd love nothing more than to tuck my head into your lap," I said, "but if I lie down now, you won't get me back up without a crane."

"I could probably rustle up a crane."

"You're very kind," I said. "I know you've got a great deal to worry about, other than me."

She stretched out her feet, kicked off her shoes, and slumped into the back of the sofa. "You're doing me a huge favor. If I'd had to spend one more *second* in that damn dining hall, watching David hop around the lawn in his new toy . . ."

"Bless you for saying that."

"The man is my oldest and dearest friend, don't get me wrong," said Dhumavati, "but sometimes I want to wring his neck."

She put her arm around me. "I want you to know I think it was absolutely ridiculous, you getting arrested. I hope they've come to their senses."

I shrugged. "I have another meeting with Detective Cartwright tomorrow morning."

"Did they tell you why?" asked Dhumavati. "I just don't understand. Do you have even the vaguest idea?"

"Unfortunately," I said, "I am not at

liberty to discuss any of this, on the advice of my attorney."

"Not even anything about who you think did it?" asked Dhumavati.

Mindful of Markham's injunctions, I said, "Oh, g'wan — you tell first."

"If I thought anyone on this campus were capable of having killed two students," said Dhumavati, "he or she would no longer be on this campus."

"Someone did, though," I said. "One of our own."

We sat with that idea for a minute.

"I don't imagine we'll be hearing a turn-in about it," I said finally.

"I don't imagine we'll be hearing a turn-in about the Xerox machine," said Dhumavati. "Not today."

"How long do these Sitting things tend to go?" I asked.

"The record was fourteen days."

"For what?"

"Somebody stole a rake."

I turned to look at her. "And you think this is a good idea? I mean, all the kids cooped in there . . . no classes, no way to get out of that room unless they've got a shrink appointment . . . two of their friends just killed . . ."

She looked away.

"I don't mean that as a bitchy question, Dhumavati." I drew my legs up onto the sofa. "Does it *help?*"

"Sitting?"

"All of it. Sitting, the meetings, the Farm."

"It's helped me." She crossed her arms over her chest. "It doesn't work for everyone. But it's given me peace, and I've been able to share that peace with a great many kids over the years. Kids no one believed had a chance in hell to survive — not them, not even their own parents — and we made sure they did."

"And that's why you're here?" I asked.

"I'm here because it saved my life, and I know mine isn't the only life this place has saved — *can* save."

I tried to look like I believed her. She deserved that much.

"I couldn't save my daughter," Dhumavati continued, "and the only way I can live with that is to fight for the lives of other children."

She rested her hand flat over the center of her chest, the way Tim always did. "When I heard about Fay and Mooney . . ."

"Dhumavati," I said, "you can't —"

"We failed them, David and I. *I* failed them."

"All of us did."

Dhumavati shook her head. "I should have asked for help. If I hadn't been so tired, none of this would have happened. David saw that months ago. He knew I needed to get away, get my head straight. I was too selfish to admit it."

"Not selfish," I said.

"Hubristic, then. Arrogant. Convinced I couldn't allow anyone else to take the reins even for a moment, because I was so indispensable. It was only when he suggested you that I allowed myself to realize how very much I needed to let go, but I'd waited too long. I can only hope your taking over for me will keep it from happening again."

"You can't be serious," I said. "How could I possibly take over for you after this week?"

"Because David and I know you had nothing to do with what happened. And because we need you."

The helicopter whined to life again outside.

"Madeline, I can't do this alone anymore," she said. "I don't have the strength."

"The strength or the conviction?"

"Both."

"Let's be honest," I said. "You've gotta know I think David is full of shit."

"So you're wondering why I'm ready to put all of this on you?"

I nodded.

"Because you'll stand up for the kids," she said, "even if it means taking on David."

"That's what you want?"

"Only until I'm ready to come back and take him on myself," she said. "And I need time for that."

"How much time?" I asked.

"A couple of months," she said. "No more. You're the only one strong enough for me to trust, even if you don't trust yourself. I think Sookie can help you with that. I've spoken to her about it, and I'd like you to do the same."

"Right now?"

"She's in her office."

"I can't," I said. "I have to go home."

"To think about it?"

"To meet with my lawyer."

"Do both," she said. "I'm depending on you. So are the kids."

27

"Well, thank the good Lord you didn't go talking to that Sookie person," said Markham after I'd related the day's events over a glass of the pinot gris he'd shown up with.

"She's a shrink," I said. "There's, like, doctor-patient privilege or something, isn't there?"

"In court, yes," he said, "but not, however, within that appalling school."

"What?"

"Madeline, every psychologist and psychiatrist employed by Santangelo has to report to him on what's discussed in their therapy sessions, on campus and off. The whole gang gathers for a weekly check-in meeting — apparently held in the man's living room each Friday evening."

Dean shook his head slowly, disgusted. "Does that include the ones who do the sessions with the kids' parents?"

"Especially them," said Markham.

"Your young researchers found this out?"

He nodded.

"Please thank them for doing such fine work," I said. "That's an incredibly useful bit of information to have."

"They're fired up about this. We are none of us liking that man, honey lamb."

"How the hell did you guys figure that out, about it not being confidential?" I asked.

"One of our intrepid staffers wondered how Santangelo managed to breeze unscathed through the forty-eight separate lawsuits brought against him since that school's inception," said Markham.

"By parents?" asked Dean.

"Parents. Employees. Erstwhile members of his psychiatric staff on three occasions. All settled out of court. All hushed up."

"Because he's got dirt on everyone," I said. "Jesus God."

"Darlin', that ol' boy's got so many folks by the short hairs," said Markham, "you gotta reckon he'd make J. Edgar Hoover squeal like a pig if they ever duked it out."

He tipped his chair back. "Which brings us to two orders of business." He tapped his fingers against the side of his wineglass, then raised it for another sip.

"First off," he said, "ix-nay on the ookie-Say from here on out."

"My pleasure," I said.

"And second?" asked Dean.

"Second — as your attorney, Madeline, I need to know what all they've got on you."

I downed some gris of my own, then cleared my throat and looked Markham in the eye. "Um . . . Sookie's hip to my whole 'I shot a man in Reno just to watch him die' thing."

"Taking into account the self-defense aspect of that ordeal," he said. "We can shake it off, should worse come to worst."

"Other than that, I can't say I've been exactly forthcoming. Last week she told me she suspected I'd been molested as a kid. I told her that was bullshit. Which it was."

"Think it through carefully, now," said Markham. "Is there anything else? Anything you wouldn't want to see in the papers?"

I stared into my wine, shuffling through the details I could recall from our sessions.

"Nada," I said. *"Rien du tout."*

Markham raised his glass in my honor, this little grin ramping up at the edge of his mouth.

"God love you for being repressed, honey lamb," he said. "WASPs rule, shrinks drool . . . chalk one up for the small preppy world."

"Ah, Markham," I replied, "you're a man after my own tiny black heart."

Dean crossed his arms. "So who else is in on these Friday-night dirt meetings?"

I shrugged. "None of the teachers that I know of."

"And how long has Sookie known about your having killed that guy, Bunny?"

"I met with her solo Friday afternoon."

"Which means she knew about it *before* Sant-ange-a-hole and company last gathered to shoot the shit," Dean said.

"Yes," I said, "it does."

"And she presumably broadcast that information before the kids got killed."

"I believe I see where your better half is going with this," said Markham.

"That makes one of us," I said.

"Somebody set you up, Madeline," Markham said. "And they put some thought into it. The only thing I couldn't put my finger on was why you looked most suitable for framing." He paused, his fingers back to using his wineglass for percussion. "When I learned about your troubles last year, the 'why' clicked into place."

"So now we need the 'who,' " I said.

"I've got a helluva big staff running

background on all concerned, but this wasn't something civilians were likely to find out, except from you. And you told Sookie."

"Like an idiot," I said.

"Maybe a smart idiot," he said. "Maybe a very *lucky* idiot."

"How so?"

"Think about it," he went on. "Sookie put you on the agenda last Friday night — ratted you out to everyone on the guest list."

"Which is lucky how?"

"You think those folks are in the habit of CC'ing their minutes to anybody else once they adjourn for the night? I sure don't."

"So you figure someone in that room picked me to take the fall?"

"We've got to surmise that the idea of saying 'Well, she's obviously unstable, Officer . . . prone to violence. Sure, and she never would've been hired a'tall had we but known she'd killed before' sounded damn good to whoever it was."

"Oh," I said, "lucky me."

"Damn right, lucky you, because that narrows the pool considerably." Markham reached for the bottle of wine and topped up his and my glasses.

"So Sookie knew," he said, "and Santangelo, and the rest of the shrinks. Now we've gotta get a bead on whether anyone else did before Tuesday night."

"Okay," I said.

"This boy Gerald," said Markham, "any way you think he would've been privy to that information?"

"He's certainly been on staff the longest," I said, "out of all us teachers. Seems pretty tight with Santangelo."

"I've gotta say I like our Mr. Gerald Jones for this, what with his having been in charge of that punch bowl," said Markham.

"And he benefits from Mooney's death, given the alleged dick-grabbing," I said.

"That he does," said Markham. "That he certainly does."

"So what do we do?"

"Tomorrow morning we make sure Detective Cartwright is apprised of the facts as we know them, ASAP."

"What else?" asked Dean.

"That poor girl's necklace," Markham said. "We need to find out how the hell it ended up in Madeline's pocket."

"I still don't know," I said.

"I'll tell you straight," he said. "Barring catastrophe, should this thing come before a grand jury, the only thing I can see giving us trouble is that necklace. The time of death is wide open. All hands on that Farm were tucked in not long after you wandered off into the snow, Madeline, and you've got some hours unaccounted for. Your two buddies found you late in the game — plenty of time for you to have sneaked Fay and Mooney up into that attic, and they liked you. They trusted you enough — plenty of people can testify to that."

"But I was passed out the whole time, when I wasn't puking my guts out. And I told the cops where I threw up, after someone dosed *me,* so they've gotta know somebody messed with my punch. Not to mention I'm the one who gave them the damn necklace in the first place."

"Except there's no way to know when you drank the punch," he said, "or when you started throwing it back up. That might've happened after you killed the kids, for all they know. It's not like the best lab in the world can narrow down time of vomit."

"So I'm supposed to have ducked outside, waited until the coast was clear, tiptoed back in, enticed the two kids up into the attic, mixed up a couple of poison cocktails, talked them into drinking the shit so as to kill them, whereupon I ripped Fay's necklace off, which I then stuck in my own jacket after Lulu picked it up and took it to Dhumavati's apartment — I guess during the time I was pretending to be either delirious or unconscious in her guest bed all night — and on top of that, I made sure my own fingerprints were all over the cups Fay and Mooney drank out of, which I left lying next to their bodies."

Markham nodded, fingers rattling along the curve of his wineglass again.

"That's ludicrous," I said. "I mean, come on."

"For a good prosecutor? That version of events would feel like manna from heaven."

"Oh *please*," I said.

"I could sell it to your average jury while standing on my head, drunk as a goat. If you weren't my client, I'd be dancing your husband round the living room right this minute, singing 'Waltz Across Texas.' "

"I don't believe it," I said.

"You *should* believe it," he said, "and let me tell you why."

"I'm all ears."

Markham pointed a finger at me. "Because poison is the favored MO of women, first off," he said, "especially when they murder kids — and most of 'em think the very best way to divert suspicion is to mix themselves a weak little dose for tossing down, after the fact."

I felt the wine coming back on me.

"The only thing you've missed," he continued, "is trying to blame it on the proverbial 'bushy-haired stranger' — preferably some fellow who's a wee tad dark-complected."

"Markham, I didn't —"

"Course not," he said, cutting me off as he reached across the table to pat my shaking hand. "But whoever did this knew how to make it look like a woman was responsible."

"Does it help that I'm probably the only teacher on campus who didn't have access to the arsenic they were using to kill rats down at the Farm?"

He laced his fingers through mine. "The lab results came back. Those children weren't killed with arsenic. There's no connection to the rat bait collected from the scene. What you all drank was cyanide. You did get a weaker dose, with some other stuff mixed in to make you hallucinate."

That explained the spiders.

"We just gotta get that necklace off the table, is all," he said. "After that, it's gonna be a cakewalk, darlin'. Just you watch."

He turned to Dean. "I want you to tuck this little lady into bed, sir, soon as I leave. Maybe a little warm milk, you got any. I want you both to get a good night's sleep, and you should rest easy as pie, because I've got all the angles covered here, and there's no need to fret over a thing."

He squeezed my hand. "I mean that with the utmost sincerity, Madeline. What I said just now wasn't meant to scare you, but I need you to know how these things play out. 'Sides which, some prosecutor tries pulling that tired old line of hooey on us in court? I'll kick his ass, eat his lunch, and charm the pants off his wife in the bargain. Poor bastard won't even know what hit 'im."

Cartwright waved us over to his desk while getting all irate with whomever he was talking to on the phone.

"Well, you tell Bobby I'd like to know what the hell they thought they were doing with a batch of C-4 up at GE in the first place! Crap like that gone *missing,* and he expects us to hunt it down? What the hell was he thinking — blow the place up, make sure nobody comes back to work?" He shook his head, looking like it was about to blow right off the top of his thick neck.

"No," he said.

"No."

He looked at me and Markham, pinching his thumb and finger together to ask for a moment, like some hitchhiker beseeching drivers for a short ride. "That's not my problem, any of it. And you can tell him I said we'll be looking over those permits with a fine-tooth damn comb . . . Oh, for chrissake, of course we'll deal with it, but I'm not about to drive right up the minute he — Get Bailey started on it. Yes, of course he's good. Best we've got for something like this."

Then he barked, "I've got an interview. Just take *care* of it," and slammed down the phone.

Markham propelled a glad hand across the desk after the requisite courtesy beat.

"Beg pardon if our arrival's made you feel rushed, Detective Cartwright," he said. "We've shown up early and certainly don't want to put you out."

Cartwright was on his feet, wrapping Markham's hand in his own meatier paw. "At your service, Counselor. It doesn't rain but it pours."

"Don't I know it," said Markham.

"Ms. Dare, we hope you're feeling the picture of health," Cartwright said, giving my hand a hail-fellow-well-met mauling in turn, coupled with a look that seemed intended to express a bashful-but-good-humored "And that you'll forgive us for that night-you-spent-puking-in-jail spot of confusion" chaser.

"Now, sir, you just let us know," Markham drawled, "should there be anything you need time to take care of this morning. I want you to know we're at your service, Ms. Dare and myself. You're responsible for a great deal, Detective . . . goes without saying . . . As such, please do not hesitate to avail yourself if it would lighten your load."

"No need, no need," said a grinning Cartwright, hands up in the air all "pshaw," fighting charm with charm.

"You're sure? You say the word, sir, we'd be happy to return at your convenience."

If Markham had had a cheekful of Red Man, he would have spat on the floor as proof of his down-home bonhomie.

"Let's just get ourselves a little peace and quiet so we can talk without further interruption," said Cartwright, the gracious host sweeping us toward the interview rooms. This time he opened the door on a bigger one, made cheery by the addition of a window. "After you, Ms. Dare." He practically bowed me in.

Bigger table in there, too. Two chairs on either side, with pens and a pad of notepaper in front of each.

"Can we get you anything?" asked Cartwright. "Coffee, soda?"

There was a pitcher of ice water on the table, four glasses.

"That water'll do me just fine, Detective," said Markham, "thank you kindly."

"Ms. Dare?"

"No, thank you." I looked out the window. Snowing.

Gentle drifting flakes, making everything beyond the glass look sweetly Grandma Moses.

Markham walked around the table to draw out a chair for me. "Madeline?"

"Let me just see what's keeping Officer Baker," said Cartwright, "then we can get things under way."

"No rush," said Markham.

Cartwright bowed again, then swung the door to behind him.

"He'll probably leave us rot for a good while now," said my attorney, shooting his cuffs. "The piker."

"How long?"

He looked at his very thin watch. "Let's say a couple hands of canasta. Too bad I left the cards in my other briefcase."

"Point being?"

"He's got to piss on his turf," said Markham. "Course, now, if I were court-appointed, we'd be talking all-day bridge tournament, heel-cooling wise."

"If you were court-appointed," I said, "I'd no doubt be smoking Bugler hand-rolleds in Framingham by now, clad head to toe in a most unbecoming shade of orange."

He grinned at me. "Your godfather's ring gets more kissable by the minute, don't it?"

I nodded, even more nervous. "Any words of wisdom you'd like to share with your client before the po-leece deign to grace us with their presence?"

"Three of 'em," he replied. *'Don't say shit.'*"

He poured us each a glass of ice water. "Just you sit back while I sing for my supper here, darlin'. We want to make sure that nice uncle Alan gets his money's worth."

28

Cartwright and Baker surprised us, coming back to the interview room after a mere ten minutes of heel-cooling on Markham's and my part.

My attorney fairly leaped to his feet, hand extended. "Officer Baker? Markham Dwight Stuyvesant, counsel for Madeline Dare."

She shook it, nonplussed.

We got resettled at the table, pens and file folders and clipboards and notepads now arrayed in front of each seat, with Baker at the helm of a tape recorder.

After the rustle and blather of preliminaries, Markham looked from Cartwright to Baker, then back.

"What we have here," he said, "is a *failure* . . . of communi*cation* . . ."

Cool Hand Stuyvesant.

Yeah, that was exactly what we needed.

But then Markham started kicking some serious ass.

"We know that my client had no compelling reason to have committed these homicides," he said, "especially when compared to some of the other members of the school's faculty."

He touched on some of the same points he'd scared me with the night before, though not all. Not by a long shot.

He revealed little that Baker and Cartwright didn't already know, but managed to nudge them toward a far wider pool of suspects all the same.

"I think you'll agree that my client is the last person whose affairs warrant further investigation," he said.

The two cops, rapt, asked a question here or there, but each inquiry seemed more like some little Hansel-and-Gretel chunk of bread thrown down in hope of their safe return, rather than any serious attempt to stop following my attorney deeper and deeper into a forest of his own design.

The guy was so good I'd have skipped along behind him myself, blithely oblivious to the possibility of bears and snakes and impending nightfall.

He slid a hint of Gerald into the mists of enchantment so subtly that the pair of them latched on to the guy, thinking his alleged guilt was their own idea.

I had no doubt that Markham could easily have charmed the pants off Baker and eaten Cartwright's lunch while he spoke, without a one of us noticing that he'd so much as twitched in his chair.

Finally, he looked at that achingly thin watch again, then grinned at us all.

"My client must return to work," he said, "and I think we can all agree that her continued employment at the Santangelo Academy is testament to that institution's utter faith in her innocence of *any* wrongdoing. In fact, she's in line for a promotion."

Hands were shaken all around.

Markham and I left the station. As we climbed into the Beamer, he winked at me and kissed his own ring.

"Dude," I said, "that was *awesome*."

"Let's not go counting any chickens," he said. "All I did was cast a few choice handfuls of grain as a temporary diversion."

"Markham, that wasn't chicken feeding, that was snake charming. Turban and all."

"What can I say, darlin'. 'Sometimes the light's all shining on me . . .' "

He hit the gas and shot us onto Route 20.

"Now you're gonna pay me back," he said, "by asking your friend Lulu what she remembers about your traveling jacket last

Tuesday night. But that's all, honey lamb. That's *all.* No meanderings from your appointed conversational task — we clear?"

"Crystal," I said as we flew back to Pittsfield.

Lulu and I were hiding out by the grape arbor, smoking and freezing our asses off on the cold ground during lunch break from Sitting.

"So listen," I said. "My attorney wants me to figure out how Fay's necklace got into my jacket. I don't have a damn clue. I mean, if you took it with you when you left the Farm at the end of that party, then how the hell could anyone else get at the thing to slip any jewelry inside?"

"I *didn't* take your jacket when I left," she said. "I didn't even know you'd left it there."

"So how'd it get up to Dhumavati's apartment?"

"Gerald," she said. "He gave it to me when I went out to wash your clothes."

"What time was that?"

"After midnight, maybe? Not exactly sure. Definitely late."

"What the hell was he doing up there? I mean, wasn't he on overnight coverage at the Farm?"

"Why don't you ask him?" said Lulu.

"Can't," I said. "Markham said I'm not allowed to talk to anyone about it. Probably piss him right off if he knew I was chatting with you, except about the necklace thing."

"So I'll ask Gerald," she said. "Piece of cake."

We heard a rustling in the trees behind us and simultaneously dropped our Camels.

Lulu threw me a breath mint just as Wiesner emerged from the woods, snow dusting his cropped blond hair.

"Got another one of those smokes for a poor wayward runaway?" he asked.

"Wiesner, honest to God," said Lulu. "You scared me to death, practically. And where the hell have you been?"

"It's a secret," he said. "And I only came out because you guys were talking about Gerald, so it's not like I'm going to come trotting back with either of you, okay?"

"We can't let you just leave," she said.

"Lulu, get real," he said, towering over her. "How the hell you gonna make me stay?"

"Um, there is that," I said.

"I mean," he said, "no one will blame you for not trying to tackle me or whatever. And I wouldn't recommend it anyway, what with my known predisposition for violence. So let's just smoke and chill for a minute, okay?

339

Then we can all just pretend we never ran into each other in the first place."

"Oh, for chrissake," she said, shrugging and handing him my pack of Camels.

"Smart move," he said, leaning down to give her a playful tap on the shoulder. "After all, I'm a dangerous man."

"You're a dangerous *boy,* Wiesner," she said. "Don't let's go putting on any airs."

He grinned at her, cigarette clenched in his teeth, then held out his hand for the lighter.

"You got enough food, wherever you are?" I asked. "Blankets and stuff?"

"Taken care of," he said, cupping the flame and pulling down a lungful of smoke. "Don't worry your pretty head."

"You should come back to school," I said. "I think Gerald's under control. Plus, it's not like you could testify against him. You weren't even in the room, right?"

"Let me tell you a little something about Gerald, Madeline," he said, "speaking of dangerous men."

Lulu reached up to pluck the lighter from his hand, then tossed it back to me.

"Go ahead, Wiesner," she said, "spill."

He turned his head to the side and blew out a plume of tar and nicotine. "Okay, start with this for spillage: I think Gerald's a

340

fucking spy."

"Wiesner, if you go off ranting about the KGB or something," I said, "I'm not above jumping you myself."

That got me a leer. "Jump me any ol' time you want. That kinda talk fires my loinage right up."

"Don't be an asshole," said Lulu. "Just tell us what the hell you mean by 'spy.' "

Wiesner sank to the ground beside us, crossing his legs Indian-style and leaning back against one of the pergola's rotting uprights.

"Gerald and I showed up here about the same time," he said, "and I gotta say, he seemed squirrelly from day one."

"Compared to what?" asked Lulu. "I mean, if you ask me, this place is pretty much ground zero, vis-à-vis Team Squirrel. Myself included, front and center."

Wiesner laughed, raising a hand to cite his own membership on the squad. "Let's just say he's above and beyond. And even weirder lately."

"I say again, weirder than what?" asked Lulu. "Weirder how?"

"Fussier. Twitchier."

"We *all* are, Wiesner," I said. "And come on, who could blame us? Fay and Mooney, all the Sitting . . ."

341

"So why's Gerald wandering all over campus in the middle of the night?" he said. "And I mean *every* night."

He took another hit of Camel. "And when he's not skulking around through the classrooms and the offices and the meeting rooms — with a flashlight, by the way, and meanwhile all dressed up in black sweats with a freaking watch cap on like he thinks he's some hokey burglar — what the hell's he doing sitting up in his apartment till dawn with piles of books on his desk, taking notes and talking into this very shpendy-looking microcassette recorder?"

"Um," I said.

"You guys wanna ask me," said Wiesner, "I think when it comes to Team Squirrel, Gerald qualifies as outright bushy-tailed varsity captain. Possibly head coach."

Not to mention, I thought, that the guy was rich enough to buy up the whole damn American Squirrel League and make it collect acorns on his lawn.

"Sounds like you've been doing a little skulking yourself, Wiesner," said Lulu.

He shrugged. "Gotta keep my hand in."

"So what's he looking for?" I asked.

"Fuck if I know," said Wiesner, stubbing out his Camel. "Maybe you should ask your attorney — after Lulu finds out what the hell Gerald was doing with your jacket that night."

He stood up and patted each of us on the head. "Think I'll be taking off now, ladies," he said, then sprinted back out into the forest.

"Who *was* that masked man?" I asked.

"And we didn't even have a chance to thank him." Lulu rose to her feet and started brushing snow off the back of her pants.

29

On the way back to the dining hall, I told Lulu the rest of what I now knew about Gerald, once we'd assured each other that Wiesner couldn't be eavesdropping.

"So I'd love to know what happened at his last gig," I said, "that he ended up here."

"Curiouser and curiouser," she said. "And what the hell is a 'special product,' anyway?"

"I dunno. Like some weird kind of algebra-extrapolation stock/bond thing. Futures or something? Risky stuff, but I guess you can make a lot of money with them."

"I'll stick to cash crops, thank you very much," she said. "Nice and tangible. Soybeans, winter wheat . . ."

"You and Dean must be cousins," I said, "somehow."

"All Methodists are cousins. It's the bond of the Jell-O salad and the pale blue American sedan."

"Not Lutherans?"

"*Lutherans?* Bite your tongue!"

"Consider it bitten," I said.

"Do you want me to ask Gerald about his career shift?"

"Lulu, *no.* Seriously, I'm not even sure you should bring up the jacket. We don't know what the guy's deal is at all. Especially now, with the whole burglar-skulking thing. Gave me the creeps, Wiesner talking about that."

"You're sure? I can be circumspect. Methodists are justly famed for their circumspection."

"Let's let Markham handle it. He's practically Samoan."

"Samoan?"

I shook my head. "Had to be there."

We trudged along in silence for a minute.

"Hey," I said, "what's today?"

"Shitty," she said.

"No, I mean day of the week."

"You know what?" she said. "All this Sitting, I don't even know."

"If it's Friday, I might like to do a little skulking of my own."

"For what?"

I told her about Santangelo's dirt meetings.

"Oh my God," she said. "You're serious?

No confidentiality?"

"Anything you wouldn't want them to know?"

She laughed. "Whining about my mother? Not a lot anyone could hold over my head, unless they threatened to reveal her secret Jell-O recipe."

"So what's the secret?"

"Shredded carrots," she said. "You can throw in mini marshmallows, if you want to get hoity-toity."

"That's *nasty.*"

"I'm not going to lose any sleep over the possibility of blackmail."

"Ew," I said, "blackmailers would pay *you* to keep that stuff under wraps."

"And don't get me started on Mother's scrapple."

"Your poor therapist! I bet she goes to those secret meetings and just uncontrollably weeps."

"Heh," said Lulu.

"Can't believe I'm about to ask this," I said, "but do you think we missed lunch?"

"Mmmm," she said, "I wonder if they have any scrapple Jell-O."

She leaned down and picked up a large pinecone from beside the path. "I can make a nice centerpiece with this."

■ ■ ■ ■

We made it before the steam tables went all verboten on us — in fact, they hadn't even started moving the salad bar back over to the wall.

I snaked myself some cottage cheese and artichoke hearts and cucumber slices and Italian dressing, with grated cheddar and even some of Santangelo's Salvation Army croutons for good measure.

When I got to the faculty table, the only place left was next to Gerald, who was fastidiously chewing each bite of his Salisbury steak and whipped potatoes thirty-two times, while Mindy babbled on about the latest pink additions to her stuffed-animal menagerie. A bunny and a puppy and two of just absolutely the *cutest* little fluffy kittens you ever *saw,* apparently. Blink blink.

I waved at Pete, but he was staring out the window and didn't wave back. Or look.

Whatever. Sitting made everyone cranky.

So, since I couldn't talk to Gerald about my jacket, or his Hamburglar deal, or anything real, I started trying to figure out a way to bring up fractals to see if I could get him chatting about his previous job.

Only let's face it, fractals are not exactly

something that come up naturally in your average conversation. I couldn't just go, "Fluffy kittens, Mindy? Funny you should mention them, because I was just thinking how they relate to the philosophical vagaries of investment banking."

We weren't exactly talking me having some whole bountylicious smorgas-copia of higher-mathematics small talk at my disposal.

I had to say something, though, before Mindy's jawing on about all those cuddwy iddoo-widdoo puddy-tats made me fwow the fuck up.

I looked around the table, desperate for inspiration. When I saw that Lulu had deposited her spiky forest swag right next to her plate, I heaved a sigh of relief.

"Hey, Lulu," I said, "okay if I play with your pinecone?"

"Have at it," she said, handing it over.

"Love these things," I said to Gerald. "They're just so damn Fibonacci, you know?"

Which was, like, the only other thing I knew about math, aside from my general suckage at the subject — that all pinecones were examples of the Fibonacci series, a string of numbers that kept appearing in nature.

I started counting the petals of the cone as they spiraled out from its base: "One, one, two, three, five," hoping to hell this would somehow coincide with fractals.

"Eight, thirteen," continued Gerald. "I love that stuff. I always used to count them when I was a kid. Did you know it works with the heads of sunflowers, too?"

"Really?" I said. "Gerald, that's fascinating. I had no idea!"

I sounded all fakey-fake, like my mom when there was a guy in the kitchen and she suddenly became incapable of opening pickle jars, but Gerald seemed pleased and flattered.

"Pineapples, Sharon fruit, and many leaf configurations," he said. "Of course, in some plants, the numbers don't belong to the sequence of F's — Fibonacci numbers — but to the sequence of G's — Lucas numbers — if not to even more anomalous sequences."

"So it's not, like, universal, then."

"Well, you couldn't really call phyllotaxis a law," he said. "It's more accurate to think of it as a fascinatingly prevalent tendency."

"Phyllotaxis? Is that anything to do with fractals?"

"You're interested in fractals?"

"Oh, I think they're inspiring," I said.

"Even though I'm not sure I fully understand the full range of their applications."

I looked deep into his eyes with a little blink blink myself.

"They're for describing things that are, like, bumpy, right?" I asked, finger to lips, the confused ingenue. "Coastlines, the stock market?"

Had Gerald looked any more ecstatic, I would've worried he was about to bend me over the table and spank me out of sheer glee.

Gotcha.

30

We were all hauling salad bar and tables back to the walls for après-lunch Sitting, but Gerald was still talking a blue streak.

"That is, the Mandelbrot set is the *subset* of the complex plane consisting of those parameters for which the *Julia* set of . . ."

His voice kept blurring in and out — phrases like "certainly include Mikhail Lyubich *and* Jean-Christophe Yoccoz, at the very least," alternating with the "Waaah, wuh-WUH waaaaah" of adult speech in Charlie Brown specials.

I was ready to throw myself at Mindy's feet and beg for enough contrapuntal iddoo-widdoo cuddwy-wuddwy that I might hope to achieve spontaneous combustion and thus end my agony.

". . . realized that prices having theoretically infinite *variance* did in fact follow a rather more Lévy-stable model," Gerald went on, "such that our comprehension of *financial* markets —"

"Financial markets?" I shrieked, grabbing the man by his cheesy lapels. "Gerald, you're a goddamn *genius!*"

He blushed, stepping back from the praise.

"Seriously," I gushed, "you're blowing me away with the staggeringly lapidary sublimeness of your erudition, here!"

"That's awfully kind of you, Madeline," he mumbled, looking down at his now bashfully pigeoned toes. "But I can't say I've made any original contribution. For goodness' sakes, Mandelbrot's 1975 *Les objets fractals: forme, hasard et dimension* alone —"

"Dude," I insisted, "don't go trying to hide your light under any bushels. You're all, like — I mean, why aren't you on Wall Street?"

I laid a gentle hand on his wrist. "Why aren't you teaching at, I don't know, Harvard?"

"Madeline, I used to imagine that I'd . . ." But he stopped there, looking like he might be on the verge of tears for a moment.

"Gerald?"

"I had no choice. My reason for coming overrode all other considerations. Money, pride, reputation . . ." And then he did tear up. Turned his head to the side so I wouldn't see.

Too late.

"Gerald," I said, "if you ever want to talk about it . . ."

"I would, I think." He looked around the shabby room, at everyone drawing its chairs back into yet another torturous circle. "I'd like to talk about it with *you*."

I sent up a little prayer of apology to Markham. "I would consider it an honor, Gerald. I really would."

"Doesn't seem like we'll have any chance of that now," he said. "Maybe we could have a cup of coffee together in my apartment after we're done with this session?"

The dining hall went quiet as people started taking their seats.

Gerald chose a place next to me on the floor, holding my hand throughout our next two hours of Sitting.

31

I spent the entire Sitting session wondering how not to accept any more Gerald-prepared beverages — especially alone in his apartment — while trying to steel myself against the desperate urge to yank my hand out of his.

It was, after all, he who'd had control of my jacket, with the consequent opportunity to plant Fay's broken necklace on my person. Gerald the spy, Gerald the probably-killer, Gerald the close personal friend of Santangelo, who'd set me up to take the probably-rap.

Gerald, the guy who creeped out Wiesner, for God's sake.

And yet he'd planted a little green tendril of doubt.

Here we'd spent all this time — me and Dean and Markham, with his brigade of hungry young associates — trying to figure out whether the man's deep dark raison-de-resignation secret was having gotten busted for dabbling in smack or groping innocent little Japanese schoolboys.

But something about the way he'd gotten all weepy made me hope he really was just a prissy, old-maidish guy in Sears, Roebuck wing tips, with his "rubbers" and his exacting OCD chewing of each bite at every meal.

I was just having a hard time maintaining my conviction that he was secretly this totally ruthless amoral killer of children and grabber of dicks. Part of me wanted to give him the benefit of Markham's lawyerly "alleged" on all of it. Not least because I could totally see how the dick-grabbing allegations had worked like a get-out-of-jail-free-card charm for Wiesner and Mooney's third roommate — a card I might have considered playing, had I ever been unlucky enough to do time here myself in my misspent youth.

Bad enough being Santangelo's hireling. We teachers could just walk out whenever the going got nasty. The kids had *Arbeit Macht* "Free to Be" day after day, with those stupid iron butterflies flopping around the gate just to rub it all in.

But when Gerald gave my hand another little squeeze, I knew for damn sure there was no way I trusted him enough to risk finding out whether any cuppa joe at his place — flagon with the dragon *or* vessel with the pestle — brimmed with "brew that is true."

Markham had said poison was most often the female weapon of choice, but Gerald wasn't exactly the butchest guy who ever came down the pike. If he *had* killed Mooney and Fay, the idea of him having done it with a gun or a knife or a blunt instrument in his soft moist grip strained credulity to the point that only dogs could hear it.

So, coffee was out, if he'd been anywhere near the carafe. And I wasn't about to go to his apartment, either.

I wondered if he'd come to Lulu's and talk there over some of her Mr. Raspberry-Hazelnut Fufu, or even up to our place in Pittsfield for Bustelo, with the side benefit of Dean's bulk backing me up.

In the end, Dhumavati's intervention during the next break period rendered my plotting pretty damn moot.

She walked up to me and Gerald and told me to follow her back into the meeting room across from the dining hall. After shutting the door behind us, she turned to me, stern. "Did you know Fay was pregnant?"

"I guess that means the autopsy results

are back?" I asked.

She ignored that. "And did you know they were planning to hit the road, she and Mooney?"

"Dhumavati, look, I —"

"What were you thinking? *Were* you thinking?"

"I was thinking that Mooney was sitting there with his hand bleeding all over me, and I figured he needed someone to talk to about why, and I didn't know what to do, since I had no idea whether or not Santangelo would react to the news by screaming at him that someone should shove the poor kid's head through a wall, so I told Mooney that *yes,* I'd wait for a few days before I told anyone."

"And do you accept any responsibility for the way that decision turned out?"

"For the fact that somebody killed them, Dhumavati? For God's sake, what the hell does one have to do with the other?"

"So you're okay with letting yourself off the hook because something even worse happened to two of our students than running away from the safety of school? I don't *think* so, Madeline."

"I *do* think so, Dhumavati. I'm sorry."

"I presume you mean you're sorry about failing to act responsibly, immediately following that conversation with Mooney."

"No. I mean I'm sorry to hear you describe what they wanted to run away *from* as 'the safety of school.' And I'm even more sorry to come to terms with the likelihood that you actually believe it. What happened to all your talk about standing up to David?"

"This has no bearing on my relationship with David."

"Of course it does. Fay and Mooney *died* here. At this school. Is that what you call safety? I want to believe you know better."

"What's at issue here is your decision to set yourself above the rules of this community."

"Rules I thought you questioned as much as I do."

"Madeline, you have to take responsibility for the consequences of the choice *you* made."

"You're going to claim with a straight face that keeping a confidence is worse than murder? Seriously, listen to yourself — that's talking *what,* like, apples and machetes?"

"No, that's talking a staff member who can't think clearly enough to protect the students in her care, or the future of this school as a whole."

"And what exactly would it have changed had I told you that Fay was pregnant? Let's presume that somehow it would have prevented her death, and Mooney's, although I don't see how. But okay, say it did, then what?"

She started to answer, but I kept going. "I'll tell you what the hell would've happened. Santangelo would've sent her home to her family so they could all gang up and force her to bring the pregnancy to term, right?"

"That wasn't your concern."

"Who the hell's concern *was* it, then? Who the hell's should it have been?"

"She was a minor, Madeline."

"Not as of Tuesday. Fay was legally an adult when she died."

"And that's what you were waiting for? That's why you kept this information to yourself?"

"I kept it to myself because I'd given Mooney my word. I agreed to respect their confidence until she turned eighteen — that was the condition he set for telling me in the first place."

"You could have told *me*."

"And what would you have done? Told David she was pregnant? Would that have changed anything?"

"We can't know that."

"Without David, she never would have gotten pregnant," I said.

"What?"

"David's the one who banned the use of birth control on campus in the first place. I mean, that's certain to keep a bunch of teenagers from fornicating and knocking each other up, right? Make sure there's no sex education. Make sure they don't have access to even condoms. There's a goddamn brilliant plan."

"Madeline, you are out of —"

"Out of what? Line? Bounds? Patience? My mind? You know better than this, don't bullshit me."

She was livid. Fuming. "That's your projection. *And* evidence of how very deeply you're in denial about your own part in the fate of those two poor children."

"I wish I *could* be in denial about my part in their fate. Because what I should have done was tell Mooney to grab Fay before that ambulance came, and run like hell. That's the only hope of safety they ever had."

"That's ridiculous. He'd almost certainly have bled to death."

"Did it make any difference in the end? I could have saved *her.* That beautiful, beautiful girl. *We* could have saved her, Dhumavati — you and me — if only we'd had the courage to break the rules just once. Can you look me in the eye and tell me that Fay's life mattered less to you than the goddamn rules do?"

I waited for her to say something, anything.

"I want you to meet with Sookie. And I want you to do it now," she replied.

"Dhumavati," I said, "you're breaking my heart."

I sat down on Sookie's love seat.

"This wasn't my idea," I said.

"Does it have to be?" Sookie asked.

I gestured toward the typewriter on her desk. There was a half-written document sticking out of its platen.

"You're obviously busy," I said.

"Dhumavati felt it was important I make time to meet with you."

"Dhumavati seems to feel it's important I open up to you about the part that my lack of spiritual and psychiatric evolution played in Mooney's and Fay's deaths."

"You seem angry."

"Ya *think?*"

"Want to talk about it?"

"My attorney has instructed me not to

discuss Fay and Mooney with anyone on campus," I said. "No offense."

"None taken," she said. "It seems like a perfectly reasonable precaution under the circumstances."

"I appreciate your saying that."

"Thank you," she said.

We looked at each other.

"So where does that leave us?" she asked. "Is there anything you'd like to discuss that your attorney didn't prohibit? I understand you've been through a lot this week."

"That's putting it mildly."

"A night in jail, the possibility you might be accused of the murders . . ."

I crossed my legs.

"It must have been tremendously upsetting," she said.

"Yes."

"Scary?"

"Please tell me that's a rhetorical question."

"Sure," she said. "What do lawyers say? 'Asked and answered'? Let's call it that."

"Let's."

She gave me "the nod."

"You don't have to do that," I said.

"What?"

"The nodding. Really. Save your breath. Or, you know, your neck or whatever, okay?"

"Okay."

We sat there.

For a good while.

Sookie crossed her legs.

I uncrossed mine.

"Is there anything I can tell *you*?" she asked.

"Such as?"

"Such as how angry *I* am?"

"About what?"

"About your having been put through all this . . . this . . . shit."

"Sookie, are you serious?"

She pointed to the typewriter. "I've written my letter of resignation."

I looked at the piece of paper.

"I was tempted to give it to Dhumavati," said Sookie, "the minute she walked you in here. And then I realized I should see if there was anything I could help you with first, while I still officially work for these people."

"I'm, um . . . wow."

"Anything, Madeline — answer your questions, talk to your lawyer, testify on your behalf — you name it."

"I admit to being shocked. Pleasantly."

"This is not what I signed on for when I worked my tail off to become a shrink. It's a travesty. And I don't mean just what

363

they're doing to you, I mean all of it."

"So, Sookie," I said, "how does that make you *feel?*"

She giggled. "Ready to blow the damn roof off this place. Where should we start?"

32

"Let's start with what you meant by 'what they're doing' to me," I said. "They who, and doing what?"

"I just can't believe it's a coincidence that all this started after you told me about what you'd gone through last year."

"Because you did the show-and-tell at Santangelo's house last Friday night?"

"You know about that?"

"I do now," I said. "A little late to matter."

"For both of us."

"And it never bothered you before, the fact that there wasn't any confidentiality? I mean, wasn't there a bit of a contrast with the other places you've worked?"

"I didn't have any other places to compare it *to*, Madeline. This was my first job out of graduate school."

"It still didn't raise any flags? Pardon my saying, but confidentiality's pretty much the cornerstone of therapy. I can't believe your professors failed to mention that."

"I thought you knew," she said. "I thought everyone knew. The kids, the parents —"

"The teachers."

"It never occurred to me that we were being pumped for information without our clients' consent. I can't believe that's legal."

"It probably isn't," I said.

"Then I guess maybe I should be making my own appointment with your attorney."

"He's expensive."

"I have a feeling I'm going to need expensive," she said, "if I ever hope to work in this field again."

I couldn't dispute that, much as I would have liked to.

"I know," she said. "I'm an idiot."

"I think that probably goes for both of us. The question is, what are we going to do about it?"

"Take them down," she said.

"If they don't take me down first."

"I won't let that happen. I don't care if it means I won't ever get a second job doing this."

"You're sure?"

"Yes."

"Okay, so let's scuttle a little confidentiality of our own. What else do they know about me? What else do you know about them?"

She thought about that.

"Start with who goes to the meetings," I said. "I presume Dhumavati and David . . . all the shrinks . . . any faculty?"

"Only two," she said. "Gerald, of course. And then lately, that new guy's been showing up too."

"Tim?" I asked, knowing full well that Sookie would have just said Tim, had he been the new guy in question.

"No," she said, "I'm talking about your 'friend' Pete."

"I'm not liking the way you just said 'friend,' Sookie. Makes me nervous."

"It should," she said. "He thinks you did it. He thinks you killed them."

It took a minute for that to sink in.

And a very bad minute it was.

"He told you guys that this Friday? What was it, last night? I don't even know what day it is anymore."

"We had an extra session this week," she said. "I suppose for damage control."

"When?"

"The night before you were taken to jail."

"Is that why?"

"Yes," she said, "I think it was. Detective Cartwright came to the meeting. With

367

another officer, a woman."

"Baker," I said.

Sookie nodded.

"Have they been back since?"

"Twice," she said. "As far as I know."

"To sit in on more meetings?"

"To talk with Pete. And Dhumavati and David. So I don't know what was said at those meetings."

"Can you find out?"

"I'll do my best," she said. "And they're coming back tomorrow morning. Apparently, Cartwright wants to talk with Gerald."

"And tonight Gerald wants to talk with me," I said.

Sookie looked thoughtful. "Are you going to take Mr. Jones up on that invitation?" she asked.

"Not alone. Not in his apartment."

"Are you saying you think *he* might have . . ." She shook her head, stunned.

"He was serving the punch the night Fay and Mooney died. Other than that, I have no idea."

"What does he want to talk about?"

"About what originally brought him here to Santangelo."

"I may be able to tell you that," she said. "In fact, I have a feeling Gerald would want me to. He recently opened up to me about it."

"You're his therapist?"

"We've been doing a lot of private sessions, which he specified would be confidential."

"How did he finagle that?"

"He pays for them. And we meet off campus."

"If you're willing to tell me, I'm presuming his reason for coming here wasn't something horrible."

"You'd be wrong," she said.

"Anything to do with the accusation that he grabbed that boy last year?"

"You know about that?"

"Wiesner told me."

"Wiesner . . . You watch yourself with that boy."

"Wiesner aside," I said, "do you think Gerald might have done any grabbing?"

"I know for a fact he didn't."

"Okay," I said. "But I still don't want to go to his apartment alone."

"Why don't I come with you?" She looked at her watch. "We could walk over right now. He should be there. He speaks with his mother every day around this time. She's in a hospice in Great Barrington. Stage-four bone cancer."

"Oh, Sookie," I said.

"They've always been close," she said. "Gerald's the eldest of seven children, and his mother was widowed when he was still very young. He helped raise the other kids."

"I had no idea."

"Gerald is a remarkable man. It's been a privilege getting to know him. Not just professionally." She checked her watch again. "I'd call, but they're probably still on the phone together."

"You're sure it would be okay for us to barge in?"

"She's in a great deal of pain. Their calls don't last very long these days."

When Gerald greeted us at the door of his apartment, it was obvious that he'd been crying.

He and Sookie hugged, and what with the way he looked at her after welcoming us inside, I began to sense why she had such absolute trust that his passions had nothing to do with young boys. Gerald was smitten with her, and she with him. They fairly glowed with it.

"Is it getting harder for her?" she asked him. "How was she today?"

"Mother's ready to go," he said. "I'm the one who can't accept it, and I can't stand the knowledge that she's suffering so greatly to make the transition easier on me. She'll wait until I'm ready. I want to be ready, able to let her go, but I'm not strong enough. Not yet."

I looked around his apartment. A lot of very good Japanese wood-block prints. Hiroshige. Hokusai. Bookshelves jammed with nonfiction hardcovers. Family photos on all the tables — group shots, mostly, in clean-lined sterling frames.

Over on his desk, there was one color eight-by-ten of a smiling dark-haired woman, taken in the early sixties, if her cat's-eye glasses were any indication. She had Gerald's jaw. His eyes. She was proudly holding up a fishing rod in one hand and a rather large walleye in the other.

Next to that shot was another of the same woman, only this time she had a laughing little girl on her lap. Beautiful-looking. Huge gray eyes, ash-blonde hair. Six years old, maybe, and holding up a minnow.

Gerald turned to me. "Sookie's told you about Mother, Madeline?"

"She has," I said. "I hope that's all right."

"Absolutely," he said. "I only wish you could both have met her before she became so ill. She is a woman of tremendous depth and courage. Always was."

"She sounds it," I said, and he smiled at me.

"May I get anything for the two of you?" he asked. "A glass of wine? Some coffee?"

"I'm fine, thank you," I said.

Sookie told him she'd love a glass of white. Gerald put some music on. Young Glenn Gould doing his 1955 take on the Goldberg Variations.

Perfect sound track for someone who loved fractals, when I thought about it — how each little piece built on the last, the way they all unfolded and sort of sparkled. *Melodies for Mandelbrot.*

Gerald had a tremendously hardcore set of speakers on that stereo. You could hear Gould humming along with himself, which I'd never been able to detect on my own cassettes *refrito* of the same recordings.

"Sure you wouldn't like anything, Madeline?" he called out from the kitchen.

"Maybe a little punch?" Sookie whispered under her breath.

"That's the kind of thing that passes for humor among shrinks?" I said, getting up to look more closely at the pictures on his desk.

"Mary," said Sookie. "Gerald's mother. And Mary-Claire."

Mary-Claire was wearing a T-shirt celebrating the Bicentennial. Not the sixties, then. Maybe his mother just took good care of her glasses. Fastidious, like her oldest son.

Gerald came back out with Sookie's wine.

"Mary-Claire was a student here," he said when he saw me looking at her photograph. "That's why I came."

33

"She was the brightest of any of us," said Gerald. "Always the head of her class. Tremendously gifted in math and science but far above average in the humanities as well. Unlike me — I was always rather one-sided academically. Mary-Claire used to tease me about that something fierce. Tried to get me to read poetry. When she was fifteen, she won a concert competition — full scholarship to study at a conservatory in Boston."

"What instrument?" I asked.

"Piano," he said. "She played stunningly. Would have given Glenn Gould a run for his money, no doubt."

Would have.

"She never got to Boston," he said. "We realized that summer that she had bi-polar disorder. Had her first psychotic break in late August, during a harrowing manic episode."

He picked up the frame and ran the tip of his finger along the edge of it. "She spent sixteen months in a hospital, then we enrolled her here."

"That was three years ago," said Sookie.

"I could afford the best care for her by then," he said. "The doctor at her hospital recommended Santangelo. From the heft of the tuition, I believed him."

"What was the name of the hospital?" I asked.

"Lake Haven," they said in unison.

"And when did Mary-Claire leave Santangelo?"

"She didn't," said Gerald.

"She died here. Two years ago," said Sookie.

"And that's when I resigned in Tokyo," said Gerald. "That's when I came here. Pretty much the first time I was ever glad to have such a common last name. You and Sookie are the only people on campus who know that Mary-Claire and I were brother and sister. Tomorrow I'll be telling Detective Cartwright."

"Gerald, I am so very sorry. What happened to her?"

"We were told she committed suicide. I don't believe it."

"Please excuse me for asking this," I said,

"but how can you be sure? I mean, considering her illness . . ."

"She was doing far, far better. Her meds were working, and she was hoping to go to the conservatory after all. She'd written to me in Japan to tell me about it. I was planning to visit the week she died."

Still, maybe she'd had another manic episode? A crash into depression afterward?

"I flew home for her funeral instead," he said. "Mother was so distraught, I couldn't leave."

"Are you sure it wasn't suicide?" I asked.

"We believed that it was at first. They did an autopsy, so we knew she was pregnant. We presumed that was why she'd done it. But then Mary-Claire's last letter to me arrived — forwarded from the office in Tokyo. She'd been raped here. That was how she got pregnant."

"Gerald, that's horrible," I said. "Do you know who did it?"

"She couldn't tell me outright."

"Why not?"

"Because she knew I wouldn't be the only one reading her letter. The kids have to leave the envelope unsealed when they write home. All mail is opened and searched, incoming and outgoing."

"But she managed to give you some idea

who was responsible?"

"She did," he said. "And I think that's why she was killed."

"One of the teachers?"

He shook his head. "David Santangelo."

I shivered. "And he killed her?"

"David wasn't here when she died. He was somewhere in Mexico."

"San Miguel de Allende," I said. "Dhumavati told me he's got a house there."

"If I'd known she was in danger . . . if I'd gotten here sooner . . ."

"You couldn't have known," I said.

"This has to end," he said. "This *place* has to end. I'm going to Cartwright as soon as I'm sure."

"And I thought you'd killed Fay and Mooney," I said. "I'm so sorry."

"Can you tell me why?" he asked. "If they've got something on me, I'll need to explain that to Cartwright as well."

"Well," I said, "there were two things. The first was that you were in charge of the punch, and the second was that you gave Lulu my jacket that night. Then, of course, you're the one who found them in that loft."

I left out the part about his having allegedly grabbed Parker's dick.

"What's the importance of your jacket?" he asked.

"I found Fay's necklace in the pocket when I was taken down to the station for questioning the next morning. The chain was broken — I knew she hadn't taken it off since Mooney gave it to her. Someone must have done that after she was killed, then planted it on me. Up until tonight, I thought you were that someone."

"There was no necklace in your pocket when I picked it up at the Farm," he said. "I wasn't sure the jacket was yours, so I checked for a wallet. You had cigarettes and a lighter and birthday candles. Nothing else. I brought it up here to hang on Lulu's doorknob. I wasn't expecting to run into her."

"Why did you leave the Farm?" I asked. "Weren't you on overnight duty?"

"That's something I'll have to tell Cartwright, too," he said, looking stricken. "I left in the middle of the night for a couple of hours. Second worst thing I've ever done."

"If you'd been there, you would have been asleep anyway," I said. "There's no way you could have prevented what happened."

"Maybe I'd have heard something," he said. "Maybe I could have stopped whoever did it. I can't forgive myself for that."

"No one else heard a thing," I said. "None

of the kids. Or Tim."

"Still," he said. "If there was any chance my having been there would have changed things . . ."

"So why did you leave?" I asked.

"He was coming here," said Sookie, "to meet me."

34

I looked at Gerald. "The fact that you were with Sookie — you alibi each other. That matters. It means that whoever really did this can't blame it on you. You have to look at it in that light — that it might mean they won't get away with it."

"You're very kind to say so," he said.

"Just honest."

"Honesty doesn't negate kindness," said Sookie.

Gerald took her hand.

"So who do we think is responsible, if not Santangelo?" I asked. "Who else stood to gain from their deaths?"

"That's what I've been trying to pin down," said Gerald.

"Someone told me you've been seen doing a little, um, research," I said. "After hours."

Gerald went pale. "Who?"

I squirmed in my chair. "Does it matter?"

"Very much. If that's common knowledge
—"

"No," I said. "I don't think anyone knows
but me and Lulu. And, well, Wiesner."

"Wiesner?" he said. "I thought he was on
the road, long since."

"I don't know where he is, but he's not
far away. He's been wandering around
campus at night. He's seen you wandering
around, too. Checking out offices, making
lots of notes here."

"Madeline," he said, "that's not comforting news."

"I know the two of you don't exactly have
a pleasant history, but he's not about to tell
anyone else. He just knew I thought you
might have . . . been involved, so he told me
about it. Now that I know you're in the
clear, I don't think it will matter, do you?"

"I guess not," he said. "Not if Wiesner's
the only one who's seen me."

"Far as I know."

A clock chimed on Gerald's desk.

Sookie looked at her watch. "I have to get
home." She got up, taking her wineglass to
the kitchen.

"Just leave that," Gerald called after her.

"I'll rinse it. Won't take a second." She
came back out and gave him a peck on the
cheek. "You two will be all right?"

"Of course," he said.

He walked her to the door. "Drive safely."

"Call me tonight," she said. "I want to know what you find out."

They kissed again, and she left.

"Didn't anybody at Santangelo know you were related to Mary-Claire?" I asked once he'd sat down again.

"I hadn't ever been here," he said. "I was so busy in Tokyo."

"But you knew she'd never mentioned you to anyone here?"

"Family always calls me Gerry," he said. "I gave Mother an allowance, so she sent the tuition checks. I was pretty confident no one would know, and I was right."

"So what exactly have you been looking for?" I asked.

"Proof," he said.

"Proof of what?"

"I'm on the verge of discovering who killed Mary-Claire. And I think knowing that will tell us who killed Fay and Mooney, too."

"You believe there's a connection?"

"I know there is," he said. "I just don't know quite enough to convince the police."

"So it's not Santangelo this time, either, is it?"

Gerald smiled at me. "Can you imagine

that man hauling his fat ass up into a loft?"

"I can't imagine him tying his own shoes."

"Not to mention that none of the kids trust him," he said. "There's no way he'd ever get Fay and Mooney to follow him anywhere in the middle of the night. Much less share any of his punch."

True enough.

"How are you planning to come by this proof?" I asked. "Another round of office-breaking?"

He pointed to the phone on his desk. "I'm expecting a call."

"From whom?"

"A detective," he said. "Someone I've had on the payroll for a very long time. After tonight I hope he'll be off the clock. So does he, I would imagine. I know he's tired of traveling, poor guy. Wants to come home."

"Where is he now?"

"South America," said Gerald. "And damn unhappy about it."

"What the hell is there to find out in South America?"

Please not Peru. Not Lulu.

"Gerald," I said, "did you know Fay was pregnant?"

He nodded, grave.

"She and Mary-Claire," I said, "they looked a lot alike, didn't they?"

He nodded again.

I remembered how reluctant Fay had been to go to Santangelo's house after Mooney punched the window. And how certain Santangelo had been that she liked cocoa with marshmallows.

"Mooney wasn't the father of Fay's baby, was he?" I asked.

"No," said Gerald. "I don't think he was."

The phone rang, and he picked it up.

"Yes," he said, "I'll accept the charges."

35

Gerald was quiet on the phone.

"And you're sure G. Landry was on that flight?" he asked.

Not Lulu, then.

"The girl who died in Indiana," he said. "Of course I remember."

He listened again for a moment. "Have them follow up with a telex. You've got the number. No, I can just explain that to Cartwright, as long as I get it in writing later."

He grabbed a pen and a message pad. "That's with the country code? Certainly, if he wants to call back. How late? I'll let him know. Thank you for the good work, Bob. You'll have your check by the time you get home."

He hung up.

"G for Gloria?" I asked.

"It's not her real name."

"Neither is Dhumavati," I said. "Please tell me what South America has to do with all of this."

"It has to do with motive," he said. "It has to do with secrets."

"What kind of secrets?"

"The kind someone would go to any lengths to protect. The kind that get people killed."

"Gerald, just *tell* me."

"I want to show you. I want to run you through the whole thing, start to finish."

"Fine," I said.

"We need to go to Sookie's office."

"Why?"

"Because that's where I've been keeping the fruits of my research. I didn't think this apartment was safe enough." He stood up. "Someone broke in not long ago. They didn't find what they wanted, but I haven't left anything important here since."

"That's why you were going into the offices at night?"

"Partly that," he said. "And partly to dig up the information I needed in order to know where I'd have to send my detective on the last leg of his travels."

"South America's a big place. Where did he go?"

"Georgetown," he said, heading for the door.

I trotted along behind him. "That's not a

particularly Latin-sounding destination."

"Perhaps because it's the capital city of a country whose official language is English," he said.

"Gerald, spit it out — *what* country?"

There was a knock on the front door.

We both froze, and he held a finger to his lips.

More knocking, and a woman's voice saying, "Gerald?"

Dhumavati.

"Is Madeline with you?" she asked. "Her husband wants her to call home."

Gerald pointed to the back door, and we both crept toward it.

He led me into the woods behind the faculty apartments.

"The Mansion's the other way," I whispered.

"There's a back entrance."

"There is?"

"It's close to the edge of the trees. They used it to sneak in runaway slaves."

"I always thought Santangelo made that up," I said.

"Lucky for us it's one of the few things he didn't."

We'd reached the edge of the road that ran between campus and the faculty apartments. I could see the school's front gates a hundred yards to our right.

Gerald waited until a lone car had gone by before he grabbed my hand to sprint across.

We bashed on through brambles and fallen boughs and snow piles for a good twenty minutes. Past the grape arbor Lulu and I frequented, Gerald bushwhacked into another overgrown patch of woods. I was panting and sweaty before the trees began to thin out again.

"Be careful where you step from here on in," he said. "Try not to make any noise."

I walked behind him, placing my feet where he had in the snow. We dropped down into a little gully, then climbed back up its far bank.

Ten paces more, and he stopped.

I could see the hulk of the Mansion ahead of us in the dark. No lights in any of its windows, just a thin splash of brightness spilling across the snow from a pair of old lanterns on either side of the front door.

Gerald led me toward a decrepit shed at the tree line, then opened the metal cellar door set into the ground beside it. He pulled me close and placed his mouth next to my ear.

"Third tread is broken," he whispered

before stepping down into what lay beneath.

There were nine steps total before my foot touched dirt.

"Stay right here," he said. "I'm going to close up behind us before I turn on my flashlight."

I heard him climb back up a few steps, then the protesting creak of old hinges as he gentled the heavy door back into place.

The flashlight that clicked on wasn't Gerald's.

Its beam came from the far side of the room, illuminating columns and dirt and spiderwebs without disclosing the identity of its owner.

Gerald turned on his own light in turn.

The face it revealed was Wiesner's.

36

"Fancy meeting you here," said Wiesner. "What brings you to my secret hideout?"

He was standing next to a sleeping bag and a small pile of canned food.

"Something important," I said.

"I bet."

"Madeline and I need to go upstairs," said Gerald. "We don't particularly have to tell anyone we saw you on the way."

"Be my guest, then," said Wiesner. "By all means."

"Gracious of you," I said.

"And you," he replied.

I followed Gerald across the room toward a narrow portal set in its far wall.

"Don't let the door hit you in that fine ass on your way out, Madeline."

I turned back to glare at him. "Shut *up,* Wiesner."

He did.

Gerald worked the latch and revealed a

staircase. I climbed it in his wake.

We came out in a pantry closet.

"There'll be enough light from outside once we get into the kitchen," said Gerald, shutting off his flashlight.

He was right. A small parking lot lay just beyond the kitchen windows, and its streetlight was plenty to navigate by.

We made our way past the old stove and through another pantry, then cut through the Mansion's formal dining room on our way to the grand front staircase. Three flights up, he slid a key into the lock of Sookie's office. We could still see dimly by the light of the parking lot below.

"Pull down the shades and close the drapes, Madeline."

When I'd done so, I couldn't see shit.

"Okay," I said, "coast is clear."

He hit the light switch by Sookie's door, blinding me for a second. When I took my hands down from my eyes, he was sitting at her desk, working another smaller key into its locked bottom drawer.

"Pull up a seat," Gerald said.

I dragged the wobbly chair over from beside the radiator and sat down next to him.

Gerald reached inside a thick file folder and took out several sheets of paper.

The first page was a xeroxed photograph depicting a dirt road with a small wooden sign posted beside it.

"Bob was calling from Guyana," I said.

I'd read the words on the sign: GREETINGS. EVERYTHING GROWS WELL IN JONESTOWN, ESPECIALLY THE CHILDREN.

I looked up at Gerald. "Dhumavati put something to that effect on the garden gate down at the Farm." I said.

"Across from the bench with the date of her daughter's death."

"November eighteenth," I said, "1978."

The remaining photos just showed piles of corpses, bloated and rotting in the jungle heat.

"Nine hundred and twelve people," said Gerald. "Of which two hundred and seventy were children. Most of the bodies were never autopsied, or even identified. The threat of disease . . ."

He didn't have to finish.

"We can nonetheless presume," I said, "that one of those kids was an eight-year-old girl named Allegra."

He nodded. "The parents made sure their children drank the punch before swallowing it themselves," he said. "They used syringes to get it down the throats of the babies.

Anyone who refused was shot, most of them with crossbows. But they'd all had a lot of practice and conditioning. Jones started running rehearsals before they'd even left the United States. He called them 'White Nights.' In Guyana, they'd make announcements over the loudspeakers in the middle of the night, calling everyone to the central pavilion."

He pulled out another Xerox, this one showing bodies grouped around a dais with a white wooden chair at its center. There was another sign nailed to a post just behind that chair.

This one read, THOSE WHO DO NOT REMEMBER THE PAST ARE CONDEMNED TO REPEAT IT.

"The needlepoint pillow on Dhumavati's sofa," I said. "The one you kept fussing with when we all had to meet in her apartment."

"Yes," he said.

"Did you know then?"

"I couldn't prove it."

"And now you can?"

"Too late," he said. "Too goddamn late."

37

"Santangelo knew," I said. "He had the bench made, and the plaque."

"They grew up together," said Gerald. "Childhood friends in Indianapolis. Dhumavati's parents were early members of Jones's church there, even before he was ordained by the Disciples of Christ. She ran away from home and followed him to San Francisco after he started telling his congregation they had to move to Northern California to escape the coming nuclear holocaust."

"Where was David?"

"His family had moved east. He went to college in New England."

"I guess he and Dhumavati kept in touch?"

"He started this school in 1978. Hired her when she showed up in January '79."

"How the hell did they get away with it? Weren't there any records?"

"She uses a social security number that can be traced to a girl who died in her teens back in Indiana. Gloria Landry."

"So what were you waiting to find out tonight from your detective?"

"The date a girl going by that name got on a plane out of Georgetown," he said.

"It was January twelfth," said Dhumavati, stepping into Sookie's office. "David left me rotting down there for two months before he wired the money."

She was wearing gloves, and of course she had a gun.

She kept it trained on Gerald as she walked over to him. Then she shoved the barrel into his mouth and pulled the trigger.

The force of it knocked him back against the wall behind Sookie's desk before he slumped over onto me. The whole back of his head was gone.

"Push him off you," said Dhumavati.

She had the gun trained on me now. "Go ahead. It's not like you're going to hurt him."

I couldn't bear the idea of shoving him onto the floor. I did my best to get out from under his weight, leaving him splayed across the seat of my chair. I couldn't stand up, just squatted on the ground next to him, soaked in his blood.

Dhumavati reached into her overcoat and pulled out a second pistol. She put the first one down on the desk.

"It's empty," she said. "So pick it up and wrap his hand around it."

"Even if this has his prints on it, they'll know he didn't kill himself," I said. "There won't be any gunshot residue on his hands."

"Maybe they'll figure *you* did it, Madeline," she said, pressing the tip of the second barrel to my head. "Since your prints will be on it, too. They might even think that was why you jumped."

"From where?"

"The roof."

I felt that second gun twitch against my scalp when she cocked the hammer. I took the first off Sookie's desk and pressed Gerald's fingers against it.

"Now get the hell up," she said, "slowly."

I rose to my feet, blood-gummed shirt sticking to my belly.

Dhumavati slid the tip of the gun to the back of my neck. "Put the papers back in that folder and pick it up."

After I had, she said, "Walk out into the hallway, then take a left."

She pressed hard, making me move quickly.

"The next door down," she said. "After the radiator."

I stopped in front of it.

"Open the thing," she said.

I did, then started to climb the narrow stairs it concealed, with her at my back.

"Stop," she said when I'd reached the fourth step.

I heard her shut the door behind us.

"Dhumavati," I said, "is protecting David really worth this much to you? Worth killing four people?"

I didn't want to think about the likelihood that she was about to make it five.

"I'm not protecting David," she said. "I'm protecting myself."

"So why does he protect *you?* You called him from Guyana, and he not only paid your way out, he gave you a job once you got here. Don't tell me he took you in out of the kindness of his heart."

"He took me in so I wouldn't tell anyone he was Allegra's father. Or that she was conceived when he raped me."

She poked me harder with the gun, and I started climbing again.

"Can you imagine people trusting their children to him," she said, "if they knew that? Especially the daughters."

"Would they have trusted you once it got

out that you killed your own child in Jonestown? David knew. That's why he had that bench made with the date of her death on it. It wasn't a gift, it was a threat."

"Our secrets keep us in stalemate," she said. "Yin and yang. Mutually assured destruction."

We'd almost reached the top of the stairs. I wanted to slow her down before we got to the door.

"Why drag me into it?" I asked. "You knew Fay was pregnant long before today. What was the point of framing me for two murders that would have looked like suicides?"

"You posed a threat to the happy equilibrium."

She gave me another shove with the gun.

"Up," she said.

I wanted to convince her there was a reason not to kill me, or at least keep her talking long enough that I could figure out how to get away from her.

I had a sudden epiphany.

"Sookie knows," I said. "Gerald told her everything. She'll tell the police."

"Sookie's already dead, Madeline," said Dhumavati. "I took care of that an hour ago."

"So that makes five people you've killed

on campus?" I said. "Don't you think six will look a little suspicious? I mean, three in one night is a lot, even for you."

"Three's nothing," she said. "Remember who you're talking to."

I shivered, thinking of the piles of bodies in Gerald's xeroxed photos. "And then what, you take off for a little R and R at David's place in San Miguel? Not like they don't have cops down there."

She laughed. "Oh, Madeline, I was never going to Mexico."

"David sure seemed to think you were."

"David thinks what I tell him to think. So you might as well go ahead and open that fucking door."

It swung outward onto a broad, chimney-studded meadow of snowy sheet copper. The waning moon had just come up above the trees. It lit everything blue-white and flawless.

There were wind-etched scallops of snow and ice all the way across the flat expanse of roof, out to its mansard edges that sloped down toward a widow's-walk railing, the iron filigree of which glittered with icicles.

Unfortunately, that fence stopped at my knees, so I didn't think it would keep me from going over the side.

"Another White Night," she said. "I'll give

you a bit of advice, something Jim said in Guyana: 'You'll have no problem with the thing if you just relax.' "

"*You* didn't relax," I said, "or we wouldn't be up on this stupid roof. What happened, you killed Allegra and then chickened out?"

"That bitch Christine kept going on and on about how we could still make the airlift to Russia, and then Jim told her" — Dhumavati frowned a little, as though she'd fumbled a word in some poem she knew by heart — "*Father* told her that we'd all die anyway.

"It was too late, because the killing had started. There would only be more congressmen." She smiled, her eyes and voice gone tender with sentiment. "And people parachuting in to butcher our children. 'It's not worth living like this,' he said, 'it's not worth living like this.' And he was right."

She might have been describing the cherished memory of her first kiss.

"If 'Father' was right," I said, "how come you're still alive?"

"I should have listened. I could have had peace. Father said, 'Death is not a fearful thing, it's living that's treacherous,' and that's the truth. He died to give us all peace, and I was too weak to understand."

There was a catch in Dhumavati's voice.

Perhaps it was evidence of some genuine regret that she'd survived Jonestown, and her daughter. More likely, it was false as her grief on the morning Fay and Mooney died, her excuse to hug me so she could slide the crescent necklace into my pocket.

"Funny how you weren't too weak to get away," I said, "once you didn't have a child slowing you down. I thought they shot anyone who didn't drink the punch."

She lost the dreamy look.

"I'd made myself part of the inner circle," she said. "Someone with the authority to give orders. You may have noticed I'm good at that."

More lights came on in the floors beneath us, projecting the glow of paned rectangles across the snowy ground four stories down.

"Guess they heard the gunshot," I said.

"It'll take them a few minutes to find Gerald. Plenty of time to finish up."

"They'll see your footprints in the snow," I said. "They'll know you were here with me."

"I ran up the minute I realized what you were going to do. I tried so hard to stop you . . ."

"So you'll say Gerald shot himself and I jumped off the building?" I asked. "And what, the cops are supposed to believe he still felt guilty about grabbing Parker's dick after the two of us killed Fay and Mooney to cover it up?"

"Something like that," she said.

"And who killed Sookie?"

"You did."

"What the hell for?"

She shrugged. "There doesn't have to be a reason. You were mentally unbalanced."

"Too many loose ends," I said.

She didn't answer that, just gestured toward the edge of the roof with the barrel of her gun.

"It's not going to look like suicide if I'm shot in the back," I said, turning to walk away from her, keeping close to the line of chimneys.

"No need," she said, crunching through the snow behind me. "I'm perfectly happy to give you a push."

I have no doubt she would in fact have been pleased as, well, punch to inflict that helpful shove if Wiesner hadn't leaped out from behind one of those chimneys and yelled, distracting Dhumavati long enough that I managed to send her over first.

She only had time to scream a little before there was this nasty wet smacking thud at the very instant her wailing stopped.

I looked away from the sight of her body

in the snow, her limbs bent in all the wrong directions like an ill-made swastika. She'd been flailing when she hit.

"Oh, Wiesner," I said, "you're the six-six-sixiest . . ."

Then my knees gave, and I crumpled down onto that ice-cold field of metal.

Wiesner came over and crouched beside me. He lifted me gently by the shoulders, cradling my head against his shoulder.

Then he leaned down and stuck his tongue in my mouth.

I bit it — just hard enough to make him yank it back behind his own teeth — and shoved him away.

"Dude," I said, "don't be an asshole. I was just starting to actually *like* you."

38

Wiesner vanished long before I reached the ground floor. One second he was behind me on the stairs, the next he was gone.

I guess he knew more of the Mansion's secrets than even Gerald had.

I found a stunned crowd at the foot of that odious grand staircase, all of them gawping up at me as I made my final descent like I was some murderous Scarlett O'Hara.

Mindy was the first to speak.

"What have you *done?*" she said. "Did you kill Dhumavati and Gerald *both?*"

She sounded so pissed I half expected her to slap me.

Disappointing that she didn't, as I would so have relished the opportunity to punch her back.

"Dhumavati did it," I said. "Dhumavati did fucking *all* of it."

"Oh, I'm *so* sure," she said, pronouncing that last word "sher."

I looked at Tim beside her, but this time he didn't tell the bitch to shut the hell up or even poke her in the arm.

More's the pity.

I started walking toward the front door, and the crowd parted to let me through.

"Tim!" whined Mindy from behind me. "Stop her!"

He didn't, which was a point in his favor.

The only thing left between me and the door was Pete.

"Pete, can't you do something?" More shrillness from Mindy. "Don't just let her get away!"

I looked him in the eye and smiled.

Made him blush.

"*Hare Rama,* candyass," I said, busting through him like he was a cheap finish line.

There was dead silence at my back until I opened the front door and stepped outside. I closed the thick slab of oak behind me, muffling the surge in volume as they turned on each other.

I walked across campus and got into my car but didn't start it up. The shakes had set in pretty bad by then, and I wanted to be alone until my teeth stopped chattering.

Once they had, I drove slowly back toward the Mansion, parking across the lawn to wait for the cops. I got out to sit on the hood with the windows rolled down, a cassette of Vivaldi playing in the tape deck.

The opening song was his "Gloria," which seemed fitting enough.

On the stroke of the very first "in excelsis Deo," Sitzman climbed up on the car next to me, wearing slippers and striped pajamas beneath his overcoat.

"You heard what happened," I said.

"Yeah, pretty much."

"The cops are on their way and everything?"

He nodded.

I pulled out my Camels and got one out for each of us.

"Promise me something," I said, lighting his.

"Name it."

"Get the hell away from this place," I said. "You deserve better. You all do."

"I appreciate that," he said.

We were quiet for a minute, smoking. There were a lot of things that still didn't make sense to me.

"You want to talk about it?" asked Sitzman, like he knew what I was thinking, how tangled up everything was in my head.

"Wiesner saved my life tonight," I said.

Sitzman took a drag. "He's cool like that

sometimes."

"And Dhumavati killed Fay and Mooney," I said.

"I know."

I snapped my head around to stare at him. "You *know?*"

"Oh, sure," he said. "For a good long time now."

"How long?"

"That girl Mary-Claire died right before I got here," he said. "All the kids were still talking about it, how they couldn't believe it was suicide."

"Why not?"

"Because she'd told too many people how excited she was about her brother coming to visit, and how she knew he'd be taking her home."

"I still don't see —"

"Look, Madeline, I didn't know right away. Let's just say I picked up on a few things over time. Saw some patterns, some possible connections . . . It all seemed pretty obvious once I saw the date on Dhumavati's bench, first time I got sent to the Farm."

I was too stunned to say anything.

"Kind of surprised me it didn't occur to you," he continued, "what with being hip to the Flavor Aid and everything. I mean, you're supposed to be a history teacher."

"Why didn't you *tell* anyone?"

He took a drag off his Camel and shrugged, expelling a smoke-blue cumulus into the cold night air. "I'm insane. Who'd've believed me?"

The first cop car screeched to a halt about twenty yards away, siren blaring. Its headlights illuminated Dhumavati's body, smashed deep into the snow.

"You never told Wiesner?" I asked.

To my relief, Sitzman shook his head.

"Did Gerald really grab that kid Parker's dick last year?" I asked.

"No," he said. "Parker just wanted to go home. So did Mooney."

"Then why'd Wiesner knock out Gerald's teeth?"

"He didn't know they were lying."

"You're sure?"

"Mooney was planning to tell him eventually, before that," he said, "but then he figured the truth would just piss Wiesner off more. We all did."

People were starting to come out of the Mansion.

"Would it've made any difference, Wiesner knowing?" Sitzman asked.

I pondered that.

If Wiesner hadn't come to my apartment to tell me about Gerald, I wouldn't have ended up at Gerald's place tonight. Without me, would he and Sookie still be alive?

But it was Dhumavati who'd sent me to see Sookie in the first place, and Sookie who'd brought me to Gerald's apartment.

Dhumavati must have known what he was going to tell me before we ever got there. Otherwise she'd have had no reason to kill Sookie, no reason to follow Gerald and me back to the Mansion with two guns in her pocket.

"No," I told Sitzman. "In the end, Wiesner knowing the truth about Gerald wouldn't have changed a thing."

"I'm glad."

"Me too," I said. "And can you promise me something else?"

"Name it."

"Should you happen to run into Wiesner, please tell him I said thank you."

"No problem," he said, flicking his cigarette out onto the lawn.

We watched more cops drive up. State police this time.

I climbed off the hood, clenched my Camel in my teeth, and reached through the Porsche's passenger window to turn off the music.

When I stood up, Sitzman was gone. You never would have known he'd been there except for his slipper prints in the snow. They were spaced farther and farther apart across the lawn, as he'd picked up speed for the woods.

I looked back toward the crowd and saw Mindy surrounded by cops, her finger raised to point at me.

■ ■ ■ ■

PART VI

■ ■ ■ ■

Madmen will justify their condition with touching loyalty, and surround it with a thousand distractive schemes. . . . When and if by their unforgivable stubbornness they finally burst through to worlds upon worlds of motionless light, they are no longer called afflicted or insane.

They are called saints.

— Mark Helprin
Winter's Tale

39

They buried Mooney and Fay in Stockbridge, side by side.

A bitter day: hard and cold and with a
lacerating wind.

Nobody but Lulu and I had come from
Santangelo to the service, or to the cemetery
afterward. Markham stood beside us, having told the firm back in Boston that he
needed several more days to wrap things
up. Dean had offered to drive us, but I
didn't want him to miss work, and he'd
already had to see me cry enough about all
of it.

Most of the kids had been taken home by
their families once the news about Dhumavati and David and all the events of the past
few weeks hit the wires.

The *Globe* and the *Times* had had the gall
to run op-eds extolling David's selfless work
on behalf of troubled children — citing his
perennial best seller, *Decrypting Your Teen-*

ager, as a constant, much needed font of comfort and enlightenment to tens of thousands of desperate parents across the country.

We were very pleased to learn that the Commonwealth of Massachusetts, had finally, nonetheless, pulled the school's license to operate.

A few homesick kids remained in the dorms even so, while the skeleton staff awaited instructions as to which institutions their parents desired to have them forwarded.

Snow eddied and whirled around us in the cemetery. Lulu and I clutched each other and wept as the officiant spoke the kindest words he was able to muster for a pair of dead kids he'd never known — first over their closed caskets in his chapel, then at the edge of their graves as we watched those dark coffins descend into the ground.

Fay's parents seemed numb with grief — her fragile pretty mother all in black, her father decked in a somber suit and tie.

Mooney's dad had been too busy to make the scene. We hadn't expected his stepmother. Someone said they were in Nassau.

Lulu announced that she despised them both, and I of course agreed.

We'd heard that David was already out on

bail, whiling away the hours by practicing takeoffs and landings from his helipad, instructor in tow.

It was our third funeral that week, following close on the service for Gerald and the one for Sookie.

No one bothered with Dhumavati's.

Gerald's mother, Mary, was scheduled for burial on Friday, and his five remaining brothers and sisters had gathered at the Red Lion Inn in Stockbridge. They'd come today, wanting to pay their respects to these children whom their eldest brother had tried so very hard to save — and to honor his courage for having done so.

When the hired priest closed his prayer book, everyone stood in line to shake hands with Fay's parents.

"She was a lovely girl," I told them. "Kind to everyone. I will miss her a great deal."

Her father teared up, shaking my hand.

I'd like to think that her mother was still too much in shock for anything to register, to so much as alight upon the delicate elegant, pink-and-gold shell she inhabited. She was so very like her daughter, except for the utter lack of feeling betrayed by those otherwise-doppelgänger gray eyes.

She smiled at me, staring off somewhere beyond my left shoulder.

415

"Thank you so very much for your gracious condolences," she said, "in our time of sorrow."

She said the very same thing to Lulu, and to each of Gerald's siblings in turn, before the chauffeur ushered Mr. and Mrs. Perry to their waiting limousine.

They'd made no further arrangements.

No reception.

No wake.

No chance for the thin crowd of their daughter's mourners to gather in her memory, out of the cold.

So as that long black car started with a purr to bear Fay's parents away, Markham invited each of us to join him for lunch back at the Red Lion Inn, having already arranged to cover the check.

"The very least those poor kids deserve, honey lamb," he said to me. "Only wish we'd had the chance to meet in person, even once, so I could've sent them off on the journey with a kind word and my hopes for a bon voyage."

"I think they know," I said. "I choose to believe that the two of them know."

"Better place awaits us all, darlin'," he said. "Sweet chariot itself's gonna swing down for to carry us home — every last weary soul."

Markham reached for my hand, warming it in both of his.

"There's not a whole lot in this life I trust," he said, "but Lordy, how I do so need to trust in a little of that."

Lulu heard him and smiled.

We were all just milling around, getting ready to walk back to our cars, but she stepped over to the head of the two graves and began to sing.

First "Swing Low" itself, for Markham, and then "Jesu, Joy of Man's Desiring."

It was a gift, the sound of her.

She made us all stand up taller.

She made sure Fay and Mooney were embarking fully blessed.

Then we shook hands, we remaining people who didn't mind the cold, didn't have any planes to catch, didn't think there was a damn thing in the world more important than what we'd come for.

And we started off toward the road, all of us happy in the knowledge that we'd have more time together, thanks to Markham.

He unlocked his car, and we climbed in: Lulu and him up front, me in the backseat. As we drove toward the cemetery gates, I could've sworn I caught a glimpse of Wiesner and Sitzman in the mirror — heads poking out from behind a putti-bedecked mausoleum's white marble, fists raised in solidarity.

I turned to look out the rear window, but the yard was empty.

Markham stood up at the head of the table, his wineglass raised. The conversation around him, already subdued, died down to nothing at all.

"I'd like to make a toast," he said, "to the memory of Fay Perry and Mooney LeChance — rose-lipped maiden, lightfoot lad — may they long be remembered for their grace, their compassion, and their very great love for one another."

"Hear hear," someone said, and we lifted our glasses to drink.

I stood up as Markham took his seat. "Here's to the memory of our dear friends Gerald Jones and Sookie Hamilton, and to Mary-Claire and Mary Jones. May we be inspired by their courage and by their kindness. They will be sorely missed."

We drank again, and when I resumed my seat, Gerald's sister Caroline reached across the table to touch my hand.

"I know my brother must have liked you a great deal," she said, "and I only wish that Mother and Mary-Claire had known you, because I'm sure they would have agreed with him, as I do."

"I wish I'd known them, and I wish I'd known Gerald better. If I could have done more . . ."

"You did what was necessary," she said. "And what was right. That's all any of us can hope to do in this life."

Across the Red Lion's dining room, I saw a man in the doorway who was searching the assembled diners for familiar faces.

"Will you excuse me for a second?" I said to Caroline. "I have a ring to kiss."

I pushed back my chair and stood up, rushing forward to greet my godfather, Uncle Alan.

I brought him back over to the table. He pulled up a chair at the corner, on Markham's left and across from me.

Markham signaled the waiter to bring another glass.

"I am so grateful for your help, Uncle Alan," I said. "I never would have expected —"

"Think nothing of it, Madeline," he said. "Least I could do."

He turned to Markham. "What remains to be wrapped up here?"

"Your goddaughter and her friends have done the heavy lifting, sir," said Markham. "I just want to make sure that justice is done as a result. This man Santangelo . . ."

Uncle Alan nodded. "Of course."

"This is on my dime, sir — the follow-up. We all feel it's important, back at the firm."

The waiter placed a wineglass in front of Uncle Alan, then filled it.

My godfather took an approving sip, then turned back to Markham. "You're to be commended on the very fine work you've done so far, young man. Most impressive."

"I appreciate your saying so."

"Do you think you'll get this Santangelo person?"

"Hope to. He's made bail, but we're going after his assets. Restitution to the families. Hard to track everything down. He owns property in Mexico, and there's been talk of his reopening the school down there."

"Wouldn't want *that*," said Uncle Alan.

"I understand he's got some people down there already," said Markham.

"How the hell would they get any students?" asked Uncle Alan. "I mean, after all this — trusting one's child to these people? Nobody in their right mind . . ."

"Desperate measures," I said, and Markham nodded sadly.

"Horrible," said Uncle Alan. "Horrible stuff."

We all drank more wine.

Uncle Alan drummed his fingers on the tablecloth, seeking a way to lighten the mood.

There wasn't one.

40

"I'm unemployed, I have no health insurance, and I'm *dying*," Lulu said before she was consumed by another horrible bout of coughing.

It went on for so long I was about to whack her between the shoulder blades, in the hope that she'd thereby gain a chance to inhale, but she shook her head at me, gasping.

"Won't help," she wheezed. "Just have to let it play out."

We were sitting in the apartment in Pittsfield. She was making collages of her photographs and paperwork from Santangelo, covering the sides of a dozen different cans she'd washed and saved for the purpose. Orange juice concentrate, V8, corned beef hash.

"These will be good for keeping things on your desk," she said. "Pencils, paper clips, what have you."

"Screwdrivers," I said, thinking of Wiesner, whom I hadn't seen head nor tail of since I'd pushed Dhumavati off the top of the Mansion.

"Do you have any more Scotch tape?" Lulu asked.

"Second drawer," I said, "left of the stove."

"You know," she said, getting up, "I still don't get why Dhumavati went to all that trouble. Not just putting the necklace in your pocket but everything else besides."

"Like framing me for murder?"

"Exactly," said Lulu, her breathing still raspy. "We know she must have overheard you talking to Sitzman about Jonestown after class — then Mooney broke the window practically simultaneously, which meant *that* whole situation was coming to a head —"

"So she's already stuck with making sure Fay's pregnancy can't threaten Santangelo," I replied, "and then she's got to worry whether I know too much about the Flavor Aid. Why not just kill me?"

"Maybe you were supposed to drink more punch."

"How stupid would that look?" I said. " 'Yes, Officer, the teenage lovers committed suicide, but only after poisoning a kindly teacher in the middle of a party, carefully ensuring her fingerprints were prominently placed on the cups they drank from hours later'?"

"Bizarre campus love triangle leads to tragedy?"

I shook my head. "If I'm such a threat, cut my brake lines or something. Get rid of me."

"So maybe she wants to punish you," said Lulu, sitting down again with a fresh roll of tape in hand. "Santangelo decides you can do her job, and she's pissed off. She's gotta take out Fay anyway, before anyone else finds out about the baby."

"And?"

"And if Mooney dies, too," she said, "she's got Gerald as a fallback suspect with plenty of motive."

"So one of us takes the rap, doesn't matter who?"

"Exactly," she said, taping a small photo over the last silvery gap on what had once been a quart-sized can of chicken broth.

"And this is because Dhumavati knew Gerald was about to finger her for Jonestown and Mary-Claire?"

Lulu's eyes snapped up to meet mine. "She did?"

"She had to," I said. "Unless she killed Sookie for sheer entertainment."

"Shit," said Lulu.

"Markham realized there must have been a bug in Gerald's apartment," I said. "Someone broke in a few weeks ago. Probably put one in Sookie's office, too, which would explain why Dhumavati confronted me about the autopsy — she needed an excuse to send me up to Sookie's. No other way she would have known where to find us all that night. And that's how she knew she had time to get Sookie out of the way while Gerald was waiting for his detective's phone call."

"Shit," said Lulu. "Did the cops find any bugs?"

I shook my head. "Someone did a good job cleaning up."

She tapped the roll of tape against her knee. "Must have been Santangelo."

"No way in hell he's going to admit it."

We both slumped down a little farther in our seats, like somebody'd turned up the gravity.

"Maybe Dhumavati was in love with him," she said, after a minute.

"Santangelo?"

"I mean, she kind of had to be, didn't she?"

I thought about that.

"She was jealous of you," said Lulu, "and

425

I bet she was jealous of those girls, too. There was no other reason for her to target you. If she knew Gerald was connected to Mary-Claire, she knew she had to kill him eventually, right? So why not frame him to begin with, or just kill him outright?"

"Dude," I said, "talk about *dark*."

But I felt the skin on my forearms tighten with recognition, and didn't have to look down to know that all the little hairs were standing straight up.

What if Dhumavati had never cared about loose ends, or getting caught, or even surviving? What if the point, all along, had been finding ways to demonstrate how very much she was ready to put at risk as proof of her devotion?

Santangelo certainly wasn't the only man for whom she'd been willing to murder a child. He was merely the last.

Whether or not she'd done it all for love, Dhumavati had told me the truth up on that roof: There didn't have to be a reason. She was just fucking nuts.

"Did I tell you I ran into Tim?" asked Lulu.

"And?"

"And he told me he and Pete were going on a road trip together."

"Where?"

"Mexico," she said.

"You're fucking kidding me!"

"David wants them on staff down at the new school. He's planning to get it up and running after New Year's, soon as he's finished up with his court stuff."

"They'd allow him to leave the country?"

"David certainly thinks so," she said, "from what Tim was saying."

" 'Free to Be,' " I said. "God, doesn't it just make you want to puke?"

"I have faith in Markham," she said.

"When are they leaving?"

"Tim wouldn't say. I think he suddenly remembered who the hell he was talking to, and the minute it sank in, he couldn't scuttle away from me fast enough."

"Mindy going, too?"

"Already down there," she said. "Canopy bed and all."

"Jesus Christ," I said. "That's just gross."

"Tell me about it."

We sat there in silence, sharing a long moment of mutual disgust.

"Do you want some coffee?" she asked when we couldn't stand it anymore.

"Love it," I said.

She got up and bustled toward the kitchen, thank God, reaching for the can of Bustelo. A convert.

"How'd it go this morning?" she called back over her shoulder as she filled the carafe under the kitchen faucet. "You feel okay about that new shrink?"

I'd had my first appointment with a doctor in Williamstown that morning. Someone who'd never even heard of Santangelo.

I still couldn't believe I was ready to give therapy another shot, but I didn't know what else to do.

"He seems okay," I said. "For a shrink."

"What'd you talk about?"

"I didn't say much at first. Just walked into his office and started crying."

"How'd he handle that?"

I laughed, not in a particularly happy way. "He watched me for a while, and then, after about five minutes, he said, 'Do you feel this way all the time?' "

"I hope you told him yes," she said.

I stood up and walked over to the window, watched the cars duking it out in the North Street rotary four stories down.

"I did," I said. " 'Fessed right up."

I turned back around, lounging against the wall with both elbows propped on the high sill.

Lulu opened a cabinet, pulling two mugs off the second shelf. "Did he ask you why?"

"You know, I figured once I admitted to

him that I was pretty much constantly weeping, we'd get right back into the whole 'and how does that make you *feel,*' routine."

"Of course." Lulu checked the progress of the brewing, then turned to lean on the pass-through, waiting for me to go on.

"Thing is," I said, "that's not how it went at all."

I walked over to the table, grabbed my Camels. "Want one?"

Lulu shook her head.

"Kind of knocked me for a loop," I said, shaking out a smoke from the near-empty pack, "his actual response."

I flicked the lighter, took a drag, exhaled. "Left field, et cetera."

She waited.

"Well," I said, "first he wanted to know how long I'd felt like this, so I said probably since I was nine years old, off and on."

"Sure," she said.

"So then he said he figured I was clinically depressed."

I tapped my ash onto the plate I'd reserved for the purpose.

"I said I'd tried therapy before," I continued, "but that I'd never really felt like it made any difference."

The coffee was done.

"Guy said he wasn't a bit surprised," I

said, settling into the sofa, "since talk therapy doesn't do crap for depression."

"No shit?" she said, shaking her head. "And after we went through all that damn Kleenex."

She filled our mugs and ferried them out to the living room.

"He told me there's this new drug," I said. "Prozac."

Lulu nestled against the armrest at the other end of the sofa, bare feet toward me, mug propped on her knees.

"Think you'll give it a try?" she asked.

I slid my mug onto the side table and arched my back so I could fish the brown plastic bottle out of my pocket.

When I'd wrestled off the childproof cap, I shook two capsules out into my palm.

Pretty little things, those pills — one end jade green, the other tinted somewhere between butter and old scrimshaw.

"I'll try anything once," I said. "You?"

"Much obliged," she said.

We plucked our respective doses from my palm, then washed them down with Bustelo.

"Ah," said Lulu, "I feel better already."

"Hard to feel worse."

She clinked my mug with hers. "Amen to that."

"You're going to stay for Thanksgiving, right?"

"I want to avoid the Jell-O salad and scrapple at home for as long as I can."

I was glad, since Markham said he'd come back out from Boston. I was hoping the two of them might hook up before she went back to work at the Econo Lodge.

Dean was still working at GE, and they said he could count on it going through December. I had a job lined up after Christmas — teaching ESL at a boarding school in Williamstown. They'd never heard of Santangelo, either, and the kids I'd met there called me Ms. Dare.

■ ■ ■ ■

PART VII

■ ■ ■ ■

Oh I have slipped the surly bonds of earth,
And danced the skies on laughter-silvered
wings . . .

John Gillespie McGee, Jr.
"High Flight"

41

Sitzman and Wiesner sat on top of the ridge, high above campus.

It had snowed again. The air was crisp and dry, sharp in their throats. Cold as you'd expect on Thanksgiving.

"What if he's not coming out?" asked Sitzman.

"He's coming out," said Wiesner. "You heard what Forchetti said."

"Maybe he changed his mind," said Sitzman. "I would. It's goddamn cold."

"Don't start going all pussy on me."

Sitzman shrugged. "I'm not. No guarantees about Santangelo."

"He's not going to change his mind," said Wiesner.

"Listen," said Sitzman, "if he doesn't come out in the next half hour —"

"There he is. I *told* you."

Sitzman squinted. "Where?"

"Dining hall." Wiesner pointed.

"I don't see him."

"He just went behind that hedge."

Below them, the fuchsia blob of Santangelo emerged from cover.

He crossed the newly plowed driveway, making for the twenty-foot square of helipad, just right of center on the snow-covered grass.

Sitzman shivered, thoughtful. "He's not going up with that instructor today, right?"

"Forchetti overheard them saying he was all set to go solo. His first time."

Santangelo paused at the lip of the concrete to admire his fancy toy, the Bell 206B-3 JetRanger III. Little snub-nosed budgie-looking thing, white with two-tone-blue stripe swooshing along its undercarriage and up to the tail boom.

The man in pink waddled around to the pilot's door and flung it wide, struggling for a second to hoist himself up into the cockpit.

"Couple more doughnuts and he'd need a forklift," said Wiesner.

The door hung open. Maybe Santangelo was taking a minute to pant a little after such exertion.

The guys on the ridge couldn't see inside to tell. They watched a pink-clad arm reach out for the door handle finally, pulling it to.

They heard a distant whine as the pilot's left hand twisted his collective's throttle grip.

No instructor, no guidance. First time.

The rotors started moving slowly, looking slightly soft until their increasing rpm's lifted them stiff, then made them blur — the pitch of the engine's shrill voice rising, as did the slender blades themselves.

The pilot raised the collective to pick up the bird, rotor disk coning, downwash blowing snow outward to denude grass, crisp and brown, across a widening circle.

The left skid was last off the ground, hanging low as tail rotor pushed craft toward the right. The fledgling pilot overcompensated with his left pedal, making the Bell's nose jerk to port.

The boys watched him wallow in the air — drifting and bouncing like a tired yo-yo — until he got the craft in trim.

With the cyclic now pushed forward, the bird nosed over to pick up airspeed, slipping the surly bonds of earth as its pilot pulled up on the collective.

"Not yet," said Sitzman.

"Not by a long shot. We want him *up* there."

Fifteen feet. Twenty.

The two-man audience didn't move.

Didn't breathe.

The chopper came level with the flat roof of the dining hall at last, then the more graceful chimneys of the Mansion.

Sixty feet and rising.

It lifted above the farthest, tallest trees in the surrounding woods.

Up, straight up.

As it drew close to the boys' eye level, the pad of Wiesner's thumb moved slowly across a button at the center of a lopsided remote he'd cobbled together out of wire and tape and solder and plastic, with batteries sticking out its side.

He touched it again, that button. A caress.

"Lifts," he said, pressing the half-inch disk of plastic downward.

At the juncture of tail boom and fuel tank, a blasting cap detonated General Electric's missing wad of C-4 explosive.

"And separates," said Wiesner as eighty gallons of aviation kerosene blossomed orange with a deep, resonant whomp.

The shock wave rocked the two boys, flattening their hair back and away from their faces. Making them scrunch their eyes shut.

When they looked again, there was little left of David Santangelo's Bell 206B-3 Jet-Ranger III, or of David Santangelo himself.

There was only the hunk of turbine housing plummeting back into those surly bonds, surrounded by a slow rain of flaming bits — none bigger than a fist — dropping and arcing and sometimes even corkscrewing down onto the glittering white expanse of campus.

Little circles of snow melted away around each on contact.

"Will you look at that," said grinning Wiesner, who, it must be remembered, really, really *liked* to blow shit up. "In excelsis David."

Sitzman shook his shaggy Saint Bernard head slowly, back and forth.

Finally, he was moved to say a single word — one syllable, so drawn out by the shock and reverence and horror with which its speaker brimmed that the sound of it seemed to linger and shimmer on the very air, until the utterance dissipated like the steamy, curling puff of breath expelled along with it.

The word was "Fuck."

ACKNOWLEDGMENTS

My thanks to:

Charles King and Lee Child, most of all.

Mandy! For the helicopter!!!! May you top the windswept heights with easy grace. (If Dwight's amenable to that kind of thing, in the *Cantina.*)

My family, especially my daughters Grace and Lila, my sister Freya, my aunt Julie and uncle Bill Hoyt, and my splendid mom, Deborah.

The wonderful people at Grand Central Publishing, who have been such a pleasure to work with: Susan Richman, Celia Johnson, Les Pockell, Jamie Raab, and Tareth Mitch. And of course the erstwhile Kristen Weber.

The excellent duo of Michelle and Catherine Lapautre.

Members of the wondrous Mysterious Writ, my writing group: Charles King, Karen Murphy, Sharon Johnson, Marilyn Mac-

Gregor, and Daisy Johnson. Without whom I would never have started the first book, or finished the second.

And of the group that will SOMEDAY meet again: Bob Young and Gaylene Givens, Dave Damianakes, Heidi Kriz.

The independent bookstores which have been so kind and supportive about my first book, and whom I hope will like my second: Mark "Bitsy Ramone" Farley (aka Bookseller to the Stars), London; Elaine and Bill Petrocelli of Book Passage, Corte Madera, California (and Karen and Hannah and Reese and all y'all cool people); Ed Kaufman and gang of M is for Mystery in San Mateo, California; Bobby and Linda at The Mystery Bookstore, Los Angeles, California; EVERYONE at Mysterious Galaxy in San Diego and at Mysteries to Die For, Thousand Oaks, California; Bill and Lynne Reed of Misty Valley Books, Chester, Vermont; Barbara Peters and the most excellent people of Poisoned Pen in Scottsdale, Arizona; and the tremendously kind staff of Houston's Murder By the Book, who very nicely did not mention having overheard me throw up a few minutes before the signing. And, last but assuredly not least, Janine and Fran and Tammy at Seattle Mystery Books — especially Janine for greeting me at Sea-Tac with my very own green plastic beach bucket, having heard about the whole throwing-up-from-nerves-right-before-the-signing-in-Houston thing. And thank you to Cody's in Berkeley, most especially the inimitable Tova Zeff.

Hillary Huber, the goddess of all things relating to voice talent, telegrams, Pucci sandals, and daughters of renegade dads. Pat Fraley for the spookily perfect music on the audio version and the wonderful stories over sushi.

Alice Hoffman my favorite newfound cousin, MBH — Mags, dude! Someday we have to figure out how *we're* related, and that goes for Auntie NZ, too . . .

My blogmates at nakedauthors.com: Patty Smiley, Paul Levine, James Grippando (at large), Jim Born, and Our J, Jacqueline Winspear.

Rae and Maggie and Deanie and Heidi and Dot and Stuart and Sneaky Thief and Janine (again) and all the cool Reacher Creatures.

My band, the Sad Anoraks: Andi Shechter (and Stu) and Shaz Wheeler and Louise Ure.

Writer peeps who have been there when most needed: Sandra Ruttan, Ken Bruen, Martha O'Connor, Joshilyn Jackson (We'll always have Paris. And Nicole.), Laura Lippman, and Cara Black.

Sarah Weinman, Jon and Ruth Jordan, David Thayer, Lesa Holstine, Elizabeth Montgomery, and Michael Leone.

Ariel Zeitlin Cooke, sister friend.

Luan Keller, who survived it with me and is an endlessly fine friend and boon companion.

Candace Andrews, friend without equal (in a good way). And of course if you hadn't worked there first, I wouldn't have a book.

And finally, Rolph Blythe. I hope it goes well for you at Gray Wolf.

The employees of Thorndike Press hope you have enjoyed this Large Print book. All our Thorndike and Wheeler Large Print titles are designed for easy reading, and all our books are made to last. Other Thorndike Press Large Print books are available at your library, through selected bookstores, or directly from us.

For information about titles, please call:
(800) 223-1244

or visit our Web site at:
http://gale.cengage.com/thorndike

To share your comments, please write:
Publisher
Thorndike Press
295 Kennedy Memorial Drive
Waterville, ME 04901